Totally Bound Publishing books by Dani Rose

Club Serenity
Free Me, Master!
Boundless Hope

I0681389

Club Serenity

BOUNDLESS HOPE

DANI ROSE

Boundless Hope
ISBN # 978-1-83943-908-7
©Copyright Dani Rose 2020
Cover Art by Louisa Maggio ©Copyright August 2020
Interior text design by Claire Siemaszkiewicz
Totally Bound Publishing

BOUNDLESS HOPE

Dedication

For Tina, my biggest cheerleader. Thank you for inspiring me and giving me the proverbial kick in the butt when I needed it.

Chapter One

The loud *umph umph* reached Kyle's ears.

He looked up from his work and a frown spread across his face. He was busy with intricate calculations and he needed peace and quiet. That was why he had chosen to work in his home office for the day.

Someone had turned up the hi-fi. He put down his papers and listened. The music wasn't coming from the adjacent living room, nor from the dungeon room of his BDSM club that was located on the far side of the building. No one was supposed to be there anyway. Not on a Wednesday afternoon. The club came to life on Fridays and went quiet again on Tuesdays, when the cleaners had done their work after a busy weekend.

So where the hell was it coming from? And who the hell was in his home?

He stormed out of his office and stalked into the living room. The hi-fi was on there all right, but the music floated in through the open patio doors. It was coming from the gardens. Someone had switched the hi-fi to the speakers there.

Kyle walked outside, music drifting to him from the lanai area. Unable to see it as it was nestled in tall bushes for privacy, he'd have to walk through the gardens to get there. Or go back indoors to enter it via the hallway.

"Too much hassle," he mumbled and strode across the slate path, veered around flowerbeds and shrubs, and crossed the wooden bridge over a bubbling stream. The landscaper he had hired was doing a good job, but he wasn't interested in plants right now. He wanted to know who had trespassed on his premises.

The closer he got to the lanai, the louder the music became.

A slight smile curved his lips as he recognized the song. He liked it, but the punk who was listening to it was going to be in serious shit.

He slowed down when he heard someone singing. *A woman. What the fuck?*

The sweet, tingling voice sang another line, followed by a husky giggle.

Was there a siren in his gardens? His dick twitched and he grinned. He had to be in dire need of a woman if a mere sexy giggle stirred his cock to life. The thought of a woman was nice though. A submissive would be better. A willing, moaning sub, her body writhing under his flogger, or underneath him as he took her.

He was hard now.

"Pathetic," he said to himself.

The woman — whoever it was — continued singing in her sparkling, sweet voice. Not the right voice for the song — nevertheless, his skin prickled.

For a minute he stood enthralled, staring at the hedge that blocked his view, as if that would magically make it disappear to reveal the singer. Then he walked around the last obstacle with a few decisive steps, only to stop dead in his tracks when he saw her. His jaw dropped.

Slender, an angel face, adorned with flaming, dark red hair that was twisted in a knot on her head. A few wavy strands had slipped free and were brushing against her cheeks. Kyle grinned when he saw the knot was kept up with a pencil. *Why bother with a clip when you have pencils?* The girl was singing into a paintbrush, the tip gleaming with red paint. Her eyes were closed as she sang her heart out in the paint brush microphone.

It made him smile, and he sized her up, intrigued. The baggy paint-stained T-shirt did nothing to hide the wonderful curves of her breasts. Worn jeans underneath enhanced her figure more than any fancy dress would have done. Long legs, good hips and a full, round ass.

A sudden desire to hold her welled up inside him. Not just hold her – he wanted to kiss her and fondle her high breasts.

He tried to rid himself of the sensation and failed. Her singing drew him even closer.

The song went on with "La-da-dis" and she started to twirl around, her hips swaying, arms up in the air.

Fuck, she is beautiful.

Her movements tugged at the knot and the pencil that held it up started to slip and dropped to the ground. Kyle sucked in a breath as her long, wavy red hair cascaded down and spilled over her back and shoulders. It caught the sunlight and sparks flew off it when she swirled around.

As he stood there, mesmerized and bewitched by the dancing redhead before him, he recalled the siren legend. It spoke of beautiful women who lived on an island surrounded by cliffs and rocks. Dangerous creatures that lured nearby sailors in with their enchanting music and voices until they crashed their boats on the rocks. Kyle could feel his boat crash underneath his feet as he was watching this beguiling creature with her flaming hair.

He held his breath as she stopped twirling, raised her arms up to the skies, threw her head back and sang the last line of the song.

A smile appeared on her face, then she lowered her arms and gaze, and looked straight at him with her green eyes that now flared wide in shock. An "Ooh!" broke from her lips and her face turned as red as the paint on the brush.

He zoomed in on her little round mouth that resembled a perfect rose bud. Thoughts of what he could make her do with that made his dick throb, and he was unable to stop it. He was a Master, but not Master of his cock.

Choosing to ignore his lust, at least for now, Kyle flashed the girl a devastating smile. She glared in turn.

"Who the hell are you and what are you doing here?" Her eyes sprayed fire as she snapped at him. "Are you some kind of perv or something?"

A corner of his mouth turned up.

"I have quite the reputation."

The statement had Sellie shocked. She didn't know the man, nor his reputation, yet the words held a promise that stirred a longing in her core. The deep timbre of his voice struck a chord inside her, soothed her, and the anger at being caught off guard melted. Yet, the calming effect was negated by his piercing blue eyes. The sense that he was able see straight through her, as if she were a clear crystal, was unsettling. And arousing. It made her want to run and hide, but a deeper part of her reveled in the unexpected buzz of the moment and wanted to stay.

Her body reacted to him in spite of her anger, and her nipples blossomed into hard peaks. They bunched even tighter when his gaze dropped to her breasts, and she cursed under her breath. Heat crept up over her face and she shifted her weight, uncertain what to say or do now that this stranger was staring at her boobs and erect nips. To make matters worse, his gaze aroused her even more, as if it was an actual touch.

Her brain was racing for something to say, anything that would make him leave, but she was tongue-tied. The man before her was too daunting.

She got out of her stupor when he started to walk toward her. The bulge in his crotch couldn't be missed, and she sucked in a breath.

No no no! Attacked on the job at a BDSM club? No way!

She put her right leg back a bit, ready to give the man a well-aimed kick to the head if he came any closer. Her heart was pounding in her chest as he kept moving and she realized she'd never reach his head. He was too tall. A blow to the knees would have to suffice.

Adrenaline was rushing through her veins, giving her the courage she needed. Yet when she met his eyes, the power in them almost paralyzing, she trembled with fear. Then her martial arts training took over and her right leg shot forward, aiming for his left knee. That would teach him to scare the bejesus out of her. She'd finish it off with a blow to the head and another in the gut when he was down on the ground.

Sellie screamed as the world turned upside down when he blocked her kick with his leg, swept her other foot out from underneath her and dropped down on his knee with her in his arms.

She stared at him in shock and the words her karate teacher used to say resonated through her mind — *'Never underestimate your enemy.'* How had she forgotten that lesson?

Why hadn't he said, *'Don't let a blond God distract you.'?*

She would've chuckled at the thought if it wasn't for the fact that the man in question held her pinned down to the ground with an ease that was frightening.

While her breathing came fast and her heart was thumping against her ribs, he looked as calm as if he was sipping an afternoon cup of tea. Or whiskey. He struck her as a whiskey kind of guy. Whose erection was pressing hard against her hip.

That got her back to planet Earth, and she started squirming and kicking. She managed to free her right hand, and she swung her arm to punch him in the face.

The man grabbed hold of her fist, which almost disappeared in his large hand. He glowered at her, his eyes colder than the Antarctic at midwinter. Her mind blanked as fear washed through her.

Kyle had had just about enough. The girl was agile and strong, and had almost succeeded in hitting him. Her legs turned out to be rather vicious and he didn't fancy getting kneed in his groin. Without further ado, he rolled on top of her, restraining her lower body with his own, rendering her legs useless. She was no match for his muscular hips and thighs. The horror and disbelief in her eyes softened his heart, but then she tried to scratch him. A growl welled up in his throat.

"Little bitch!"

He grabbed both her hands and pulled her arms over her head, holding her wrists with just one hand.

The position arched her breasts up and they pushed against his chest.

His cock pulsed. Against her mound. What an unfortunate position to be in, having his dick right where it wanted to be, yet not being able to do with it what he wanted to do.

The girl was panting underneath him while he hadn't even broken a sweat, although the struggle had turned up the heat in his core. Excitement coursed through him and he had to suppress the animalistic urge to take his prey now that he had her subdued.

While he tried to get a grip of himself, he looked her over. Her hair was spread out like a fan, the strands highlighted by the sun as if it was on fire.

He wondered if she'd have red pubes or if she'd be bald. He'd appreciate either. Seeing sparks fly off her pussy curls when he lowered his head to indulge between her long legs held a lot of appeal. He groaned.

Fury shot from her emerald eyes. Images of them glazing over after he'd ripped off her jeans to hammer his cock balls-deep into her cunt flooded his brain. For a split second, the sensation of fucking her was so real it was near unbearable. His vision blurred and his erection strained against the zipper of his slacks.

He hauled in a deep breath.

"Get off me, you bastard!" the girl hissed.

His eyes darted to her mouth. Perfect and round and beautiful, yet spewing out such foul words. A ball gag would sort that problem. His dick jerked as if to agree, and he gritted his teeth to keep from kissing her. He should stand up before this got out of hand. Facing sexual harassment charges wasn't on his bucket list. The courts would have a field day with a BDSM Master harassing an innocent woman.

"Get off me, fucking pervert!" Powerful words, but they sounded like a plea for him to let go of her.

His gaze was still on her mouth that had spewed out the profanities. He couldn't shake the thought of a ball gag and how it would make that gorgeous red rosebud appear even fuller. The way she stared at him, vulnerable yet angry, made him want to devour her, yank off her clothes and take her.

"Can I kiss you?" Kyle's voice was hoarse.

He pushed himself up a bit. The movement shifted his hips, and her eyes widened when his erection pressed into her pussy even more. A moan escaped her.

"I take that as a yes," Kyle said, leaned in and took her mouth with a hunger that shook him. The girl opened her lips, and he swept in with his tongue, finding hers, tangling and caressing. She mewled into his mouth and rubbed her crotch against his hard cock. He thrust forward in response, and her needy whine set his core alight. Somewhere in the back of his mind, he knew he was but a hairbreadth away from crossing a line from which there was no turning back. With great effort he tapped into his willpower, and he was about to withdraw when she wrapped her legs around him, robbing him of his last shred of sanity. A deep grunt came from him and he intensified the kiss. He craved to feel her, the warmth of her skin, the fullness of her breasts, and he slid his hand down to slip it under her shirt.

"What the fuck is this?"

Kyle growled as he lifted his head to find out who'd interrupted him while he was taking his pleasure from the fiery siren underneath him.

His gaze met the ruthless eyes that belonged to Cal, one of his club Masters.

"I'm taking care of a trespasser," Kyle snapped.

Cal raised an eyebrow and smirked.

"Hey, it don't confront me none if you want to play role games with the hired help, but—"

"Hired help?" Kyle interrupted, and shook his head in an attempt to clear his brain.

He glanced at the girl. Her eyes were still dazed, her lips red and swollen from their kiss. She was so hot and fuckable. Regret flowed through him. He sighed and tangled his fingers in her hair, the strands soft and silky, suppressing the urge to wrap it around his wrist and take her mouth again.

He managed to control himself, and used his Dom-gaze to bring her back to reality. It worked all right—it always did. A visible shock ran through her, the expression of surrender alluring.

"No more fighting, understand?" Kyle's voice came out a low rumble, her "okay" a mere squeak.

Kyle got up, grabbed the girl's hand and pulled her to her feet. He looked at Cal, paying heed to the girl from the corner of his eye in case she'd start kicking again.

"Hired help?" he demanded.

"Yeah, the girl works for the landscaping company. They hired her to paint the trompe-l'oeil." Cal tilted his head toward the lanai wall. "I let her in since you were busy."

Kyle glanced over his shoulder at the beginnings of a painted archway with a seascape in the middle.

Kyle swallowed hard. He'd forced himself upon a fucking painter. She had been willing enough, but Marie, the owner of the landscaping company he'd gotten in to do his gardens, was going to have his hide if she found out. She had very strict work ethics. As did he. Until this redhead had gotten under his skin and had caused him to crash his proverbial boat on the cliffs, resulting in him almost getting his rocks off on her. In his boxers at that.

"What did you want, Cal?" Kyle grumbled.

"It'll keep. You deal with the hired help first," Cal said as he gestured at the redhead.

Kyle turned to her. The poor thing was trembling. He must have scared the hell out of her, coming on so strong, so fast. And he was sure she was shaken up by her own powerful reaction to him.

He gave her a warm smile.

"I'm sorry, miss. I had by no means intended to..." He had to clear his throat. *Plunder you. Ravish you. Fuck you.*

Cal's deep laughter filled the air. "Mr. Eloquent stuck for words. I'll be damned!"

Kyle scowled at his friend, who shrugged and sauntered away, laughing still.

"I'm sorry, miss," Kyle continued. "That should never have happened. I'm Kyle Pearson. I own this mansion."

Ten minutes later Sellie was sipping a cappuccino at a robust oak table in the kitchen. She glanced around the spacious room. Anthracite worktops, cream cupboard doors, shiny chrome equipment. The only thing that seemed out of place was a pink tea towel on a hook on the wall. Sunlight came in through large windows and gave the room a sense of home. His home.

She fidgeted in the chair and clenched her fingers around her cup. Being here was too intimate. After what had just happened, she needed some distance and time to sort out her feelings. Her reaction to this God had been extreme. She knew herself to be a passionate woman with a healthy appetite for sex, but the way she had reacted to him was ridiculous. No man had ever overwhelmed her the way he did, and it had been an amazing turn-on. But to end up rolling on the ground with her lips glued to a guy she'd held for a pervert, ready and willing to spread her legs for him, was concerning at best.

He had invited her in for a drink with the words, *'Please allow me to make up for my rudeness, miss.'* Not invading her personal space, he had been very polite, and his expression had shown genuine regret about what had happened.

Nevertheless, she had objected to entering his home.

'No, thank you. My clothes have paint on them.' She'd fumbled with the hem of her shirt and hadn't been able to keep her voice from trembling.

Kyle had been adamant that she come in for something to drink though, and she'd found that, in spite of her spirited nature, she was no match for him. Whereas she was capable of having fervent bouts of strength, he had a steadfast aura of power and self-confidence. It had taken him less than a minute to get her to come inside.

Once indoors, she had introduced herself to him, using her full name.

'I'm Seline.'

His reaction had been a bit odd. He had lifted an eyebrow and mumbled, *'A moon goddess. Not a siren.'* He'd shaken his head as if to rid himself of some image, then smiled. *'Nice to meet you, Seline.'*

She'd stared at him in wonder when he took her hand, raised it to his mouth and brushed the back of it with his lips.

'Enchanté,' he'd said, his voice soft. His eyes had met hers, the open admiration in them stabbing. Her heart

had done a somersault in her chest, a triple one when he'd given her a smile that melted her spine.

The man was downright overwhelming. A one hundred percent sexual energy man who pushed all her buttons in one go, putting her system into overdrive. And now he was the most charming suitor making romantic gestures. No man had ever kissed her hand before.

Then he'd pulled back a chair, the spell broken and the moment lost. She wasn't sure whether to be glad for it or not.

"Please be seated, Seline."

While he was busy making the cappuccinos, Sellie observed him as nonchalantly as possible. The way he moved around was more than interesting — relaxed but with the typical focus of a man who knew what he was doing. And where to find everything. Rich or not, she bet he cooked his own food. She had no doubt he'd whip up a six-course meal with the same ease that he was making the cappuccinos. He was in total control of everything all the time — not even a piece of equipment would dare defy his authority. He was Lord of the Manor, all right. And the sheer speed and agility with which he had taken her down in the garden proved he was King of the Jungle just the same. A dangerous man. A swift and lethal predator one minute, elegant, courteous and cordial the next.

Then he was done. He put their drinks on the table and excused himself for a minute.

"I've gotten paint on my shirt. I'll be right back, Seline," he said with a half-smile.

She nodded and couldn't help but perv on his butt when he stalked out of the kitchen. Muscular and firm like the rest of him. The man looked good.

"Everything about him feels good too," she whispered.

She'd had an up close and personal encounter to be able to vouch for that. Her eyes unfocused as she visualized him.

Golden blond hair, hypnotizing blue eyes, full lips, straight nose and a masculine jawline. To-die-for broad shoulders, and she had seen chest hair peek through the opening of his shirt. She guesstimated he was six-foot-two. He towered over her, despite her own five-foot-ten. A new experience for her—she was used to having to look down, not up. She was certain she'd never been around a man as tall as Kyle. The effect it had on her was peculiar. It roused both her femininity and her libido. Maybe that didn't have as much to do with his height as it did with him. Or both.

"Women must drop at his feet wherever he goes," she mumbled. Either in adoration or by being overwhelmed by the King of the Jungle.

She giggled. That title suited him down to the ground.

When Kyle came back into the kitchen, she gawked like a schoolgirl. He had changed into a tight black T-shirt that hugged his shoulders and chest, the short sleeves snug around his bulging biceps and triceps. The man was built like a brick shithouse.

You know that, Sellie, you've been squirming under him!

Her cheeks warmed as the memory of his hard erection between her legs flooded her and a jolt shot through her core.

Her skin prickled as she sensed his gaze on her, and when she dared to glance up, her heart hammering, she saw apprehension in his eyes. He knew what she was thinking about?

A burning heat crept up over her face and she dropped her gaze, only to end up staring at the bulge in his pants.

She tried to force herself to turn her head, but her body refused to obey. Her shoulder muscles tightened and she clutched the cup on the table.

"Seline, breathe." His smooth voice calmed her down a bit. "I am not going to jump you."

Kyle sighed when she cast him a 'Yeah, right!' glance.

"Seline—"

"Sellie," she interrupted, grimacing. "I prefer to be called Sellie."

Kyle mouthed it, like he was tasting it on his tongue and lips, and nodded.

As if she needed his approval. Yet warmth washed through her that her name pleased him.

"All right, Sellie it is. I'm sorry about what happened earlier on," Kyle said. "I don't make a habit out of jumping women."

"I doubt you'd need to. I bet they all jump you!" Sellie blurted.

Kyle chuckled.

"Well, it was you who made the first move, girl. How could I resist?" His eyes gleamed with pleasure.

Sellie blinked, dumbfounded. Her mouth fell open when she realized he was right. She snapped it shut and giggled.

Kyle held his breath as she transformed before him as if she were a butterfly. Mischief danced in her eyes, then her laughter resonated through the air like tiny silver bells in an afternoon breeze.

His slacks were having a hard time containing his erection. He had better steer the conversation to calmer, less dangerous waters.

"How did you end up working for Marie?" he asked.

The girl opened up and was beaming when she talked about her work and her passion, painting. All of the earlier shyness melted away, her movements became freer and she used her hands to create images of what she was explaining. Every now and then, her slender fingers brushed a defiant curl behind her ear.

Kyle could do nothing but stare and was surprised to find he had to force himself to listen to her story. He was gifted with the ability to observe, listen and detect, all at the same time, but with her all his usual reactions were different, like a fish out of water depending on her for his air to breathe. He blinked and focused on her words instead of lips.

"My friend had heard that Marie needed a painter and she told her about me," Sellie said. "I owe Rebecca for being able to do the work I love."

Kyle sat back in his chair and frowned.

"Rebecca? Are you talking about Rebecca Williams?"

"Yes. Rebecca and I go way back. We used to take art classes together and we hit it off." Sellie smiled. "Somehow we lost touch though, busy with life. But we're still friends. Last week she said she got married and all."

For a moment he was speechless and lost in thought. He wondered how much Rebecca had told her about her relationship and what Sellie would know about BDSM. It was possible that Rebecca had decided to keep it a secret. Maybe she'd figured Sellie wouldn't understand as she was younger. He guessed Sellie was around thirty-two, whereas Rebecca was forty-two. But that didn't put Sellie at a virgin or novice age.

Since Sellie hadn't recognized Cal, nor he her, they hadn't met. Kyle was intrigued.

He picked up his cup and drank the cappuccino. As he glanced at Sellie over the rim, he met her confused expression. From his peripheral view, he noticed how she held her hands in her lap and her arms against her body.

He set the cup back on the table and put a smile on his face.

"I'm sorry," he apologized. "I was thinking how peculiar it is we both know Rebecca."

He got himself a half-hearted smile. Although he realized the timing was off, he decided to ask the question that was burning in his mind.

"How much did she tell you about their relationship?" he asked as nonchalantly as possible.

Sellie went poker-faced and her back stiffened.

"That they're very much in love," she answered. "Anyway, thanks for the coffee. I've got to go on with my work. My brushes are getting hard out there."

She moved her chair back, nodded and walked out of the kitchen.

"Way to go," he muttered.

Chapter Two

Kyle rested his elbows on the matte glass top of his desk and twiddled his pen. After a relaxed drive to his office in town earlier that day, he'd been in good spirits. He liked being at the office. Being able to rely on his secretary was great and made work a lot easier. He let his gaze go through the spacious room with a glass conference table that matched his desk. Plush champagne-colored carpeting dampened footsteps and speech. Near the windows were two white leather chairs that he often used when he had to read intricate material. A couple of ferns and orchids added a more personal touch to the otherwise modern interior. His morning had been busy, lunch hasty, and he still had plenty to do, but he found it impossible to concentrate. His mind kept drifting and each time he found himself thinking of home, and her. He sighed.

A week had gone by since he'd last seen Sellie. A new client had kept him busy and had required him to go into town daily. By the time he'd gotten home, she'd been gone. No reminder of her presence other than paint pots in a neat stack set in a corner, the cleaned brushes on top of them.

Every day he walked over to the lanai to check out the progress of the trompe-l'oeil. It was beautiful. Although it wasn't finished, it was obvious she was a good painter with a great eye for detail, composition, colors and light.

Kyle was toying with the idea of commissioning another wall painting. An indoor mural this time, in the dungeon. Between one of the arches on the walls would be great. As yet, he wasn't sure how to approach Sellie about the matter. He assumed she'd been informed that the mansion harbored a posh BDSM club. But knowing about it and seeing it for real were two different things. The club room tended to be pretty daunting to people who weren't into the scene. The sight of whips, stocks, chains, ropes and whatnot could give vanilla—non-BDSM people—the creeps.

He'd have to take his chances with her. She was spirited enough, and he doubted she was the kind of woman who'd shy away from the less common things in life. Apart from that, it was business, not personal.

"Oh, cut the crap," he said out loud. "You want her in your dungeon."

He pulled a face. Indeed he did. But he wanted a mural in there too. For a minute he sat back in his black leather desk chair and stared out of the large window. Being an architect, he always appreciated the city skyline, but this afternoon it didn't interest him much. Neither did the pile of work in front of him. He grinned. In his forties, and haunted by green eyes and red hair. He leaned forward, reached for the intercom on his desk and pressed a button.

"Karen, please clear my agenda for the afternoon." Even as he was speaking he started shutting down his computer.

"What about your three o'clock meeting, Mr. Pearson?" his secretary asked.

"Reschedule it."

He snapped his laptop shut, grabbed some files and walked out of the office.

It didn't take him long to get to his car and pull out of the building's garage. Traffic wasn't too busy at this time of day and he hummed as he drove home. His car was fast and comfortable, with plenty of space for his long legs. Even though his mind was on getting from A to B, he did enjoy the ride and how the car reacted when he sped up. Its acceleration was quite astounding, which was one of the reasons he'd bought it. He always appreciated it for the machine it was, but now its feel and reactions were almost visceral and it reminded him of Sellie. Like his car, she needed but a little nudge to be off. Passionate and fast, giving him her all without hesitation. Both had wonderful curves.

He grinned, realizing he was in deep shit. Going home early because he wanted to see her, dreaming of her at night, getting hard just thinking about her and now comparing his car to her.

He forced himself to focus on driving and heed the speed limit, and before long he entered the driveway to his mansion. After he'd grabbed his laptop and files from the passenger seat, he stalked straight to his home office and dumped the items on his desk. As he made his way to the patio doors, he loosened his tie and shirt. They seemed tight and uncomfortable. He thought of changing into something more casual, but his desire to see her was stronger and he started to walk through the garden.

His heart skipped a beat when he got to the lanai and found her absorbed in painting.

The covered patio was his favorite place to be, and her being there added to that vibe. Something in his gut seemed to unwind and his shoulder muscles relaxed. He put his hands in his pockets and took his time to enjoy the view. Not just her, but the setting as well. Her and the setting. Her.

"Fuck it," he swore, ripped his gaze from Sellie and focused on the lanai. It had a wooden roof supported by oak columns. To the right was a Moroccan style fireplace, partially behind furniture that was moved out of the way. They had large, white sheets over them to protect them from paint. The potted cypresses and the dark pink bougainvillea — his pride and joy — were nowhere to be seen.

He frowned and scanned the covered shapes in front of the hearth for the tall silhouettes of the plants. He failed to spot any.

A movement caught his attention, and he forgot all about the plants when he watched her get on tiptoes, reaching up with a brush to paint a cloud in the imaginary sky. Her top rode up with her shoulders, revealing the wonderful curves of her ass and waistline. He feasted his eyes as she shifted her weight, causing the muscles in her butt to flex. Unaware of her intruder, she put her left hand up to wipe away some paint with a cloth. Now she was on tiptoes with both arms up in the air, her perky ass taunting him, the sight way too kinky. His mind filled in the blanks and envisioned cuffs and chains around her wrists and ankles, her butt bared for him to spank.

Without thought, his hands clenched and unclenched as if readying himself for the action. A low groan broke from him as he could almost see her firm flesh shake after each slap. Heat rose from his groin and his dick stirred. He cursed, tore his gaze away from her luscious body, took a few deep breaths and rolled his shoulders.

Needing to break from this spell, he stepped closer, expecting she'd hear him, but she didn't react. He cleared his throat. Nothing. Then he said her name and a shock ran through her body. She almost lost her balance when she turned around, wide-eyed and clutching the brush in front of her as if it were a buoy.

"Sellie, there's something I'd like to discuss with you."

Realizing that sounded quite serious, he flashed her a warm smile, yet when their gazes met, hers was filled with concern. It tugged at his heart. He hadn't meant to alarm her.

"Sellie..." His vocal cords failed him when her nipples bloomed under her top. The heat in his lower body turned up a notch and an overwhelming sexual tension sizzled between them like lightning after a hot summer's day. It took most of his willpower to not drop his gaze to her heaving chest. A deep pink spread across her cheeks.

"Talk about what?" Her words came out husky, and his dick responded with a twitch, leaving him semi-hard.

In an attempt to distract himself, Kyle gestured at the mural.

"It's about your work," he said. "Why don't you come to talk about it? I make a hell of a cappuccino."

"My work?" She tilted her head, her expression tense.

"Don't worry, I'm happy with your work," Kyle assured her. "So much so that I want to commission another one."

Her whole face lit up and she tossed the brush to the ground, leaving a sprinkling of blue paint on the sheet that covered the hardwood patio floor.

"That's great!" she beamed and clapped her hands together. "You made my day!"

A silly grin pulled at Kyle's lips and he was certain he just got an inch taller.

"Glad you're glad! Let's go in and discuss it."

Not much later they were in his kitchen, chitchatting over cappuccinos. Out of the blue, she changed the subject from a movie they both liked to the matter at hand with a "Now tell me!" Her eyes sparkled with enthusiasm.

For a second he stared at her, his hand with his cup midway between the table and his lips. He opened his mouth, but no sound came out. He closed it and chuckled. The woman had succeeded at getting him off-balance, which he considered quite the feat. He tended to be the one to render people off-kilter, something he very much enjoyed. *Part of a Master's territory.* Now he found himself tongue-tied by a sexy girl.

"Well, I'd like another mural. Indoors. But..." Kyle wasn't quite sure how to phrase it. Then he figured it was best to be straightforward. "Are you aware of the nature of my business?"

Sellie lowered her gaze and her fair skin turned an oh-so-charming red, telling him that she did indeed know.

He smiled and decided to not beat around the bush. If she was going to be working in there, she'd find out anyway.

"Serenity is a members-only BDSM club and I'd love a wall painting in there."

"All right, but I-I don't know much about it."

As she glanced up he saw a question in her eyes. Was it possible that she was interested?

The girl's face went tomato red. Okay, maybe she wasn't all that interested. Mild disappointment trickled through him as a rather horrified glimmer appeared in her eyes. It made him wonder what distorted view she held about BDSM. He suspected it would be much like the default one. About people being forced to do abnormal things, wear rubber masks and get hurt while being tied up. And it was obvious that didn't appeal to her at all.

He sighed, a bit annoyed that there was so little understanding about what BDSM truly entailed. The girl seemed equally annoyed.

"I'd need to see the setting," Sellie explained with a snap in her voice. "To get a feel of what the room needs."

I'll tell you what it needs! A gorgeous redhead with flaming hair in chains and under my command.

Kyle shook his head to get the image out of his mind. His stirring manhood didn't help much. *Dammit.*

The heat that shimmied in the air between them affected Sellie. Granted, she wasn't sure what was going through his head, but there was no doubt about it being sexual. Hot. A sudden need rose from her core.

She had to focus on the task at hand. On Work. Money. Not her needy pussy.

"Do you have something in mind?" she asked.

The suggestive nature of her question sank in the second the words had left her lips.

Sexual power radiated off the blue-eyed lion sitting across from her, enveloping and enthralling her. Sellie wished he'd throw the table out of the way and plunder her. Rip her clothes off and bury himself inside her.

Lord knew she was wet enough. She hadn't been with a man in months. The closest she'd come to intimacy had been when she was squirming under Kyle, his erection pressing against her most sensitive spot. A jolt zinged through her clit.

He cleared his throat and spoke up.

"Well, I best show you the room."

Sellie blinked, suppressed the pang of disappointment of him going back to business as if nothing had happened. Had she misjudged the situation and let her own hormones cloud her vision?

"I have no specific ideas about the painting," Kyle continued. "I'll leave that up to you, but before you start, I do want to see a drawing of what you intend to do."

Sellie didn't want to speak, not trusting her voice, and she nodded instead.

"It'll have to be classy, an enhancement of the feel of the dungeon," he went on. "You can work from Mondays through Thursdays. You will have to clear out your items on Thursdays, as the club will be busy during the weekend. We can't have pots of paint in there."

Sellie thought of a Dom chasing after a naked woman with a whip, then accidentally putting his foot in a paint bucket, screaming bloody murder as he fell facedown to the floor.

Amusement flowed through her and she tried to stifle the giggle that bubbled up in her chest, failed, and broke into laughter.

There was no way for Kyle to know why she was laughing, but he smiled nonetheless. When she fell quiet, he asked, "What was so funny?"

She avoided looking at him. "Erm... Just some funny accident with paint pots when erm...people are doing…erm… Well, whatever it is they do in there," Sellie stammered.

Her face was burning and she was grateful he didn't press for more details.

When they walked through the house to the club, she got nervous. This would be her first visit to a BDSM club, escorted by a powerful hunk of a man. There was no one else around — if he wanted to do not-so-honorable things to her, she was on her own.

Her heart was pounding when they got to a heavy wooden door. Kyle opened it.

"Ladies first," he said with a smile.

Sellie mumbled a thank-you. All of a sudden, she was curious to find out what a BDSM club would be like, and she stepped inside the dungeon room.

"Wow!" She was tongue-tied. The room was beautiful! The artist in her woke up and she took in the play of the sunlight coming in through windows high up on the walls, the shadows that were cast on the dark wood floor and furniture. One wall had stained glass windows, and she loved the soft glow coming from them. Rafters adorned the ceilings, and there were niches, plants, and a huge oval bar to the left of the room, with lots of dark wood and shiny copper.

She walked around, taking in the walls and how the light hit them, trying to decide which wall would be best for a mural. As she was strolling around the room, her hands absentmindedly slid over furniture. Leather sofas, the smooth wooden surface of the bar, and some weird item that stood a few meters off the wall.

After Sellie had walked around the entire room, she'd decided which wall would be best for a mural. She turned around to Kyle to discuss it. A shiver ran up her spine. He was still standing at the entrance, leaning against the doorjamb. His hands in the pockets of his jeans and his legs crossed at the ankles, emphasizing the bulge in his groin. His posture was casual, but his eyes contradicted that message. The eyes of a hungry lion, King of the Jungle—he was King, she was in his jungle. Tremors shook her. Her brain screamed for her to get the hell out of there, but her pussy ached for him to leap through the room and…

"Well, what do you think?" Kyle asked in a hoarse voice.

Gorgeous! Hot! Please take me! Hard!

Sellie swallowed. She opened her mouth to answer, but no sound came out.

He pushed himself off the doorjamb and stalked toward her, pinning her with his gaze. She couldn't tear her eyes away from him. When he stood in front of her, she had to raise her head. He was so tall.

"It's big. Looks great. Impressive," Sellie mumbled.

Was she talking about his groin or the room? She wasn't sure.

Kyle's soft, low laughter sent quivers through her belly. He tugged a lock of her hair.

"Let me show you which wall I have in mind," he said, and curved his fingers around her upper arm to turn her around. As they walked to the other side of the room, he put his hand on the small of her back.

When they stood in front of a wall, he pointed at an archway.

"I think that would be a great place for a mural," he said.

Sellie chewed on her bottom lip. The angle of the light coming in was all wrong for this wall.

"You'd have lights on during club nights, right?" she asked, and when he confirmed, "Can you switch them on for me, please?"

"Yes, ma'am," Kyle said and walked away.

"Wow!" Sellie exclaimed when the dungeon lit up. Whoever had done the lighting in this place had sure as heck known what they were doing.

Some areas were highlighted, while others were bathed in soft light. As she faced the wall again, she had to agree it was the best spot in the entire room for a mural. It'd be seen from almost every corner of the room, except from the more secluded areas. She nodded and told him she'd start brainstorming and run ideas by him as soon as she had something worked out.

Sellie noticed a peculiar glint in Kyle's eyes as he walked her out of the room, and it confused her. What was with the man? Distant one minute, a mind-boggling aphrodisiac the next. She had difficulty working him out. It'd be best for her own sanity and well-being to stay out of his way as much as possible. No matter how strong she was, she sensed that deep down she was no match for him, and she wasn't up for biting off more than she could chew. If ever she'd get involved again, the man had to be easygoing and calm. Anything but volatile and dangerous like Kyle.

She mumbled something she hoped would be polite and hurried back to the safety of the lanai.

Chapter Three

Sellie was in the clubroom working on the mural. She'd come a long way with the one on the lanai, and Kyle had wanted her to make the painting in the dungeon her first priority. She had time to work on the trompe-l'oeil outdoors on Fridays to finish it off.

In the meantime, Sellie had learned that her friend Rebecca worked for Kyle at the office. That made her wonder about Rebecca. Would she be into this weird BDSM stuff with her husband? She found that creepy. Maybe she should talk to Rebecca about it and find out a bit more.

At first she had been awkward in the dungeon. Being there with Kyle had been disconcerting, but being there on her own was downright awkward. As if she was trespassing on his jungle. Knowing Rebecca was in the vicinity was reassuring.

She decided to focus on her work and to heed her surroundings as little as possible. That was easier said than done. A little voice in the back of her head kept nagging, wanted her to put down her brush and wander around.

Sellie frowned, not understanding why the room held so much appeal. BDSM was not her thing—she wanted nothing to do with it. In spite of that, the vibe of the place seemed to sneak up on her like a living, breathing entity.

"God damn it!" she cursed. "Leave me alone!"

Her voice bounced off the walls and hearing it made her smile. She rolled her shoulders and stretched her neck muscles. Getting her energy flow going always helped clear her mind. A deep breath to finish it off, then she got to work.

She painted for two hours straight before she put her brush away and stepped back to get an overall view of the initial setup of the painting.

"Wonderful!" she beamed. "Time for a coffee break."

She made herself a cappuccino in the kitchenette, and as she sipped, she thought about going outdoors to relax. It was a warm and sunny day, the gardens were beautiful and some fresh air and stretching her legs held a lot of appeal. In spite of that, she found herself staring at the heavy wooden doors that granted access to the clubroom. She'd left them open, and from where she was standing she could see the bar. Sunlight hit its shining copper railing and it sparkled as if to say "Please come in!" The unspoken invitation woke her curiosity and she wandered into the room. A sense of mystery welcomed her like a warm embrace, both exciting and daunting. She swallowed, torn between her I-want-nothing-to-do-with-this part and the darker half of her personality that was intrigued. As she put her cup on the bar and strolled toward a large wooden cross, she was almost shocked to notice she was aroused. Even though she didn't know what the equipment was called, she sure as hell was smart enough to work out how it was to be used. A shiver ran down her spine.

Then her eye caught a stand with different types of whips, and items that had a handle with a lot of strands dangling off them. Coiled ropes were hanging on the wall next to it. Different kinds as well. Being a tactile person, she brushed over some of the ropes. Next, she turned to the rack, and couldn't resist running the leather strands over her fingers. Not the ones with knots in them, but the ones with soft, leather strips. Sellie took a thick one off its hook and ran the tails over the skin of her forearm. It tickled, the softness almost a caress. She ran it over her arm again.

"It's a deer skin flogger." Kyle's soft voice came from behind her.

Sellie startled. *How long has he been there?*

He strolled around her, his intent gaze on her.

"May I?" he asked, and took the flogger from her hands. He traced it over her arms, collar bones and shoulders, and the sweet sensations raised goose bumps on her entire body.

"Deer skin is very, very soft," Kyle whispered as he ran the flogger along the side of her neck. Shivers zinged across her nerves. She'd had no idea her neck was so sensitive that butterfly touches on it would melt her spine. A protesting moan fled her when he moved the strands to another area, letting them graze over her breasts, tickling her now hard nipples.

Sellie had closed her eyes, and as he moved up again, closer and closer to her neck, a whispered "Please!" fled her lips.

He pressed a kiss to the side of her neck and jolts of pleasure shot out from it through her entire body. Her knees got weak and she clung to him for support, hoping that for the love of God he wouldn't stop.

"Kyle, where are you?"

Sellie blinked at the sound of Rebecca's voice. Kyle cursed under his breath, tossed the flogger over the stand and cupped Sellie's face.

"Are you all right, sweetie?" he asked.

"Yes. Yes. I'm fine," Sellie mumbled, and walked away from Kyle and the floggers, back to her paint and brushes. Her legs were shaking and her hands trembled. She was anything but all right. Crash-landing on planet Earth after she'd jumped out of an airplane without a parachute seemed a better description. She almost giggled. The situation was ridiculous. Getting caught by her friend as she was making out with her boss in a BDSM dungeon had not been on her bucket-list.

Her breathing still came fast as Rebecca entered the room.

"I need you to have a... Oh, hi, Sellie!" Rebecca said, beaming as usual.

Before Sellie had time to reply, something odd happened. Rebecca had been smiling as she entered the room, but now she was glaring at Kyle. Sellie couldn't see Kyle's reaction, but judging from the expression on Rebecca's face the silent exchange was far from pleasant.

She tilted her head, trying to work out what the heck was going on between the two. Then Kyle stalked out of the room without saying a word.

Rebecca came toward her and it was clear to Sellie she was off-kilter. But when she asked her about the mural, her voice was steady.

Even though she was curious about what was going on between Rebecca and Kyle, she didn't ask. Not now.

Her own intermezzo with him, the intimacy of the moment and her own reaction to it, had her confused. Her body was in a state of arousal, her mind in mild shock.

Somehow she succeeded in focusing on Rebecca. Her friend was safe territory, and as it was, she needed that to find her feet again. She sensed Rebecca had the exact same problem and was using this moment to stabilize herself as well. They chatted for a bit, smiled and laughed, but when both got back to work, Sellie couldn't remember a single word of what they'd talked about.

She did, however, decide to steer clear from wandering through the dungeon. And she should stay away from Kyle as well.

It took her quite some time to recover from the intimate moment. The vibe between them was too overwhelming, and it seemed neither was able to control it. Just seeing the man was enough to put her senses in overdrive—having him tease her with a flogger was too much. She worked for him, and instead of wanting to drape herself all over him, she should focus on her work. And she did.

* * * *

Rebecca sighed. What was supposed to have been another day at the office was turning into one of those days. No matter what she was doing, she found it impossible to concentrate. It wasn't the work, nor the office itself. Lord knew Kyle had spent enough on it. The black leather desk chair was wonderful. She wasn't too keen on the white L-shaped desk, but it offered plenty of space, which she did appreciate. The office computers were mega fast, and when she'd complained the printer took forever to print a single page, he'd had another one delivered the next day. Apart from the luxurious furniture and equipment, the room was spacious and light, with cream-colored walls and hardwood flooring. Two plants on small tables gave it a bit of a homey touch.

None of that pleased her today. *It isn't easy to be comfortable when you have a butt plug up your ass.* She needed a break and went to the little kitchenette to get herself a drink. Thank goodness it was located next to the office so she didn't have to go far. As she was pouring out coffee, Sellie came in.

"Oh, pour me a cup, please," Sellie said. "How are you doing?"

Rebecca forced a smile and handed her a cup.

"I'm fine, thanks. Busy day. I'm sorry, I have to get on with work. I'll catch up soon, okay?"

Sellie frowned and Rebecca gave her another smile before making her way back to the office. She tried her hardest to walk normally, but the damned anal plug kept moving, and she was glad to get to her chair. As she lowered herself onto it while supporting herself with her arms on the desk, Sellie appeared in the doorway.

"Are you sure you are okay?" she asked, an eyebrow raised.

Rebecca's cheeks began to burn. *Dammit.* She hadn't wanted her friend to see her like this.

"Yes, I'm fine. It's just… My stomach is a bit upset. I must've eaten something wrong," Rebecca replied without making eye contact. "But I'm fine, really!"

"Okay," Sellie said. "Are you sure?"

Rebecca almost cursed out loud. It was great to have a friend who cared, but all she wanted right now was for Sellie to leave so she could suffer in silence. She realized Sellie wasn't going to give up just like that. Rebecca put on her best poker face and looked her in the eyes.

"Yes, yes, I'm sure," she said.

A sigh of relief escaped her when Sellie smiled and left with an "Okay, back to work it is!"

Rebecca rested her head against the chair and closed her eyes as she thought about what had gone down the day before, the cause of her misery today.

The minute she'd walked into the dungeon, she had sensed something was off. Taking on Kyle wasn't a smart move, but she had gotten protective of her friend, who didn't know the first thing about BDSM. Nevertheless, Rebecca hadn't dared to tell him off, but she sure as heck had done so with her gaze.

She chuckled as she recalled how she'd glared at Kyle, sending him the message to leave her friend alone. The result had been far from pleasant. His death-look had mortified her and she'd almost dropped to her knees to beg him for forgiveness. Cal, her Master, had intimidation down to a science, but Master Kyle could vie with him for the first place with ease. And a sub questioning and glaring at a Master was not smart. She had begged him with her eyes not to tell Cal, but Kyle's gaze had been cold as ice. And as he'd walked past her, he'd said in an undertone for her ears only, "You'll have to wait and see. Sub."

Right then and there, she'd known she was in trouble.

And indeed Kyle had told her Master she'd been rude. And Cal, being the strict Master he was, had enjoyed punishing her. The man sure as heck had a hard hand. And large butt plugs.

The damn thing had had her on tiptoes all day long. Cal had made her go to work with it so Kyle would see he'd taken care of his insolent sub. Kyle was working from home today, and every time he saw her, his lips curled up in a knowing smile.

Damn bastard!

Although Cal tended to be strict as a Master, she loved him to bits. How she wished for Sellie to find a similar, loving relationship. Just not with Kyle. Not that there was anything wrong with the man. As a matter of fact, he was great. But he was also a Master. One that had proved to be unfit for a vanilla relationship. He had tried that with her friend Olivia, and it hadn't worked out. Rebecca didn't want Sellie to head for disaster, but for now she was unsure how to prevent it. And should she? In all honesty, it wasn't any of her business, yet as a friend she felt she was obliged to do something. Then again, thinking of the vibe between those two in the dungeon... It had radiated lust and attraction.

I think it's too late. Dammit.

"I may not be able to stop it, but I sure as hell will help you along, Sellie!" she mumbled.

Chapter Four

Kyle walked into the dungeon and found Sellie sitting on the ground, her legs spread, leaning forward to work on the mural. She was sucked into painting and it seemed she was on a roll. She was working on a detail, making a very thin, fine line. He understood that she needed her focus, so he didn't say anything.

When she was finished with it, she got up and started stepping backward to check the result. Her head tilted left, right. She took a few more steps back. By now she should be able to see him from the corner of her eye, but it was plain that she was on another planet as she didn't acknowledge his presence.

Kyle smiled. She reminded him of a Mistress who was tuned in to her sub, seeing every little movement and reaction. A kind of tunnel vision during play. Sellie seemed to be in a similar mindset, focused on her painting.

She took another step back, and Kyle had to move aside so she wouldn't bump into him. He was amused, but didn't want to be in her way and he said a soft, "Sorry."

Instead of facing him, she absentmindedly handed him the dirty rag she was holding, and mumbled, "That's all right, I always wanted a paint roadie."

Kyle's full, deep laugh filled the air. He watched her crash land on planet Earth. He couldn't see her expression, but the way her muscles tensed said it all. As did the way she turned around, her eyes wide.

"I'm sorry, I didn't mean..." The paint brush slipped from her hand and dropped to the floor.

"Shit!"

As she bent over to pick it up, Kyle leaned down to clean off the paint with the rag she'd handed him. Their heads almost bashed together and they both jerked up. His face was barely an inch from hers when she looked at him with huge eyes. The brush slid out of her hand and he simply dropped the rag. Heat flared up from his core and a soft moan broke from her. Kyle took her mouth. He tangled his hand in her hair to pull her head back, forcing her to open her mouth, and he plunged in. Hard and deep, demanding.

A possessive hunger washed through him, making his head spin. He cupped her ass and yanked her against his erection. She moaned, her body quivering in his arms. A groan came from him when she pushed her legs off the ground and wrapped them around him. He tilted his hips and rubbed his cock over her crotch. She threw her head back and mewled, "Please, don't stop!"

"I don't intend to!" Kyle growled, then nipped the slope of her neck, and she whimpered. He pulled her even closer, wanting to feel more of her. It still wasn't enough. With Sellie draped around his body, he walked to a secluded corner and set her down on a thick rug.

"Damn, you're gorgeous," he whispered, and kissed her again. He only stopped to yank her top over her head and unhook her bra. Her breasts spilled free — full breasts with a slight scoop at the top and a delicious curve of the lower breast. They were crowned with velvety pink areolae and nipples that begged to be teased. He captured one in his mouth and sucked it.

"Oooh... Kyle, please..." Sellie said softly, "I want you. Now."

Her hands tangled in his hair, trying to pull his head up.

Demanding little thing! Bossy brat! A woman pulling his hair to make him do things to her almost made Kyle slip into his Master mode. He'd give her what she wanted, though. This time. He wasn't thinking of dragging this out. His balls were aching and his cock was about to rip his zipper to shreds.

He uncurled her fingers and moved them out of his hair. His gaze met hers, and his dick jerked when he saw her need. She offered him her lips, begging him to take them.

He couldn't possibly resist? With one swift movement he slid her legs out from under her and put her on the rug. He yanked her jeans off, then her thong. Short, trimmed-to-be-neat red pubic hair sparkled in the light. Kyle growled. He preferred bald, but as it was, he found the tiny red curls sexy as hell. She reached out her arms.

"Please, Kyle, please!" she begged him, her eyes dazed with need.

"Give me a second, love," he grunted, undid his slacks and grabbed a condom from a small stand nearby. He sheathed his cock and positioned himself on top of her. She wrapped her legs around his hips, opening her pussy for him.

Kyle circled the tip of his cock through her wetness. She was more than ready to receive him.

"How do you want me, baby?" he asked, his voice thick with lust.

"Hard! Please, take me hard, Kyle!"

His dick throbbed in agreement. He took her mouth first, then hammered himself balls-deep into her slick pussy. She screamed at the brutal intrusion and exploded underneath him. Her body spasmed and shook, and her cunt clamped down on his cock like a hot, wet fist.

Kyle clenched his jaws, fighting not to lose control. When most of the shocks had gone, he thrust inside her again, deep and hard, starting a steady rhythm. He moved his hips to find the sweet spot inside her, that one point every woman had that was ever so sensitive and tended to make it easier for them to come.

"Ooooh yes! God, Kyle, yes! Yes!"

Hearing, feeling and seeing her passionate response made him groan. He hammered into her it until another orgasm ripped her body apart.

Kyle waited for it to pass, a sheen of sweat on his forehead as it took all his control not to empty his balls when her pussy convulsed around his cock, trying to milk him. When the convulsions turned to gentler, rippling aftershocks, he put her legs over his shoulders, opening her further. He gave her his full length, getting even deeper now. A cry broke from her as he impaled her.

"Ooohh...Kyle...yess!" She rolled her head back and forth.

Damned spitfire was going to be the death of him! Her begging drove him wild and he couldn't hold it any longer. He hammered into her with fast thrusts until his balls tightened to the point of pain. His vision blurred as the fire at the bottom of his spine exploded and seared outward and up. His hard thrusts threw her over the edge a third time. As her cunt started sucking him dry, hot spurts of fire shot up and out of his cock. His orgasmic roar drowned out her shrill cries. Then he took her mouth in a hot, intimate, post-orgasm kiss.

Chapter Five

Kyle thought he was going nuts. It had been two weeks since he and Sellie had given in to their desire, and he found it had done nothing to lessen the need. As a matter of fact, it had gotten worse.

It was impossible to forget her gorgeous red hair, the green eyes that could shoot fire, her delicious rose bud mouth that tasted so good on his own lips. He'd tried to rid himself of the image of her lush body underneath him, her husky cries, the way her tight pussy had welcomed his cock, and had failed.

She hadn't held anything back, but instead had wrapped herself around him, and had given him her all when he had taken her.

The little spitfire kept haunting him, day and night. Every other woman he'd ever met in his life seemed bland in comparison to this siren.

He'd decided he wanted to see her again. He had to. Not at the club, though, but in a more personal setting.

He wanted to woo her. Flirt with her. It'd have to be special. *She* was special.

But how the hell would he go about it? It'd been clear that she was vanilla, and being vanilla and having to do without kink and BDSM wasn't going to work for him.

Lord knew he had tried with Olivia, whom he had met at Cal and Rebecca's wedding. They'd dated for a while and both had tried to accommodate the other. Olivia had tried some BDSM things and he'd tried to be more vanilla. In the end it had made neither of them happy. He'd liked the girl well enough, but it hadn't worked for him, so they'd parted as friends.

What to do with Sellie? Like Olivia, she wasn't familiar with BDSM. He could ask her out, get to know her a bit better then address the issue. But he figured that'd be leading her on. The alternative would be to contact her, go see her and be open about it.

Hi, Sellie, I can't forget you. I'd like to get to know you better.

That part was okay, but the next not so much.

I can't wait to tie you up and whip your sexy ass before I fuck you.

He sighed, realizing he'd have to do something or he'd lose his marbles.

* * * *

Kyle went over to Sellie's with a bunch of orange roses—a dark orange that reminded him of the color of her hair.

He rang the doorbell and waited. The door swung open and there she was.

His beautiful siren, her hair undone, flaming in the sunlight. She wore a tight top that hugged her breasts and hot-pants that set off her creamy long legs.

Within a few seconds he was hard as rock.

Her eyes got wide, her lips parted and a soft sigh of relief came over them as if she'd been waiting all this time to see him again.

Kyle groaned in response and fought the urge to pull her into his arms and take her mouth. Her everything.

He cleared his throat and reached out his hand with the roses.

"Can we talk?" he asked, sounding a little hoarse.

Sellie's expression revealed her hesitation. Kyle wasn't really surprised. Talk would mean letting him in. Talk would be civil. But the vibe between them was anything but civil. No matter how hard he tried to suppress his attraction and urges, he was quite sure it oozed out of him.

All he could think of, and had been thinking of the last few weeks, was him on top of her, making her come again and again. He pushed the thoughts away.

"I promise I'll behave. But I do like to talk," Kyle said with a polite smile.

The brief glint of disappointment in her eyes didn't go unnoticed. It took all his control not to lower his eyes and stare at her breasts, but he knew — sensed — her nipples were hard and that she was as aroused as he was. He wasn't so sure anymore that he could behave.

Then Sellie nodded, took the flowers from him and stepped aside to let him in. Not wanting to give her time to change her mind, he walked past her into the narrow hallway. His upper arm brushed over her breasts, making her gasp. Kyle mumbled an excuse.

Talk, Kyle. Not plunder!

Sellie swallowed hard. How did a man get her so needy without even saying or doing anything much? This was going to be difficult. The aura of power that exuded from him filled the entire hallway, as did his large frame.

She closed the front door and invited him to go into the living room. No way was she going to walk past him and risk touching him. Hauling in a breath, she followed him into her own home.

"Please sit down," she said and walked into the kitchen to put the roses in a vase. They were beautiful and smelled really nice too. She put her nose in them to inhale the sweet scent.

"They reminded me of your hair."

The soft words sent a tremor through her and made her blush.

"Thank you. They're beautiful." Her voice shook a little.

"So are you!"

She sensed his presence behind her. He was very close. The skin on her back started to tingle as if he'd touched her.

"Sellie," he whispered.

She turned around.

"Please, Kyle…" she started. Then their eyes locked and her voice trailed off. She was breathless, mesmerized by his blue eyes and the fire in them.

"Please, what? Please leave? Please talk?" Kyle's face was level, but his voice was a little throaty. The lust she heard in it sent need spiraling up from her core.

"Please take me!"

He groaned and pulled her against his hard body, a hand behind her head and the other on her ass. The second their lips touched, fire seared through her body. Sellie moaned into his mouth when Kyle pushed his pelvis forward as he plundered her mouth with his tongue.

She pushed herself off the ground and wrapped her legs around him so she could feel his erection against her pussy. Another moan came from her.

Right when she was about to lose her sanity, Kyle pulled back.

"We need to talk," he panted into her hair. Sellie keened a protest and bucked her hips, pressing her crotch against his raging hard-on.

"No. Yes... Please. Kyle, please!"

He growled when she brushed her breasts over his chest. Then he peeled her off him, had them both stripped in a heartbeat, got a condom out of his wallet and put her with her ass on the edge of the kitchen counter. She wrapped her arms around his neck and offered him her lips.

"I'd love to see that rosebud around my cock." His deep voice sounded thick with lust. The words and the thought sent a tiny jolt through her clit. She'd love to suck him, to tease and please him, to get him to the edge of orgasm over and over, yet not allow him to come. She peered at him through her lashes and smiled her sexiest smile.

"Where have you been all my life?" he mumbled.

He took her mouth, and when he ran his fingers over her inner thighs, close to her needy pussy, she spread her legs for him. He went up, traced over her mound, down again over her labia. Her breath hitched as he slid toward her entrance, slow and teasing, not touching her aching clit. Desire washed through her. She was so wet. Then he slid part of his finger inside her and held it still. Her brain turned to mush.

Kyle let go of her lips.

"Next time I want you bald," he whispered.

He put his thumb next to her clit and stimulated the sensitive area, and a mewl broke from her lips.

"I'd love to lick your bald pussy." As if to demonstrate, he lapped erotically over her cheekbone, all the while moving his thumb right up against her clit. Her vagina clamped down on his finger.

"Please, Kyle!"

He continued teasing her with his fingers, ignoring her plea.

"Will you be bald for my mouth next time, Sellie?" he mumbled in her ear, licking the sensitive inside. A shiver ran up her spine. "Shave those pretty curls so I can lick and taste the flesh of your cunt?"

Her pussy clenched again and he laughed.

"Yes. Yes. I will."

Her head was spinning. She didn't care. If he wanted her bald, she'd be bald. Right now she wanted him to…

He rammed his finger deep inside her tight pussy and her cry bounced off the kitchen walls. He held her stable with one arm, finger-fucking her while his thumb started rubbing over her clit.

"Brace yourself, baby," he growled. "You're going to come for me, and come hard."

He worked her pussy, and her need rose until her entire body seemed to burn. Her clit swelled against his thumb.

Then he bent his head and sucked a nipple into his mouth, and she exploded. Her body shook out of her control. Her shrill cries of exquisite pleasure rang in her ears. Before the last aftershock had left her body, he sheathed himself in the condom and buried his cock to the root inside her. Sellie whined.

"Oh damn, no! Too much," she slurred and dug her fingernails into his biceps.

Kyle withdrew a little, his breathing ragged.

"No, don't! Don't!" she begged, blind with passion.

"Don't what, Sellie? You want me to stop?"

"No! Damn, no! More!"

His low groan made her shiver. He pulled back, then gave her every inch of his length.

"I love it when a woman begs me." His voice had gone low with desire.

Then he took her hard. Ruthless. Taking and plundering with his cock, her hungry, wet cunt receiving. Each time he thrust into her, her clit throbbed and her pussy clenched, the slides driving her to the point of no return.

She put her feet on his ass to get him even deeper, and to have his body move over her nub. Glorious heat spread up and out from her core. Her clit was throbbing, her leg muscles began to tremble and her nipples tingled and got so hard it almost hurt. The sensation of nearing the zenith of climax blanked her mind. Time seemed to stand still as her entire being and body craved that one thrust to send her over the edge. He rammed his cock deep inside her cunt and the fire in her lower body exploded.

"Yesss, ooooh yesss!"

The pressure release pushed up tongues of fire that seared her as she came. She could do nothing but surrender to her need. She cried out in joy as exhilarating shocks of pleasure raced over her nerves and made her spasm, again and again.

His orgasmic roar sent another heat wave through her and a wonderful sense of possessiveness filled her when he came inside her.

The waves turned to ripples and she shuddered as he fucked the last aftershocks out of her.

When his legs were strong enough to carry him again, he pulled out and got rid of the condom. He drew her into his arms and held her for long, wonderful minutes. Her soft body felt so good against his, a perfect fit. He breathed in the scent of her shampoo. A fresh aroma that reminded him of the ocean.

"Siren," he mumbled.

Sellie glanced up, still a little dazed. The look of a completely sated woman.

"What?" she asked.

"You. That's what you are," he said softly, tugging a strand of her red hair. "My sexy, fiery siren."

She giggled.

"Sounds more like a fury to me," she said, and pressed a kiss to his chest.

"Oh yes, that's you all right." He grinned. "And I'm not complaining."

Sellie's cheeks got pink, but she didn't shy away from his gaze.

"I wouldn't think so. I'm quite sure even my neighbors lit a cigarette when they heard you roar a few minutes ago!" she said with a cheeky smile.

"Behave, woman!" He attempted to sound serious, but even he heard the amusement in his own voice. "I'm quite sure your sexy shrieks made them light an entire pack!"

Even though her cheeks were dark red now as she recalled how loud she'd been, she started laughing.

Kyle's insides melted when he heard the sparkling sound.

And he admired her spirit, how she didn't try to hide her shyness. He ran his fingers over her cheek.

"Let's talk, Sellie. And we best get dressed. If we don't, I fear I'm going to take you again!"

Sellie sucked in a breath and her gaze dropped to his groin. Kyle chuckled.

"Not there yet, but if you keep looking at me like that, it won't take long."

They both got dressed and Sellie got them something to drink, then they sat down at the dinner table.

"I'm going to be direct, Sellie. I want to see you again," Kyle started.

"Yes. I'd like that too," she said.

"But… You know about the club. I own it. I am part of it. I am a Master, Sellie," he continued. "I've given vanilla relationships a whirl, but it doesn't work out for me. It's not…fulfilling. I need more."

He observed her as she took his words in and didn't miss the shiver that went through her body. His heart hammered in his chest as he waited for her reply. The woman was smart—she'd work it out. She'd known he was a Master. She had seen the dungeon.

"H-how…how m-much more?" she stammered.

Kyle let out a soft sigh of relief. At least she hadn't said no right away.

Yet he hesitated to answer the question. Telling her he'd not only like to tie her up, but fancied spanking, flogging, the occasional caning, specific forms of humiliation, public play, nipple and pussy clamps, and so on would sound horrible without context and understanding. But he didn't want to lie or beat around the bush either.

"A lot more," he said, his voice soft. The glint of lust in her eyes surprised him. Then again, not really. She was spirited enough to be able to enjoy at least mild BDSM activities. All of a sudden, he was quite sure she'd get aroused by a spanking, if the timing and setting were right. And he hoped that—with the right guidance—she could enjoy a lot more. But she'd have to make an informed decision.

"Explain." Not much more than a whisper, but the interest in her eyes was encouraging. He decided to give it to her straight.

"I want it all. Your total submission, mind, body and soul. Not always. That's called 24/7 and I'm not into that. But when I play, I want it all."

Her breath hitched and her nipples blossomed. His cock jerked. Then the spark in her eyes turned to trepidation.

"I don't like to be forced to wear masks and have the shit whipped out of me!"

Kyle sensed she was pulling back from him.

"It's not about that, Sellie. Not for me. Some people may enjoy that, but I'm not one of them," he said and smiled to reassure her. "There are many flavors, like with regular sex. Some like it rough, some like it tender, or anything in between. In BDSM it's not so different."

Kyle took a sip of his coffee.

"You want me to explain a bit more?" he asked.

She nodded.

About an hour later, he finished. He had told her enough to make sure she knew a lot more about BDSM than she had when he'd turned up on her doorstep. No matter how fast her brain worked, he was quite sure she needed some time to let it sink in. They sat in silence for a bit and Kyle assessed her — her cheeks were hot, her breathing a little fast. He sensed her excitement and decided to be bold.

"Are you wet, Sellie?" he asked, as casual as if he was asking about the weather.

She gave him a shocked look, turned a crimson red and got up from her chair.

"I think it's time for you to go," she said in a voice so sharp it could have cut him. She picked up her empty cup, walked into the kitchen and put it on the worktop. When she turned around, he stood right in front of her, got even closer, pinning her between him and the worktop. Deliberately looming over her.

"Answer the question, Sellie. Are you wet?" He put his Master-power into his penetrating stare and was pleased to see her eyes widen.

"You cannot —" she started.

"I can, and I will check for myself if you don't answer!" He managed to bite back *sub*.

"You wouldn't!" she gasped. He didn't speak, just held her with his gaze. "I am not one of your subs!"

Kyle cupped her chin, bent his head so his face was an inch from hers.

"Answer!" He kept his voice soft, like a caress, aware that it contradicted the power he'd put in his eyes. A shiver went through her.

"Yes," she whispered.

"Thank you, Sellie," he said and pulled her in his arms. He felt how she calmed down, her muscles relaxing as she melted against him. He smiled into her hair. *A beautiful, submissive woman.*

"I will do as you've asked and go. Is it okay if I contact you again?" he asked.

She nodded. "Yes."

He heard the eagerness in her voice and his heart jumped for joy that she wanted more. Kyle took himself a sweet, tender kiss. He withdrew and looked her over, her expression easy to read. She was wet and ready, yearning for his touch. Exactly how he liked to see a woman. But now it was his cue to go and leave her aching for him.

With the words, "Speak to you soon, siren," he left her standing there.

Chapter Six

Rebecca had had a busy day in the office and she was happy to go home. Kyle had left in the afternoon and Sellie had been working in the dungeon all day. Rebecca cleaned up her desk and walked into the kitchenette to grab herself a cup of coffee before leaving. Sellie was doing the same thing.

"Ah, there you are!" Rebecca said with a smile. "Kyle asked me to give you this."

She handed Sellie a package, and when her friend blushed, both curiosity and concern welled up in Rebecca. Sellie's reaction and body language told her that the package wasn't work related.

"Sellie, it's not really any of my business, but I care about you," she started, not certain how to open a conversation about BDSM with a vanilla girl. It had been difficult enough with her friend Olivia at the time. And was it okay for her to address the issue, or would that be an infringement of Kyle's privacy?

She sighed. *Might as well cut the crap.*

"Are you aware that Kyle is into BDSM?" she asked.

Sellie's cheeks got a crimson red now and she dropped her gaze.

"He has told me," she replied. "Explained some things to me. But it's all..."

"Overwhelming? Confusing? Mind-boggling?" Rebecca asked, a smile pulling at her lips, happy that Kyle had at least told her something. "Sellie, I think we should get together and talk. Cal and I... Well..."

Sellie's eyes got wide, then they danced with laughter.

"I should have known." She chuckled. "Getting me a job here, you working here. Normally speaking, I'm pretty good at doing the math, but you sure as heck had me fooled!"

Rebecca laughed.

"I'm sorry, but not everyone is open-minded," she said. "But now the cat is out of the bag... How about we go out for drinks tomorrow? We can talk about it. I'll answer any question you have."

Sellie agreed, looking eager to hear more about the ins and outs of BDSM.

"My package," Sellie mumbled.

"You want me to leave?" Rebecca asked.

Sellie shook her head, tore open the envelope, reached inside and took out a book. An erotic BDSM novel. And a note. After she'd read it, she read it out to Rebecca.

"If you want to learn more, understand me better, please read this book. Kyle."

Rebecca hummed, pleased that the note was not too personal and didn't say anything that pressured Sellie. It was more of a request with no strings attached, no matter what she'd decide to do with it.

Sellie eyed Rebecca.

"He wants me to read this book," she mumbled.

"And he made me give it to you. Sneaky bastard!" Rebecca replied. Kyle knew how protective and helpful Rebecca was, and she realized he was using her as a middleman to raise the subject with Sellie. After all, hearing that her friend was into the lifestyle as well would make opening up to it easier for her. And thus for Kyle as well.

"You think he deliberately gave it to you so you…?"

"Oh, I don't think, I know! You have no idea what these men are like!" Rebecca laughed. "I'd say you best get reading tonight, and we go for drinks tomorrow — if you want to, that is?"

Sellie very much wanted that. She started to collect her things to go home. In the doorway she turned around.

"Oh, and you've got a lot of explaining to do, Becca!" she said with a cheeky smile. "Keeping such sexy things from me!"

Rebecca just grinned.

Chapter Seven

After dinner, Sellie curled up on the sofa with the book. Soon she was sucked into the story. Some things she read about turned her off, other things turned her on. She completely lost track of time until she started to yawn a lot and one glance at the clock said it was close to four a.m.

Damn, I have to get to bed! She had an early start, having to go over to the club to work on the mural. She brushed her teeth, got into a nightie and slipped into bed. Her hand drifted toward her crotch. She was still aroused and she knew she wouldn't be able to sleep if she didn't please herself. After a really good orgasm, she fell asleep with a smile on her face.

She was sure no more than five minutes had gone by when the alarm went off. She groaned. She pressed the snooze button and turned around, wanting a few more minutes.

As if struck by lightning, Sellie sat up in bed in one go, wide awake, and checked the time.

Oh. My. God! Eleven o'clock. Shit.

She rushed out of bed, had a quick shower and drove over to the club. She walked in and barged straight into Kyle's solid frame. He knocked the wind out of her.

"I'm sorry. I really am. I just... I-I," she stammered.

A corner of Kyle's mouth turned up as he took her in, hair tousled, eyes still a bit sleepy, heat rising up from her neck and onto her cheeks. Guilt and embarrassment washed through her.

"That good, huh!" Not a question.

She got that he was referring to the book, and her cheeks got even warmer. He chuckled.

"Kitchen. Cappuccino." Not a question either.

"But the painting..." she objected.

"Can wait." He turned around and walked to the kitchen, certain she would follow.

Rebecca was in the office and Sellie caught her eyes. They gleamed with laughter. Sellie glared. Rebecca shrugged.

"Get used to it," she said with a smile.

Sellie walked into the kitchen.

"I do not like..."

Before there was time to finish her sentence, Kyle was looming over her, pinning her with nothing but his piercing blue eyes. Sellie's mouth went dry and her pussy got wet.

"You don't like what?" he asked, his voice soft.

Her brain cells had melted, making it impossible for her to remember what she was going to say. She could do nothing but stand there motionless and look into his eyes. *Such strong eyes.* He smiled a knowing smile, then his gaze let her go. Relief as well as a sense of loss washed through her.

Kyle pulled back a chair, inviting her to take a seat. Somehow her legs still seemed to work and she sat down at the table.

A few minutes later he put a cappuccino and a sandwich in front of her.

"I don't—"

"I think you do," he interrupted again.

Her temperament woke up now. She did not like to be interrupted, nor have decisions made for her about when she should eat.

"Woman, you didn't even comb your hair. I doubt you had breakfast," he said with a slight smile as he lifted his arm with a theatrical movement to glance at his watch. "Oh, lunch."

Sellie felt like an overripe tomato, and completely off-kilter, unable to fathom whether he was addressing her as her boss, her lover, or a friend. Was he putting her in her place as her employer for being late or simply toying with her as a sub-to-be?

The book had taught her that this was what Doms could do to their subs. But where reading about it had been arousing and seemed like a whole lot of fun, having it happen to her turned out to be somewhat different. A lot different. She didn't like it one bit. She didn't like to feel tongue-tied, overwhelmed and confused, nor being made self-conscious about her appearance. She combed her fingers through her hair in an attempt to make it look a bit better.

All the while he sat there, observing her.

"Stop doing that! I'm not your guinea pig!" she snapped.

She expected and hoped for some reaction, him getting up. Anything. Anything to make him stop studying her like she was some test rat in a lab.

The only reaction she got out of him was a glint in his eyes. One she couldn't read.

"I'm way past guinea pigs, Sellie. I go for what I want. And I want it all." His voice was so soft it was barely audible, and both that and the words sent a quiver through her.

His unspoken *'And I want you!'* lingered between them and the air seemed to thicken around her, heavy, laden with his power and desire. She couldn't escape from it, had to breathe it in. It made her head spin and her core glow.

Although she wasn't a lightweight herself, when opposing Kyle, she seemed more like a domesticated cat facing a lion. He could tease, toy, tempt and overwhelm her at will, and she knew that if she gave her consent, he would. Her lower body got melty and butterflies danced in her stomach. Something inside her wanted him to do that. Longed for him to make her, take her, devour her. Yet when he did, like right now, it was...awkward. Scary as hell, but exciting and arousing at the same time.

Her feelings were all over the place. This was all so confusing.

"Eat, Sellie."

Her stomach growled in response. Damn, she was hungry! She let out a breath, grabbed the sandwich and started to eat. Somehow the air seemed to lift, as if he could not only control her responses, but the elements as well.

Kyle sat in silence while she ate the BLT sandwich he'd made her.

"God, that was good!" She let out a content sigh when she'd swallowed the last bite.

Kyle leaned forward and wiped a tiny bit of BBQ sauce from her lips with his finger. He held it in front of her mouth and, without thinking, she licked it off. The sensation was so erotic and time seemed to stand still as she looked into his eyes. The heat in them seared her and her insides tingled.

"Time to get to work, Sellie." His hot breath brushed over her wet lips.

Damn. She needed to get away from him and his overwhelming aura of power. Right now!

She pushed the chair back so fast it almost tumbled to the ground, and she all but ran from the kitchen, his soft laugh following her all the way to the dungeon.

* * * *

It took her quite some time to get going with the painting. At some point Rebecca called her for a break and a drink. They talked about their meeting that night, and agreed on a time and place.

"Hang in there, girlfriend," Rebecca said before they both went back to work. "From what I can tell, you're doing great!"

"I beg to differ on that one, but thank you!" Sellie grinned. "I got the sneaking suspicion I ain't seen nothing yet."

Although Rebecca's nod wasn't too reassuring, she managed to forget about it all when she was working. After a while, her stomach told her she needed food. Sellie sighed. She couldn't go home yet. She'd missed out on an entire morning — she couldn't afford to miss out on pay, and it was her own fault for not going to bed on time.

"Time to clean up."

Kyle's voice. Sellie spun around and saw him standing in the doorway, resting his shoulder against the doorjamb.

"But I should —"

"Stop. Right now." The command in his voice had her nailed to the floor. It didn't take her long to snap out of her stupor, and fury bubbled up inside her about being interrupted by him yet again. She did not like it one bit, and she almost spat it out.

"I know. It's irritating, isn't it." Kyle pushed himself off the doorjamb and sauntered over to her.

As he strode closer, slow but agile, he assessed her. And the hunger in his gaze showed he was pleased with what he saw. It was most unsettling. And annoying that he could get under her skin with the blink of an eye.

"I'm not some meek puppy that you can order around." Why didn't she sound the least bit strong?

As he towered over her, the warmth from his body penetrating hers, her brain turned to mush.

"I don't want a meek puppy, Sellie." His low, smooth voice made her core quiver. "I want a fiery siren."

Kyle wrapped a strand of red hair around his index finger and tugged, then traced over her trembling bottom lip.

"I want that beautiful rosebud to beg." The words barely audible, but powerful nonetheless. "Begging for my cock. Your soft velvety lips around me. Sucking me."

A soft mewl broke from her.

"I don't beg," she whispered.

"You will."

She knew he was right. It was only a matter of time. Sellie swallowed hard. She should get away from him. Run and hide. But she was transfixed by his eyes and his touch.

Minutes went by before he spoke again.

"Go home, Sellie. I'll see you tomorrow."

With that, he turned and strode out, leaving her hot and bothered and trembling all over. Again.

Chapter Eight

"So how does it all work? Are people who like this sick in the head? Do they have mental problems? If I am interested in it, does that mean I'm not sane?"

Sellie fired a whole lot of questions at Rebecca, who raised her hands in the air.

"Hold up, girl." She laughed. "One at the time, please!"

They waited as their drinks arrived.

Rebecca tried to explain as best as she could and answer all of Sellie's questions. Which took quite some time, as she kept asking more.

Rebecca told her about her first steps in the realms of BDSM, after a bad experience with a partner a few years before that.

"I met Kyle in a diner, he offered me a job, and from there on it was one roller-coaster ride. Please don't get offended, it's been a while ago, but first…first Kyle and I thought there was something between us."

A hint of jealousy stung Sellie, but she realized it was ridiculous even to go there about something that had happened way before she had met Kyle.

Rebecca was open to Sellie about what had gone down, how they had found out it didn't work between them and how Kyle had then introduced her to Cal, who had swept her off her feet. Literally. And how he had given her a good walloping after she'd bitten his lip.

Both Sellie and Rebecca laughed about the story.

"It bloody hurt like hell, but then I...I submitted. Something opened up inside me, and I felt set free. It was the most glorious sensation, so intense and liberating!"

Sellie saw the spark in her friend's eyes. It was the look of a woman who belonged and was home. An odd sense of longing stabbed her heart. She wanted that as well.

A soft glow came over Rebecca as she spoke of her wedding, the handfasting and the collaring ceremony.

"Wow, that sounds awesome!" Sellie exclaimed. "You lucky girl!"

"Oh, I am. Very lucky indeed." The love in Rebecca's gaze made Sellie smile. She knew she wanted that too. The love, the sense of belonging. But with Kyle it would come hand in hand with submission. And like he'd said, he wanted it all. And she wasn't sure about that yet.

"So...I don't mean to pry, but I'm dying to learn more," Sellie said. "Do you submit often? And does he always spank you to get you there?"

Rebecca giggled.

"We play regularly, and yes, when we do I submit. But no, spanking isn't always on the menu. Yes, he does spank me at times, but a Master has a lot more tools than just his hands," she said. "You know, his biggest tool is his mind. His intent. His desire to lead, to protect and nurture. To make sure you get what you need. Mind you, not what you want, but what you need. Of course you have to be with the right partner. There has to be a click, attraction, so you desire to please him and he desires to lead you. He takes, and by doing so he gives. If you got that, you fulfill each other's needs. You still can be a pain in the ass every now and then, though. But know that when you are, he will be one too. Oh, some of the things I've done and said!"

Rebecca's laugh was infectious and Sellie couldn't help but grin.

"Meaning you don't roll over and play sub?" she asked.

"Hell no!" Rebecca chuckled. "I can be a real troublemaker. And Cal can be strict, but sometimes he enjoys giving me just enough rope to hang myself with. And we're not always in Dom/sub mode either. I have my work, so does he. I'm not under his authority or command 24/7. Often we're much like every other couple in love. But it's not restricted to the bedroom either. Sometimes it simply comes up. The fact it can happen anytime, anywhere, is part of the thrill to me. If it had defined borders, like bedroom-only, I think I'd get bored. I like my Master to be inventive, flexible, playful, and to pick up on the dynamic of the moment."

"I'd like to see this Cal of yours," Sellie replied.

Rebecca grabbed her phone and showed her a picture of Cal and herself.

"Oh my goodness!" Sellie gasped.

Her friend appeared confused. "What?"

"I've seen him!" Sellie recovered from her shock and started laughing until her stomach hurt. She was still hiccupping when she told Rebecca about her first encounter with Kyle, and how Cal had walked in on them, Kyle on top of her, passionately kissing each other.

Now Rebecca shook with laughter as well.

"But your man, he's erm... Quite something. Daunting," Sellie said, remembering the dark-haired man.

"I call him Wolf Man." Rebecca's eyes got dreamy.

"Isn't that typical. I think of Kyle as a lion. Or King of the Jungle." Sellie chuckled. "But please don't ever tell him!"

"These men are like wild animals, aren't they?" Rebecca agreed. "I get the lion, but why King of the Jungle?"

"Have you not seen how he moves through the dungeon? It is his domain, his home. His jungle. He reigns there."

"Very clever!" Rebecca was impressed. Her friend had picked up a lot more than she was aware of. Even though other people played at the club, it was still Kyle's place. It was open and inviting to everyone, but there was something in Kyle's gait that stood out whenever he moved through the dungeon. Without making any effort to imprint his ownership on anything or anyone, it just oozed out of him. It was still his jungle.

Now that they were so openly sharing, Rebecca decided to tell Sellie the story of the infamous butt plug she was made to wear the other day.

"You remember when I walked in on you and Kyle? I sensed something had gone down between you two, and I glared at him."

When she'd finished the story, Sellie let out a shocked "Oh my God! That's awful!" Now she understood why Rebecca had wobbled the way she had, and she swallowed.

"I don't think I'm cut out for this," she said, sounding troubled.

"Punishment isn't always fun, but they never give you more than you can bear. They will push your limits, yes, but no is no. Cal would never whip me extremely hard, because I don't want that. I don't like severe pain." Rebecca grabbed Sellie's hand and stroked it with her fingers.

"Sellie, I'm not going to lie to you. It's not all pleasure and great sex. Punishment from time to time is part of it. Not for the heck of it. In context. With a reason. And somehow you will find you need that too. If you're a sub."

"I need another drink," Sellie mumbled with a sigh.

They ordered new drinks and chatted about other things for a while, but soon the conversation circled back to sex and BDSM.

Rebecca gave her a cheeky smile and leaned forward.

"There's more to that butt plug story," she said with a husky laugh. "A butt plug is quite arousing, and by the time I got home, I was turned on beyond belief. Cal was aware of that, of course. Next, the asshole made me wait, teased me and aroused me even more. In the end, when he… Gosh, just thinking about it almost makes me come again!"

Excitement had colored her cheeks a cute pink. Sellie giggled.

"That sounds quite...sexy." She heard the curiosity and wonder in her own voice.

"Well, since we're quite open with one another... Have you ever had anal sex?" When Sellie nodded, she continued. "Think of being with Kyle, flirting, teasing, working each other up, and him doing his Master thing. He's done it to you, so you know what I mean. And then, when you're all excited, he would start playing with that other part of you and puts a butt plug in there. Doesn't have to be a large one—there are small ones too. Think of it, imagine it. Would that really be so bad?"

The heat that crept up from Sellie's chest to her face spoke for itself.

"That's what I mean." Rebecca sounded husky. "Some things appear to be off-putting or scary when you read or hear about them, but when you receive them in the right setting, with the right person, they are oh-so-exciting. And it's like that with many things."

"I get your point," Sellie replied. "You're telling me to not be so quick to judge."

Rebecca nodded.

"Yes. Take your time. It's clear you are interested. Intrigued even," she said. "Kyle is trustworthy, knows what he's doing, and he will never force himself upon you. You cannot be in safer hands to explore BDSM. And that in itself is valuable. There are a lot of idiots out there, wannabe Masters and Doms, who wouldn't hesitate to prey on a sub. With Kyle you needn't worry about that."

Sellie wrinkled her nose.

"He said he'd want it all."

Rebecca laughed.

"Yes. He would! And he will!" She grinned. "Oh, Sellie, you should see the expression on your face. Priceless! But I think you want him to take it all! As a matter of fact, I'm almost convinced of it."

Sellie lowered her gaze, uncomfortable with her friend's accurate assessment.

"Ow, sweetie, don't do that," Rebecca said softly as she grabbed Sellie's hand and squeezed it. "It's okay. I need the same thing from my Master. And there's thousands of people like us."

Sellie looked up, tears pooling in her eyes.

"You're right. And it's becoming clear that I want that too. But it's so damned scary!" she whispered. "He's so strong! I may be a newbie, but I do know he will ask a lot. Everything. I don't want to change into someone else and turn into some meek puppy!"

"Sellie, you won't! Do I seem like a meek puppy to you? Kyle will take, and yes, he will demand a lot. But instead of reducing you to a spineless woman, he'll help you grow and develop. It'll make you open up and set you free. He won't ask for more than you are willing to give. But he will push you for sure. Because often you aren't aware of how much you want and need to give in order to be whole. Trust me on that, Sellie!"

Sellie took in a shuddering breath.

"My intuition tells me you're spot on. But it's still scary!" she sighed.

"Well, it wouldn't be right if you walked in there, inexperienced, yet being confident about it all. It's part of it," Rebecca said.

"I guess you're right," Sellie mumbled. "So what do I do next?"

"You go for it. Kyle won't throw you in the deep end. Trust, girl. Even though he's a Master, has he done anything so far that you didn't want? Did he lose control at any point? No, I didn't think so. So trust him. He'll take you by the hand and let you explore at a pace you can deal with," Rebecca smiled. "And don't underestimate the knowledge you have acquired in this short time. You're an eager student."

They both laughed, ordered new drinks and talked about more lighthearted things until it was time to go home.

Before they got into their cars, they hugged each other.

"Thank you, Rebecca! You're worth your weight in gold," Sellie said.

"You're welcome, Sellie! You go get your Master!"

Chapter Nine

Thursday had gone by. She'd made good progress with the mural in the dungeon. By four p.m. she had gotten everything out of the club so no Master or Dom would trip over paint pots on Friday night. The thought still made her giggle.

The lanai trompe-l'oeil, a beautiful painting of arches with an ocean view, was finished, meaning she had Friday off. Which was perfect considering the plans she had. Rebecca had come up with it, and Cal had agreed to cooperate.

Sellie arrived at the club at ten p.m. sharp. Cal and Rebecca arrived at the same time. The man intimidated her right away. He looked different from when she'd seen him in the garden the first time, when Kyle had been on top of her. It was obvious he was in Master-mode now.

He took her in, introduced himself as Master Cal, and his dark eyes seemed to see straight through her. She tried to hold herself under his assessment, but found she couldn't, and lowered her gaze. He put his hand under her chin, tilted her face up and smiled at her, almost gentle.

"You'll be fine, sweetie. Don't worry," he mumbled.

Sellie nodded.

"Thank you," she whispered.

They walked in, then had to spend some time at the reception desk as she had to read a pile of forms and sign them. Master Cal insisted she read them all, and she did. She was impressed, and overwhelmed, by the club rules and regulations on behavior, safety, Dungeon Masters, alcohol and drugs, and so on. When she signed the forms, her hand was trembling a bit.

Sellie had been informed that she would be Master Cal's guest, as the club was members only.

When the paperwork was done, Master Cal said, "Rebecca has requested to spend some time with you and introduce you to other subs. I've agreed, but you got one hour. After that, I will require my sub myself."

Sellie nodded again, then rushed to say, "Thank you!"

Master Cal raised an eyebrow.

"You have to address Dominants the right way, Sellie. Starting now." The soft-spoken command shook her.

"Thank you, S-Sir," she stammered. *Damn, it was awkward to say that!*

Master Cal made an approving sound.

"Good. Let's go." And to Rebecca, "One hour, sub! Not a minute longer!"

"Yes, Sir, thank you!" Rebecca replied with a grateful smile.

Master Cal went into the dungeon and the girls entered the dressing room. As Sellie put her coat in a locker, Rebecca whistled.

"Girl, you look a treat! Turn around, let me see you!"

Sellie blushed but did what Rebecca had asked her to do. She'd gone for a siren costume as a way to let Kyle know that she wanted to be his and was willing to set foot into the realms of BDSM with him. And she was darned proud of her fiery gold siren costume with iridescent turquoise fish scales on the skirt. The bra top had two golden cups resembling shells and thanks to transparent straps it seemed to be held in place by nothing but her breasts.

The long, form-fitting skirt rode low on her hips and even the tiniest of movements set off sparks of gold and turquoise.

"That is one of the sexiest outfits I've ever seen in my life," Rebecca cheered. "But how on Earth can you walk in it?"

Sellie grinned as she stepped forward, revealing two long splits that stopped a few inches short of her crotch.

Rebecca's jaw dropped. "Kyle is going to have a heart attack when he sees you!"

"You think it's too much?" Sellie frowned. Maybe she should've gone for something simpler. A latex dress, for instance.

"No freaking way! You're going to steal the show," Rebecca exclaimed. "Besides, this has 'Sellie' written all over it. Kyle will love it."

For an instant Sellie hesitated, then blurted, "There's more, and I need your help with it."

She rummaged in her bag and dug up three pieces of filigree jewelry, inlaid with faux gems.

"What on earth is that?" Rebecca asked as she touched the items.

"For my arms and one for my leg." Sellie beamed as she held them out.

"Gosh, you're going for it, aren't you?"

Rebecca helped her with the filigree upper-arm cuffs. Next, she fastened the leg jewelry that ran from Sellie's knee to her ankle. It wasn't visible when she stood still, but as soon as she moved, the splits opened up and the jewelry flashed to life.

"What about shoes?" Rebecca pointed at Sellie's bare feet.

Sellie shook her head.

"All set now?" Rebecca asked.

"One last thing, hang on!" Sellie's tone was full of excitement. "Be honest and tell me if you like it or not!"

She undid her hairclip and her locks tumbled down her back, showing off strands that were dip-dyed in various colors. Some were neon green, others aqua, yellow and indigo, making her red hair appear even brighter.

Rebecca sucked in a breath.

"Damn, girl! You got taste. Your hair is on fire!"

Sellie laughed.

"That was the idea." She smiled. "Kyle called me 'siren' a few times, so, well…"

"Ah, you're already dressing to impress your Master." Rebecca giggled.

Sellie's face flushed.

"I hadn't thought of it like that." She chewed on her bottom lip. "I wish I'd gone for something different now."

"Oh, nonsense. Kyle is going to love it. As will everybody else, so be prepared, you're going to get a lot of attention," Rebecca warned. "You ready?"

"Not really," Sellie mumbled. Now that the moment was here, she wasn't so sure anymore that this was a good idea.

"Well, we have to go," Rebecca decided. "I've only got an hour, remember. And I don't want to piss Cal off when he's doing me a favor."

Sellie nodded, nervous as hell.

"Let's do it."

She walked to the door with more bravura than she had, and they entered the dungeon side by side.

The moment the door closed behind them, Sellie wanted to run back out.

"Fuck, the dungeon's different now," she cursed under her breath.

"Yep, it is!" Rebecca agreed, grabbed her friend's arm and guided her toward the bar.

"Crap, I'm not sure..." Sellie objected as everybody seemed to be gawking.

"Yes, you are!" Rebecca stepped back and faced her. "Take a breath. That's right. Another one. Good. You're a strong woman. Tap into that."

Sellie calmed down a bit, drawing strength from Rebecca's resolve and confidence. The sounds she heard alone were unsettling. Moans, screams, whips being used, clanking chains. Sounds and smells of arousal and sex. And on top of that, the visual input. There were people taking her in, submissives and slaves walking around half naked, and Masters and Doms dressed to intimidate. Sellie dared to glance around the dungeon and saw people being tied up, someone suspended in ropes, a woman being taken by two men, a half-naked man on his knees with his head between the legs of a woman who was sat on a throne.

"Breathe, Sellie." Rebecca's voice again.

"I-I… I'm good. I-I think," Sellie stammered.

"Okay, let's get a drink, then I'll show you around in the more quiet areas, introduce you to some of the other single subs so that when I'm with Cal, you can…"

While Rebecca was talking, Sellie spotted Kyle halfway across the dungeon. He was to-die-for sexy in dark brown leathers that hugged his muscular thighs. Her gaze went up to the black V-neck shirt that emphasized his broad shoulders and chest and his muscular arms. The arms that felt so good around her, the chest with the crisp golden hair that rubbed over her nipples when he took her. The man she wanted to be with.

When she glanced at his face, she knew she'd fallen head over heels in love with Kyle. But in here he was Master Kyle. Her heart was pounding, her cheeks had gotten warm with arousal and somehow her bra top seemed too small for her breasts.

How she loved his masculine jawline, not smoothly shaven now but with a bit of stubble, and his lips that were so firm when he kissed her.

She started to move closer, as if drawn toward him by an invisible force. He chose that exact moment to spin around, and their eyes locked. A shiver ran up her spine as she stood there, transfixed by the electricity that surged between them, even over that distance.

The awe and appreciation in his expression melted her insides and tingling sensations shot through her. Then something about him changed, and a corner of his mouth turned up as comprehension blossomed in his gaze. A sudden possessiveness radiated off him.

Oh hell, he gets it. She'd wanted that, but in her enthusiasm it had eluded her that it would give him carte blanche to be her Master. Now that his full-blown attention was upon her, she felt like a fish out of water. Her heart was racing as she almost panicked, realizing she'd underestimated the implications of being exposed to a dominant's power. Her legs almost gave out underneath her when Kyle started moving. He stalked closer and closer, agile and dominant, never breaking the eye contact, pinning her with his gaze like a predator would.

It was scary as hell, yet the sensation of being overpowered sent delicious tremors through her body. An urgent heat rose from her core and her pussy dampened. She wanted to be his prey, his everything. When he stopped in front of her, tall and handsome, she was lightheaded and yearning for him to kiss her, to take her, to take from her. Anything and everything.

"Has your boat crashed on the rocks yet?" A mere whisper, her cheeks warm.

Kyle groaned, fisted her hair, tipped her head back and took her mouth. His lips demanded she open up for him and he swept in. The kiss was so hot and intense that her head spun and she clung to him for balance. He splayed his fingers over her behind and pulled her against his erection, and she moaned.

When he withdrew, she needed the strong arm around her hips for support to keep her stable. She glanced up at him, having difficulty focusing.

"My boat crashed the second I laid eyes on you, girl," he said, sounding hoarse. "I think it's beyond repair. And I will punish you for that."

The promise sent a shiver down her spine as both lust and mild fear welled up inside her. Kyle brushed a finger over her jawline, making her quiver.

"Don't worry, siren girl, you will enjoy it," he whispered. "But for now you'll need these."

He took leather handcuffs from his belt and had put them on her before she could even react or object. She stared at them, not sure what to think of it, then glanced up at Kyle.

"I'm not..." She swallowed, not sure what to say, still bedazzled by him, the situation and the vibe between them.

He ran his knuckles over her cheek.

"For now you can see it as a means to protect other people here," he said, his voice soft.

"What do you mean?" Sellie asked, confused.

"If someone so much as looks at you, I am liable to kill them." His voice held a low, threatening tone. "At least with cuffs on it is clear you are taken."

What a daunting thought. And arousing as hell.

"I want you, Sellie. Tonight. Here." Sheer dominance shone in his eyes and voice. It wasn't a request. No question. He was just going to take her.

She swallowed, and her bottom lip trembled when she whispered, "Okay."

His mouth curled up in a lazy smile that turned her bones to mush.

"But I think my woman needs a drink first." Not a request either. *Isn't he supposed to take it slow? Go easy on me?*

She was about to protest against his course of action when he put a finger over her lips.

"No, Sellie. You can handle it. Do you trust me?"

She nodded.

"Good. Drinks it is." He laid his hand on the small of her back and guided her to the bar. He asked her what her poison was, ordered it and handed it to her.

Right at that moment, Master Cal and Rebecca came over.

"Well, I see you caught yourself a very sexy mermaid, Kyle," Cal said with a smile.

"Yes, I like fishing," Master Kyle replied. "Takes patience, but sometimes the catch is astounding. When a man finds a singing siren in his nets, he can do nothing but help himself to it!"

Sellie's cheeks burned and she glared at Master Kyle.

"Ah, a siren, I see," Master Cal said, his eyes gleaming with humor. "Quite dangerous creatures."

"Indeed they are! That's why I intend to tie her up. Just to be sure." Master Kyle gave her a wicked smile.

Sellie's jaw dropped. Kyle tapped the tip of her nose.

"An open mouth is very tempting for a Master, Sellie," Master Kyle said, deadpan. "I quite enjoy ball gags."

She snapped her jaw shut and glowered at him. He raised an eyebrow, the sudden steel in his eyes cutting through her like a knife, and she lowered her gaze.

"Seems you've got some work set out for you." Master Cal chuckled.

"Yes, it would appear so." Master Kyle grinned. "But I like a challenge. Especially one as beautiful as this."

"So you reckon your catch will make a good sub? Beg and moan?" Master Cal asked.

Sellie couldn't believe they were talking about her as if she weren't there. She expected Kyle to warn Master Cal to not push it, but instead he laughed.

"Hell yes! She will beg. And moan. Before the night is through," Kyle said, then faced her. The raw lust in his eyes sent a jolt through her core.

"Hell no!" she intervened in a sharp voice. "I will not."

Kyle wrapped his arm around her waist, drew her flush against his side and traced a finger over the upper curve of her breasts. Her breathing hitched a little, and she knew he'd noticed it when he laughed.

"Oh, sugar, we're going to have a lot of fun." His deep voice as much a caress as his finger. "And you will beg for me."

She flashed him a defiant gaze, but he smiled a knowing smile, not in the least affected by her resistance.

"Well, I think it's time I get my own sub to beg," Master Cal said. He tugged a strand of Rebecca's hair. "I'm thinking nipple clamps."

He slid a hand under Rebecca's low-cut top and squeezed her nipple. A soft mewl broke from her lips.

"Nope, you like that a bit too much." Cal rubbed his chin, as if thinking what to do next. "Figging would be nice."

His wife's eyes got large.

"Not figging, God no!"

Cal grinned.

"You're lucky, girl. I didn't bring ginger root with me." He smiled at her. "But I'd like to test the new pussy clamps. Nice and tight, then redden your sexy ass until you beg me to take you. Let's find out where you want me tonight."

Cal wished Kyle and Sellie a lot of fun and walked off with his loved one in tow.

Sellie took a deep breath. That had been intense, to say the least. Cal sure was intimidating. Blunt as hell. Keen, and sharp like a knife. As was Kyle, yet both men expressed it in a different style.

She sipped from her drink and glanced at Kyle from under her eyelashes. His strong gaze was upon her and he seemed as content as a lion who knew he'd subdued his prey, ready to start toying before he devoured it.

"Kyle," she started, then his dominant stare shut her up.

"I assume you entered as Master Cal's guest. Did he not instruct you, sub?"

Sellie swallowed. *Dammit.* She knew what he wanted — demanded, rather. It wasn't the done thing to call him by his name. Not in here. And new sub or not, the stern set of his jaw made clear he was not going to relent on it. Her insides clenched, as if joining the resistance in her mind. How could she call him Sir? The man she'd had sex with, arguments and more sex. And had fallen in love with. Kyle. She hadn't anticipated that saying that one word would be so difficult.

"Sir." She almost spat it out, trying to suppress the fury that flowed through her.

Kyle chuckled and the corners of his eyes crinkled. Then, within a split second, his face appeared chiseled and hard.

"Try again, sub." The snap in his command almost made her jump as she was caught off guard by the quick change in reaction.

"Sir," she whispered, her eyes down.

"Better. Now look at me and say it again."

Her gaze lifted and a tremor went through her when their eyes locked. She didn't like this at all. It was awkward as hell, but her pussy was quite happy and very wet.

"Sir," she said. Her clit throbbed when his gaze fired with possessiveness. Then his shoulder muscles seemed to relax. A tiny movement, but she saw it and she realized he needed this. He was pleased. And she found that she needed to please him. Her insides unclenched and a strange softness settled in her abdomen.

"Sir," she whispered again, as if to taste it.

Kyle pulled her in his arms.

"That's right, girl," he mumbled against her lips. He nibbled her bottom lip, and when she opened her mouth, he swept in. He kissed her, soft and sweet, but she wanted more. Much more. Overwhelming desire coursed through her veins, followed by the need to please and give, and in turn to be pleased and given. She melted against him and kissed him like a fury on fire. He groaned and took her deeper, plundering her. Hard and demanding. A soft mewl broke from her when he drew her against his erection. The throbbing between her legs increased and her mind blanked. All she could think of was how much she wanted him to take her, to lift her up, lower her over his cock until she screamed her joy to the world.

When he pulled back, his breathing was as ragged as hers.

"Finish your drink."

Sellie blinked, dazed from the hot kiss.

"Now!" A shiver coursed through her and she picked up her glass to do as she was told.

"Playtime."

No smile, just that gleam in his eyes. Lust. Fire. Dominance.

"Ready?"

"No," she whispered, getting the jitters, and shook her head.

"Tough shit."

There was a blur of black and brown, and before her brain had even registered what had happened, he walked off with her in his arms, into his jungle, with strong, confident strides.

Oh. My. God.

Chapter Ten

It was a wonderful sensation to be carried, but Sellie was too nervous to enjoy it. As Kyle wound his way through the club with her in his arms, she tried to see where he was taking her.

She had no idea how far into the dungeon they'd gotten when he put her down.

"Kyle. Sir," she started. One brief glance shut her up and she let him go about his business as he attached the handcuffs to chains, spreading her arms in a horizontal line. Her breasts arched forward, pushing against the cups of her top, and he ran his finger over the swell.

"Gorgeous!"

Sellie felt more cold chains against the bare skin of her back and legs and she turned her head to find out what it was.

"It's a spiderweb," he said. "But tonight I prefer to think of it as a fishing net with my siren in it."

"I don't think I like this." Sellie yanked on the cuffs, but they didn't budge.

Kyle stepped closer, his bulge touching her lower belly, his chest pressing against her breasts. He kissed the soft curve of her neck and nipped it. She hissed, then sucked in air as he traced his wet tongue over the side of her neck toward her ear. A quiver went through her and she moved her head to the side to give him access.

"Kyle, please." Her voice was husky.

"Begging already!" He tugged a strand of her hair. "But it's Master Kyle. My Lord, Liege or Sire is also acceptable."

"My Liege?" Sellie stared at him in disbelief.

"Yes, subbie, what's up?" Kyle's eyes glinted with pleasure as he put his hand on her behind to knead it.

"I didn't mean you!" she snapped.

His hand landed on her ass cheek.

Smack!

"I do not fancy that tone of voice."

Sellie blinked and she jerked at the cuffs again.

"Aren't you supposed to go easy on me?" she asked, not certain whether she was angry or afraid.

"I am, sub. Treating your Master with respect is the very first step. Addressing him properly is part of that." Kyle's soft, deep voice felt like warm honey trickling over her skin. "So far I have done nothing any odd love couple wouldn't do. I've used handcuffs, slapped your ass and kissed you. You, on the other hand…"

Sellie realized he had a good point. The rules had been explained to her — she knew about the respect and the use of titles. She had chosen to experience this, yet before they'd even started, she was about to screw things up.

"I'm sorry, Kyle. Sir," she whispered.

"You're forgiven, Sellie. This time." The warning in his voice couldn't be missed.

"Yes. Yes, Sir." It remained weird to call him Sir, but the funny flutters in her stomach when she did were pleasurable. And she loved how his eyes lit up each time she said it.

"Good. You've heard of safe words?" he asked.

"I have. Sir."

"Excellent. For now yours is *red*. Use that and everything stops. Use it wisely, not prematurely. Understood?"

"Yes, Sir," she answered. Although there was a slight tremor in her voice, anticipation began to well up from her core.

"You don't speak at all," he said. "Unless you need to use your safe word. You may moan, mewl or cry. When you have an urgent question, you can use *yellow*."

When she nodded her reply, Kyle hummed. With his foot, he urged her feet apart. He began to caress her, tickling and teasing, sensitizing her belly, her back, her face, her arms, until every inch of her skin was tingling. Sellie's eyelids closed by themselves, her breathing sped up and her body yearned for his touch, begging for more.

"So fucking beautiful!" he mumbled as he let his fingers circle over her legs and down to her ankles. Then he traced his fingers up over the oh-so-sensitive inner sides of her thighs. Sweet anticipation pulsed through her pussy when he neared her crotch. She ached to be touched there.

Kyle's soft laugh reached her ears. The fabric of her skirt was moved aside and Sellie peered through her lashes, needing to see what he was going to do. A husky sound escaped her when Kyle bent his head. He licked over the soft skin of her thigh, drawing sensual circles and leaving a sizzling trail of fire in his wake as he moved up and up and up. She tilted her hips. Just a few more inches. He went higher still, less than an inch from her pussy now, his tongue hot and wet. Her heart seemed to stop, time stood still, everything moved in slow motion as she waited, hoped, needed...

His tongue flicked over her clit. Once. A throaty moan broke from her. She yanked on the cuffs. How she wanted to grab his head and push it against her pussy! His tongue had felt so good, even over the satin fabric of her G-string.

Please, rip it off!

Kyle's low laugh made her insides quiver.

"Greedy, sub! I will take it off, but not yet."

Sellie couldn't recall saying that out loud, nor did she really care.

Kyle got up, looming over her.

"I will taste your pussy tonight, subbie," he said, sounding hoarse. "And you'll come."

Sellie was about to object, but remembered she wasn't to speak, so she shook her head instead. She wanted to be made to come, but not with all those people around.

Kyle flashed her a smile and rounded the spiderweb so he stood behind her. He reached through the openings, splayed his fingers over her breasts and held them.

"I want to feel your nipples." His whispered words were low and arousing.

A longing sigh fled her lips as he slid his hands underneath the bra top and cupped her breasts. She moaned and arched her chest, pushing her breasts into his hands. Her nipples jutted hard into his palms, and he kneaded, sending waves of pleasure straight to her pussy. He worked her up until her breasts were full, the skin almost too tight. He inched his way toward her hard buds and toyed with them, rolled them between his fingers then tugged. Heat seared from her nipples to her core. Then Kyle pulled harder and she moaned. The pain made her clit jolt, and she wriggled her body and bucked her hips. With expert fingers he undid the bra top and removed the shoulder straps, baring her breasts. Anticipation and need sent a shiver up her spine.

"You like it, Sellie?" he asked, his voice hoarse.

She gave a vigorous nod, biting back a "*yes!*"

He cupped his hands under her breasts, weighing them, lifting them.

"Look up, Sellie." A soft command, but a command nonetheless.

She complied, and her breath hitched when she saw a group of people around the spiderweb, watching from a respectful distance.

"Lord have mercy on me." A mere whisper.

"I love that title, but mercy I have not," he said, and pulled at her nipples. Hard.

Sellie tilted her head back and her loud, husky whine mingled with his low growl.

"That's my girl," he muttered.

He pushed his cock against her buttocks and pinched her nips. A keening cry broke from her and she almost came right then and there. Her mind had blanked — she was lost in the moment and all the wonderful sensations. All she knew was that she craved more.

Kyle eased the pressure on her nipples, then let go. He circled the spiderweb and stood in front of her.

"Beautiful," he mumbled and took her lips for a sweet kiss.

When he withdrew, he ran his knuckles over her cheek. For a brief moment, he considered getting out a flogger. He remembered all too well how fascinated she'd been by them when she had first seen them, and the thought of his flogger on her skin sure as hell was enticing. Hearing and watching the tails land on her body was something he'd dreamed of. He wouldn't flog her too hard as she wasn't used to it yet, but it'd be arousing nonetheless. Then he decided against it. He'd put her through quite a lot as it was. Being tied up, exposed and played with in public was enough for now.

"Time to get you down, Sellie. We'll continue elsewhere," he said. He knew that if he went on, she'd come, and he didn't want to make her climax in front of an audience. He was quite sure she could enjoy that, but doing that the first time she was here could scare her off. He preferred to be careful with her and thought it best to finish their play in a more private setting.

But then he met her gaze. There was disbelief in it. And disappointment? He narrowed his eyes. Had he misjudged the situation? Underestimated her?

"Do you want to go on, Sellie? You may answer."

"Not…not if you don't!" Her eyes filled with tears. She'd omitted the 'Sir' and he sensed that she felt rejected. Hurt. He read it in her eyes as well.

Kyle cursed under his breath. Clearly 'experienced Master' didn't mean jack when playing with such a passionate woman. Maybe his short relationship with Olivia had made him too careful.

He stepped closer, put his hands on Sellie's behind and lifted her up a bit.

"Wrap your legs around me," he said, and she complied without a second's hesitation. His erection pressed against her pussy.

"I'm hard for you. I am not rejecting you. I want you. Damn, do I want you!" His voice was rough. "And yes, I'd love to continue, to take you here, make you beg and scream. I'm goddamned proud to have you in my cuffs. But we have quite the audience and I don't want to push you, Sellie."

Her eyes shone with joy at his words.

"I have my safeword, asshole!" she grumbled. "I didn't use it, did I?"

He stared at her, dumbfounded, then the corners of his mouth curled up and a laugh rumbled through his chest.

"I didn't know I'd chosen myself such a wussy Master," she said, a mischievous spark in her eyes.

"I didn't know I'd chosen myself such a sassy, mouthy sub!" he gave back, amusement trickling through him. He was glad she'd bounced back so fast from that little dip.

She tilted her hips, rubbing over his hard cock, and he groaned.

"I'm not mouthy, I'm just—"

"Horny?" he interrupted, and chuckled when she blushed. Then he got serious. "How much more do you want?"

"A lot. Do...do what you do," she whispered.

He looked into her eyes and saw a hunger there that equaled his own.

"Sellie, if we go on, it will be full on. I will not hold back, and I won't stop unless you use your safeword."

"Okay. Sir," she replied.

"Good!" His voice sounded a little rough.

Kyle put her down, grabbed a chair from the edge of the scene area, undid the cuffs from the spiderweb and walked her toward the chair. He sat down and yanked her face down over his lap without further ado. She let out a startled cry. He shifted her until she had no leverage whatsoever, anchoring her legs with his. When she tried to get up, he pushed her back down with a hand on her upper back. Ignoring her protests, he moved her skirt out of the way and made an approving sound when he saw her round ass, the thin turquoise strap from her G-string between the cheeks. He caressed them, enjoying the softness of her skin.

"Now let's see," he muttered, but loud enough for her to hear. "I'm an asshole, a wussy Master, you've neglected to call me Sir several times. That calls for punishment."

Smack!

Sellie yelped, most likely more from shock than pain. Kyle chuckled.

"Just warming your beautiful skin, sweetie," he said. *Smack! Smack!*

He alternated between her buttocks until they'd gotten a nice pink glow. Kyle stroked over the now warm skin of her ass.

"Now you're prepped and ready for your punishment, sub."

Sellie was shocked. She'd thought he was done.

"Please. It hurts!" she said, a plea in her voice.

"No, it doesn't. Not yet."

A tremor went through her.

"Tell me how much you think you deserve. Feel free to be greedy. That will please your Master."

I have to tell him how many times to wallop me?

Sellie hadn't a clue, and tried to remember things from the book she'd read. Would three be okay? She had a sneaking suspicion that he'd only laugh at that. Maybe ten? Or twenty? Could she handle twenty?

"Sir, please advise. I'm not sure," she whispered, embarrassed that she didn't know what would be correct.

"Very good to ask me, Sellie. I'm proud of you." He pressed a soft kiss on her spine.

She shook, touched by his kiss and his words. Something in her lower belly started to glow.

"Do you think ten will suffice?"

"Yes, Sir, I think ten is…good," she mumbled, not having a clue whether it would be or not.

"Excellent. You can count for me after each one. Out loud," he said, and without waiting for a reply, he slapped her ass.

Sellie let out a cry, shocked that he'd hit her that hard.

"That hurt, goddammit!" she spat out.

"Wrong answer, girl."

Smack!

"Ouch. Damn. One," she said through her teeth.

Smack!

Sellie cursed under her breath. Never had she expected a spanking to be this painful.

"Two," she hastened to say, then whispered, "Bastard."

He chuckled as stroked her behind, which helped to ease the pain, then slapped her ass again. Sellie sucked in air as a white-hot flash shot over her nerves, the sting so sharp that her eyes filled with tears.

"I don't think—" she started.

"Don't think. Count." The timbre of his voice made her core quiver. "Or safeword."

Like hell she was going to do that. She wasn't going to give up on this.

"Three, Sir."

His hard hand landed on her ass again and a sob welled up in her throat as she realized she wanted this, needed it, even though it hurt.

After the sixth her mind blanked. His mumbling words soothed her, kept her stable. Pain zinged from her ass to her pussy and turned into pleasure.

The last slap came, an even harder one, and her cry echoed through the dungeon.

Kyle lifted her up, put her on his lap and pulled her against his chest. Her body was trembling within the circle of his arms.

"I-I… Kyle, my Lord, p-please, I need… P-please!" she stammered against his shoulder. Her mushy brain couldn't find the words to express what was going through her. She wasn't sure she understood herself. Although the spanking had been a punishment, it had turned her on. Her ass was aching, her pussy was wet and she was close to tears, but at the same time she knew this wasn't enough.

Kyle pulled her head back by her hair and looked into her dazed green eyes, which begged him. His cock pulsed when he saw her need. Need for more, and her Master. Her Lord—he fucking loved that title.

This thing in his lower abdomen roared to life. Full blast. He needed more as well. He had sensed the woman had gotten turned on by his hard hand, and it sure as hell had moved him too, but he hadn't thought she'd be ready for more serious things this soon. Although he should've expected it, she was spirited enough. He hadn't expected to feel the way he did himself either. The way she reacted to him, and how she'd been writhing and moaning as he had slapped her hard, had stirred up things inside that he hadn't felt in a long time. If at all. It came as a complete surprise and it shook him, yet something seemed to click into place.

Explore later, Kyle. Focus.

He lifted her off his lap and got up.

"You're going to please me, girl." He grabbed her by the hair, earning himself a husky moan, and led her toward the spiderweb. He cuffed her to it, her arms raised in a vee this time, which he knew would make her feel far more vulnerable than with her arms spread horizontally.

Her breasts arched forward, seeming even fuller. Kyle bent his head, sucked a nipple into his mouth and pulled, let go of the swollen bud and moved his attention to the other one, enjoying the sounds of passion coming from her. He slid his hand under her skirt and her G-string, and he loosely put his index finger on the swollen nub between her labia. Her hips jerked when he touched her there, and a long whine escaped her. He didn't put any pressure on her clit though, just held his finger there—annoyingly arousing, but nothing more than that. At the same time, he kept working her nipples with his mouth, alternating between pain and pleasure, licking, lapping, teasing, sucking. Her hips moved out of control as she tried to get more pressure on her clit. He didn't give her that.

"Please! Please, my Lord!" Her plea was music to his ears and the title stoked up the fire in his groin, making his cock pulse.

He let go of her nipple, leaving it swollen and red.

"Do you want to come, Sellie?"

"Yes, Master." Her voice slurred a bit.

He smiled, aware that she wanted release and not being asked awkward questions about it. But that was part of the fun.

Kyle let his fingers leisurely trace over her breasts and around her swollen nipples in slow, erotic circles. His other finger was still on her clit.

"You want to come here in the club?" Kyle asked. He knew the answer—there was no alternative. She was beyond caring about their audience—she had to come.

"Yes. Please let me come for you, Master," she whispered, her eyes begging him.

Her words shook him. In her innocence, she had gone for the jugular, expressing her desire to please him instead of asking for her own satisfaction. She begged to come for him, to have him take it from her for his pleasure, at his will and at his command. For a moment he was caught off guard. No woman had ever moved him the way Sellie did, not even his ex-wife, whom he'd loved to bits. But this siren was of a different caliber from any woman he'd ever encountered in his life. He realized in that split second that he was playing with fire and that his heart was at stake. Scary as fuck, but he was drawn to her like a moth to a flame. There was no escaping nor denying it, and he wasn't sure he wanted to either. Somehow they worked. Everything was right between them, as if they were the perfect dancers that moved to the same tune.

"You may come for me," he growled and moved his finger over her swollen clit, faster and harder until it engorged even further. Wanting to give her more pleasure, he put his mouth around her nipple and sucked. Her leg muscles began to tremble and she bucked her hips. Hearing and seeing a woman this close to orgasm blew his mind each and every time. Sensing the total surrender to her physical cravings, and knowing he was the one who'd got her there, and the ecstasy that oozed out of her, made his cock so hard it was painful. His balls were throbbing with a need equal to hers.

Then she reached the zenith, plunged over the edge and came. Her body shook out of control on the web and her shrill cries of exquisite joy filled the air as he forced every last spasm and aftershock out of her.

Kyle put a finger under her chin, tilting her face up.

"That pleased me a lot, Sellie. So much so that I want it again." His voice was hoarse.

"Yes, if it pleases you," she said, throaty from her orgasm. "Please, make me, take me for your pleasure."

"That I will," he whispered against her lips. "You may not come until I tell you to."

Sellie blinked. He smiled at her, aware how difficult that would be for her considering he knew how to arouse her. And he'd enjoy drawing it out. To watch and hear her struggle not to come until he allowed her to would ratchet his need for control higher and higher. And he'd push her until she was torn between her physical craving to come and her mental desire to please him by not climaxing.

First he took a kiss, sweet and hot and full of promise. Then he withdrew, reached under her skirt and pulled her G-string down over her legs. He helped her step out of it and threw it aside. With his foot he pushed her feet apart, so far that she had to raise herself onto her toes. He slid his hand under her skirt again. Her pussy lips had parted and her clit was exposed for his touch.

For now he left the front strip of her skirt in place, although he was dying to see her shaven pussy. So far he'd only seen her with red curls, and he longed to put his mouth on her bare flesh and to feel how she'd react to his touch on her creamy, bald pussy lips.

It'd have to wait. First he'd tease, play and torture her. And after she'd climaxed, he'd fuck her brains out. His balls were so damn tight they ached. So did his cock. His need for release was high, but he fought his urge to take her right then and there.

He focused his attention on her and moved his hands and mouth all over her body, arousing, pinching, caressing, sucking, tickling and teasing every bit of naked skin. Her nipples were red and swollen from his tugging fingers and sucking mouth. Her eyes had glazed over, and he sensed she was floating on clouds. She moved her hips in an instinctive plea to be touched there. While he drew sexy circles around her belly button with his tongue, he splayed one hand on her ass, kneading. He knew she was still sore from the spanking, but didn't care. It would only add to her desire. A moan broke from her when he let his other hand slide between her legs. He tugged at her labia and pinched them, making her whimper. He slid toward her soaking wet entrance, traced a finger over her swollen inner lips. Then he pushed a finger inside her, and her vagina walls clamped down.

"I love your tight cunt," he mumbled. Her pussy clenched again and he laughed. He moved his finger in and out. Too slow to get her off, enough to keep her aroused.

"I can't wait to bury my cock in you. Hard. Deep. No mercy," he said. "You want that, Sellie?"

"Yes! Oh God, yes!" Her leg muscles quivered out of control and her pussy began to ripple around his finger as she got close to climaxing.

"No orgasm!" His hard command snapped her out of it. As he watched her struggle to not come, he had to fight the urge to get his cock out and make himself come all over her. Her breathing was fast, her chest heaving with the effort to suppress orgasm. After a while, her muscles relaxed and he sensed it was ebbing away, only to rise again at the speed of light when he started to work her pussy.

A long wail broke from her, the sound of a woman in dire need. His cock jerked in response, wanting to act upon her mating call.

Kyle growled, knowing he couldn't wait much longer. He moved her skirt out of the way and draped it through an opening of the web. A groan welled up in his throat when he saw her bald pussy, her swollen labia spread apart, her engorged clit gleaming with the juices he had rubbed over it with his finger.

He got down in front of her and pushed a finger inside her, so slow that it'd be torture. He pulled out and put two fingers inside her tight cunt.

"Come for me now!" he commanded, rammed his fingers deep inside her, and she came like a comet, crying out over and over.

Without giving her time to recover, he put his mouth on her clit and started licking it. He slid over it and circled around it while pressing against the sides, sending little quivers through her legs.

He licked through her slit toward her swollen inner lips, traced over them with the point of his tongue, then went back and licked up against the nub that peeped out from its hood.

Her entire body shook and her knees buckled.

"Yes, oh damn, yes!"

Kyle grinned and kept licking, teasing, giving her pussy-torture with his mouth. Soon she was on the edge of coming again, and he kept her there for sweet minutes, enjoying her wails and pleas, while sensing with his entire being how she fought not to climax.

Then he gave her permission to come, and he sucked her clit into his mouth. The chains clanked from the sheer force of her orgasm, and her body shook on the web as she rode the waves of pleasure.

"Kyle. Please! I need you!" Her shrill cry for him made him get up and sheath himself in a condom so fast it surprised him that the damn thing didn't tear. He fisted the base of his shaft, put the head against her entrance and rammed himself home with one hard thrust. He growled like an animal in heat, drowning out her cry.

He cupped her ass, lifted her off the ground, and she put her legs around him. No time to play and drag things out. Pure blind lust raged through him, a hunger so ferocious that it seared his body. He took her hard, hammering inside her cunt, which tried to grab hold of him each time he pulled back, only to slam into her again.

The sounds of sheer desire that broke from her drove him wild. His balls were about to explode. They were so full that it was unbearable to wait any longer.

"Come with me," he groaned. Her cunt tightened even more, like a slick vise around his cock.

A few more thrusts and she came hard. Her pussy clamped down on him, rippling, milking. A low, guttural growl broke from him as his balls exploded and pumped up his seed in glorious, mind-blowing jets. He buried himself deep inside her sucking cunt with each spurt, and knew right then and there that he wanted to spend the rest of his life with this woman.

Chapter Eleven

Kyle held her for eternity, basking in the afterglow of orgasm, one so intense and good that he needed a bit of time to find his bearings again. He loved the feel of her soft body against him, the way her head rested in the crook of his neck, how her ragged breathing faded back to normal.

"Kyle," she mumbled in his skin.

"Hmmm, yes?"

"I...I think I love you."

He sucked in a breath and his heart almost jumped out of his chest. His arms tightened around her, hugging her even closer.

Trust his spirited girl to be so open and honest. He knew she was vulnerable right now, and after what they'd shared, he couldn't lie to her. Nor did he want to risk losing her by holding back. He was aware it was soon, way too soon maybe, but he knew his own heart. He wanted her. He hadn't planned on telling her, not yet. He'd wanted to let things develop and grow, but her statement had him cornered now. He chuckled. Master Kyle trapped by a sub after their first scene together. Not a sub — *his* sub. Fucked if he was going to let her go, fucked if he was going to lose her.

"I'm sorry —" she started.

"Don't be," he interrupted. "Please, never be sorry for being honest, babe. Look at me."

She complied and his eyes penetrated hers.

"I love you, Sellie," he said, his voice laden with emotion.

Tears pooled in her eyes. Thank goodness she hadn't asked "Really?" He so disliked it when a woman questioned every statement a man made.

He smiled at her.

"Damn, I want to kiss you, but I have to get you down from the web. Can you stand on your feet?"

Sellie nodded and put her feet on the ground. When he was sure she was stable, he got rid of the condom and closed his leathers. He had the cuffs undone from the chains within seconds and he embraced her. She wrapped her arms around his neck and offered him her mouth. He accepted with a groan and started a slow kiss, savoring the feel of her velvety lips, her taste and her eager tongue that tangled with his.

With a contented sigh, he released her and peeled her arms off him. He gathered her clothes, put them in her hands, got a soft blanket from a pile at the edge of the scene area and wrapped her in it. After grazing her cheek with his fingers, he swung her up into his arms and carried her to a sitting area.

He gestured for a waitress to come over and ordered two drinks, two bottles of water and a large plate of finger food and chocolate. When the girl got back with their order, he made her put it on the sofa next to him so he could get to it. Sellie was still snuggling — she hadn't landed yet. He opened a bottle of water and gave it to her.

"Drink, girl."

She accepted the bottle and drank. Kyle fed her little bits of chocolate, happy to sit there with her in his lap, all soft and sated. Keeping one arm around her, he drank his own bottle of water and helped himself to some chocolate.

At some point she began to stir, lifted her head and smiled at him. Kyle pressed a soft kiss on her lips. *Damn, it's good to sit with a willing, happy sub in my arms!*

He almost regretted it that she was landing and sat up to glance around, finding her bearings and checking out where he'd taken her. Then she spotted the plate with finger foods and her stomach growled. Kyle laughed.

"BDSM is hard work, isn't it?"

Her eyes shone as she smiled back at him.

"Don't look at me like that, woman," he grumbled.

"Like what?" she asked.

"Like a woman who successfully wore out her man." He grinned. "I'm so going to fuck you again in a minute!"

Sellie's cheeks got red as a spark of lust lit her gaze. She averted her eyes, but he'd seen it.

"It pleases me that you want more, greedy sub," he teased. "But first you need to eat a bit."

He took a mini quiche from the plate and held it in front of her mouth.

"Open for me, girl," he said, the suggestion making her blush again. Yet she did as she was told and he put the tiny quiche in her mouth, brushing over her lips and tongue. As she closed her mouth around his fingers, she glanced at him from under her lashes.

His dick started to come to life.

He loved the soft feeling of her lips on his skin, almost feeling those same soft lips around his cock, pursing, her mouth sucking. He groaned as he thought of what he wanted next. But now they both needed other sustenance. He kept feeding her little tidbits, paying attention to which ones she liked and which she didn't. He didn't give her the ones she disliked twice. In between, he enjoyed some of the delicious finger foods himself, and also drank. When she'd finished her water, he gave her a mint julep.

His gaze was glued to her as she took a sip. Her expression almost orgasmic as she let the liquid roll through her mouth.

Then she swallowed and her tongue flicked over her upper lip to lick off the bourbon. Kyle followed the movement with his gaze while he slid his hand underneath the blanket to cup her breast. He loved her firm breasts, and he kneaded and caressed them, and rubbed her nipple with his palm.

"Kyle," she said, breathless.

"What happened to 'my Lord'?" he asked.

"He came and got limp." She giggled, a twinkle of mischief in her eyes.

A corner of his mouth turned up. *Quick-witted little thing.* He let go of her breast, grabbed her hand and put it on his crotch. Her eyes widened.

"He came and wants more."

A shudder went through her body, making the blanket slide off her shoulders. She tried to grab it, but he stopped her before she could pull it up.

"Leave it," he commanded. "You have a beautiful body. I like seeing it."

He put his hand on her breast again and started fondling it, teasing her nipple with back-and-forth strokes of his thumb.

"Kyle..." she started.

"Don't tell me you've already forgotten, sub." He let out an exaggerated sigh to keep it lighthearted, but he was dead serious. "It's either Sir or Master Kyle, and you may call me my Lord too. I must admit I like that coming from your gorgeous lips."

Before she could reply, he put a mushroom stuffed with crab in her mouth. She tried to speak but it came out muffled.

"Don't talk with your mouth full, sugar. Not polite." He grinned.

Sellie chewed and swallowed the mushroom.

"Then stop putting things in my mouth," she grumbled.

"I intend to put a lot more in there," he said as he moved a slice of mango over her bottom lip, tickling and teasing. Her little sigh pleased him, and he traced the silky, slippery fruit toward the corner of her mouth and followed the cupid bow of her upper lip. A soft mewl escaped her and her eyes closed.

Kyle moved the slice into her mouth, over her tongue, sensitizing it.

"Think of my cock sliding in and out your mouth," he whispered. "Soft and smooth and hard underneath, filling your mouth, sliding over your wet, hot tongue."

He moved the slice of mango in and out, enjoying how she was caught up in their erotic game, her breasts heaving, her lips a little swollen from excitement.

"Show me how you'd use your tongue on my cock."
His voice had gotten lower and hoarser.

Sellie glanced up at him, her eyes glowing with
arousal as she started moving her tongue over the
mango. She licked it, traced over it with the point of her
tongue and swirled around it.

Kyle grunted and his cock jerked as if to tell him it
wanted to be in that sexy, hot mouth. He pulled out the
slice, and she closed her lips around it, sucking, trying
to get it back in. Fire lit her green eyes, along with the
satisfied glow of a woman who knew she could — and
had — aroused her man.

God, he wanted to come in her mouth. Now. Have
her suck him dry. Her eyes told him she wanted that
too.

"With or without condom?" He knew what he
wanted, but he had to ask her.

Sellie blinked, almost disappointed by the intrusion
of his question.

"Why do I have to make all the decisions, my Lord?"
she asked, emphasizing *my Lord*.

"Because in the end the sub is in control," he replied.
"A Master can only take what you allow him to. And
since we haven't discussed any details yet, I have to
ask."

"Great," she mumbled.

"Isn't it!" He grinned. "Get up, girl."

The sudden snap in his command made her jump off
his lap. Uncomfortable about her nakedness, she tried
to cover herself and put her hands over her breasts. She
realized she did that odd thing women did when they
were caught naked — covering their breasts, not their

sex. However weird it might be, she couldn't help herself.

Kyle's hot gaze seared her, made her pussy throb and her nipples harden in taut peaks. She glared at him, but he just smiled at her awkwardness.

"Go over to that stand and get a condom."

She looked behind her and saw the stand several meters away. The thought of walking stark naked to it wasn't particularly appealing.

"Yes, my Lord, anything you say, my Lord," she said in a mocking tone of voice.

The threat in his piercing eyes almost had her running to the stand, grabbing a condom and rushing back. Her breasts jostled, which was painful, but he seemed to enjoy the view. She stood in front of him and handed him the condom. Kyle put it on the sofa next to him without taking his eyes of her. Heat rose up from her neck and onto her cheeks.

"Beautiful, sexy siren," he said, reached out and slid a finger through her pussy. Heat zinged across her nerves as he rubbed over her clit. He moved toward her wet entrance, then thrust inside. Sellie gasped. Kyle pulled out his finger and licked it off. His wicked smile made her heart do a triple somersault in her chest.

"I like knowing you're so eager to suck your Master's cock," he said and opened his leathers. "On your knees."

She stared at him for a few seconds, then complied, and he handed her the condom.

"If you want to use it, go ahead."

"Me? I have never… I can't!" she objected.

"Then it's time you learn," he said as he held his hard cock by the base.

"But I don't want to use a —" she said with a defiant spark in her eyes.

"Too bad. Do it. Now, Sellie," he replied, pinning her with his strong gaze.

Her hands trembled as she tore open the condom wrapper. She glanced up at him, still hoping he was going to do it for her, but his expression was level. No inclination whatsoever that he was going to help her out. She sighed and her gaze dropped to his dick for the very first time, and her eyes got wide. He was huge! No wonder he could give her such intense orgasms.

"It flatters a man when a woman is speechless as she sees his cock." He grinned.

Up to that moment her cheeks had been warm, now they burned.

"Don't worry, girl. I'm equally impressed with you," he muttered and brushed his knuckles over her breasts.

"Don't distract me," she grumbled. "This is hard enough as it is."

"I know, I'm so hard it hurts," he replied with both humor and lust in his voice.

"Asshole," she said and tried to focus on the job at hand. She put the condom on the head of his dick, fumbling as she tried to get it to roll down.

She was quite sure he was an expert at it. As a matter of fact, she had seen him put one on at the speed of light not that long ago. *Bastard for making me feel so awkward.*

From the corner of her eyes, she saw Kyle's shoulders shaking with laughter as her fingers were fluttering over his shaft, trying to get the condom on properly.

Sellie glanced up and glowered at him. It was plain he found it amusing to watch her fumble.

"Don't worry, your touch is very arousing, sweetie." His voice was a little hoarse in spite of his laughter.

She wasn't convinced and his amusement irritated her.

"I'm so sorry," she said in a tone of voice that made clear she was far from sorry. "I simply can't—"

"You're doing fine, sweetheart," he interrupted with a sexy smile. "If you don't hurry up, I may even come before I've had your lips around me."

Her cheeks were burning, yet somehow she was pleased that her fingers turned him on, clumsy or not. Then the condom slipped into place and she gave him a smug look.

"Good. Excellent job!" He smiled as he pulled the condom off and dropped it on the floor.

Sellie stared at the condom. She couldn't believe it. He'd made her do that for the heck of it?

His eyes gleamed with amusement and a deep laugh rumbled through his chest. Sellie bent her head, took his cock into her mouth and sucked hard. The laughter stopped and he groaned.

Yeah, that shut you up, didn't it?

She giggled and swirled her tongue around the tip, then sucked at it, loving how it swelled in her mouth.

"Little bitch!" he panted. She giggled again, and he moaned. "Suck me, oh damn, yes!"

As she pleasured him, she got more and more excited herself. She teased him, brought him to the edge of orgasm then let it ebb away only to work him up again. Then she repeated the whole thing, loving how he groaned each time. She knew he couldn't take it anymore when he grabbed her by her hair and pulled her head up.

The fire in his gaze sent a jolt through her clit. Her pussy was wet and aching with the need to have him inside her.

"No more teasing," he growled. Without breaking the eye contact, she stuck out her tongue and licked up his shaft as if it were a popsicle.

"No, Sir," she whispered, knowing full well what effect the visual was having on him. Again she licked up his shaft and rubbed over the sensitive frenulum at the underside. A quiver ran through him and his cock jerked against her tongue. She circled over the head, loving that she could turn him on, make him needy. A sense of power and control came over her as she put her lips around his cock to tease him a bit more. Then something in his gaze changed and his lips curved up in a wicked smile. Her breath hitched when he gave her his most intimidating Dom-look. Within a split second he had taken her new-found control away from her. And how foolish to think she could dominate a Master.

"Drink me. All of me," he commanded.

"I had planned to," she replied. "I am greedy that way."

Lust lit up his eyes and her pussy clenched in response. Dominance oozed out of his every pore and seeped into her aura. Something shifted inside her and she had a hard time holding herself under his gaze that seemed to penetrate every fiber of her being. No matter how intimidating it was, she couldn't break the eye contact. She swallowed hard, entangled in his web of power, unable to break free from it and not sure whether she wanted to. A sudden need to have all control taken from her rose inside her. The added effect of his hand in her hair, holding her, sent a quiver through her body.

"Please let me pleasure you, Master," she whispered.

"That you shall, girl." He lowered her head over his cock and she sucked him into her mouth. As she tightened her lips around the shaft, he swelled even more, and she sensed he was close. Very close.

"Are you ready for me?" he asked, panting.

She mumbled around his dick and went up and down faster, kneading his balls with her hand. Before long he erupted with a guttural groan. His body shook with the force of orgasm and his cock jerked in her mouth. Hot spurts shot out of the tip and Sellie accepted his juices with pleasure.

* * * *

Sellie cuddled up to him, with the blanket draped over her, basking in his presence and warmth. The way he touched her, so loving and gentle, was overpowering. The bond between them was getting deeper and deeper and for now it was wonderful to sit and be. No words were necessary. Not yet.

After a while, Kyle ordered drinks, non-alcoholic beverages this time, and more finger foods, which he fed her. He caressed her cheeks and he gave her a lazy smile.

"You look like a big cat," she whispered. "A large, sated cat. A lion."

He huffed a laugh. "A brand-new fairy tale. The Lion and the Siren. Unusual combination, but proving to be quite sexy!"

Sellie giggled, letting her soft fingers tickle over his five o'clock shadow. With a content sigh she burrowed even closer to his warm body and buried her head in the hollow of his neck, her arms around his solid chest.

When their drinks and finger foods had gone, Kyle lifted her off his lap and got up as well. He gathered her clothes, put them in her arms and swung her up.

"Time to leave the party," he said. "I want to be alone with you."

He walked toward Rafe, who was standing close to the bar.

"Club's yours for the rest of the night, Rafe."

A corner of Rafe's mouth curled up as he eyed her, making her blush.

"No problem. Have fun!" He grinned.

Sellie's cheeks were burning now and she hid her face against Kyle's chest.

"Asshole," she muttered.

Kyle snorted a laugh while he strode out of the dungeon with her. "You don't want to annoy Master Rafe, girl. You may not like it so much. He can be quite the pervert."

"Is there a Master who isn't?" she asked.

"We all got our specialties," Kyle answered with a mysterious smile. Sellie decided not to ask what his specialty was.

He put her down when they got to the dressing rooms.

"Get your things." He brushed a kiss across her lips.

A few minutes later she came out with a bag and her coat. He slung the bag over his shoulder, wrapped the coat around her, picked her up in his arms again and started walking toward his private quarters.

"I can walk myself," she protested.

"I know. I like carrying you." He rubbed his cheek over hers, grazing her with his stubble. She winced.

"Don't worry, I'll shave before I lick your cunt," he said, sounding a little hoarse.

"Kyle!" Sellie gave him a half mocking, half sincere, shocked look. She found it a bit off to hear him say such crude things when they were not engaged in a sexual setting. It somehow seemed to clash with him being such an elegant, smooth, charming man. Even dressed as a Master in leathers, she couldn't quite erase that gentleman image from her mind.

"What? You have a problem with sex talk?" Kyle asked.

"No, but... Maybe a little. It's odd, I mean you are..." She stumbled over her words, not sure how to tell a hunk of a man that he seemed too elegant for sex talk.

A laugh rumbled through his chest.

"Sellie, I may be a gentleman, but saying 'Dear, I'd love cunnilingus tonight' is pushing it!"

She grinned. "I guess you're like the lady in the parlor."

Kyle raised an eyebrow, a corner of his mouth tipping up.

"Go on?"

She blushed but didn't lower her gaze.

"A gentleman in the parlor, a chef in the kitchen, and a..." she started, but couldn't finish the sentence. Her gaze did drop now, her cheeks warm.

"Yes? A what?" he asked, amusement in his voice.

What was she to say? *A god in the bedroom? Lord in the bedroom?* She drew a blank.

"Gigolo!" she blurted.

"Gigolo?" He almost sounded shocked. Then his loud laughter echoed through the hallway. Sellie laughed with him, realizing what a daft comparison it had been. He fell silent and she locked eyes with him. A tremor ran through her.

"Oh fuck," she mumbled. What had she been thinking? That she could toy with this potent man?

His only response was a smile.

"I meant Lord," she attempted. "Lion?"

Kyle chuckled as he carried her straight to the bedroom, put her down and tilted her face up.

"This Lion is hungry and needs to feed, honey. I'm thinking pussy." The glint in his eyes sure as heck was that of a predator on the prowl. It melted her core and a hot fire started to flare up from her lower belly.

He yanked off the coat and blanket and looked her over, burning her flesh with his gaze. His hand slid between her legs, sending jolts through her when he grazed her labia. He swirled a finger toward her entrance.

"Definitely eating pussy tonight! I am going to enjoy your cunt." His now deep voice and rough words sent a shiver up her spine.

"Kyle!" she exclaimed, more embarrassed than shocked.

"Gentleman Kyle is gone." He almost growled now.

He put his hands on her shoulders and pushed her so hard that she fell onto the bed, her legs dangling off it. She let out a startled cry and crawled backward to get away from him.

"You said you'd shave," she objected, realizing it was a meaningless comment, made to distract him. No, herself.

"I will. After I've eaten."

He just stood there, keeping her fixated with his piercing eyes, overpowering her with his dominant aura, with an ease that was concerning. It aroused her beyond belief.

He stepped closer.

"Oh God," she mumbled and pushed herself off with her feet on the mattress to get farther away.

Kyle grabbed her ankle and yanked her toward him. He pushed her legs up and out, and curved his hands around her thighs, holding her still. Her pussy tilted up, throbbing and aching for his touch, his mouth. Yet her mind objected to being restrained and she tried to free herself from his grip. Then his death-look was upon her, all her willpower seeped from her body and she yielded to his will. To him. The possessiveness that lit up his eyes as she surrendered affected her and a soft mewl came over her lips. He dragged his gaze from hers and lowered it to her pussy. A quiver ran through her and he smiled. *The jerk!* There she was, her entire private area in view and opened up like a flower with his eyes on it. Her pussy didn't mind — her clit throbbed and need shot up from her core.

Then his mouth was on her slit. Her entire body jerked at the touch and she moaned. He licked upward from her vagina and found her clit. Her hips bucked when he rubbed his tongue over it. Then he went wild between her legs — licking, lapping, teasing, flicking, pushing, sucking. Her brain shut down on her and all her blood rushed to her core, eager to join the party that was going on there.

He brought her to the brink of ecstasy again and again until she was begging him to let her come. The next time she was hovering over the delicate edge of orgasm, long wails of need escaping her lips, he pushed a finger up her anus and she came hard, thrashing and screaming.

Chapter Twelve

Kyle woke up with his woman's back against his chest. During the night he'd wrapped his arm around her, his hand cupping her breast as if even in sleep he wanted to make clear she was his. He closed his eyes, reveling in the feeling of waking up with a warm woman in his arms. Not just any woman — Sellie. A content sigh came over his lips. He moved his hand over her breast, the palm rubbing, and her nipple jutted. The sensation made him hard as a rock and he groaned as his erection pushed against her soft bottom. He let go of her breast and drifted toward the vee between her legs. Her breathing sped up a little.

"What are you doing?" she whispered.

"Checking if breakfast is ready," he answered, and his finger found her clit. "I want you, Sellie."

She spread her legs a bit, giving him room to move his finger over her nub.

"I think it's ready, but please make sure." Her voice, smoky from sleep and arousal, stirred up the heat in his loins.

He moved his finger through her pussy toward her entrance and pushed a finger inside. Her vagina walls clenched, and she moaned, telling him her tissues were tender after last night.

"A bit sore, are we? I did fuck you hard, didn't I?" he mumbled, pulling out of her pussy.

"Do you have to be so... Ooh!" Her hips jerked as his finger flicked over her clit, then she continued. "So rude!"

Making sure to go slow, he slid his finger inside her again.

"But, baby, I think you love me being rude," he whispered. He kissed the side of her neck, then nipped. She mewled, enticing him to trace his tongue over the spot he'd bitten.

"You taste so good. Whether it's your skin or your cunt," he groaned. Her pussy clamped down on his finger, and he laughed. "Yes, you do like a bit of rude with your sex."

He got himself a protesting huff, but her ragged breathing was all the confirmation he needed.

"I want you, Kyle. In me."

The urgent plea in her voice made his balls clench and he pushed his cock against her ass.

"There's no place I'd rather be!" He sounded hoarse. "But best get you a little wetter before I make you mine again. I don't want to hurt you."

Her cunt clenched around his finger when he reminded her of his size and her tender tissues, and he grinned. Knowing how much she longed for him made him feel utterly masculine.

Without warning, he thrust his finger inside her, so deep and hard that a wail broke from her lips. His cock twitched in response.

"Yes, oh, Kyle!" She moved her hips as if to beg him for more. Not wanting to rush, he started to finger-fuck her, knowing by her wet pussy that she needed more. He'd give her more. So much more. He had plenty of hot, solid steel, desperate to plunge balls-deep into her wet, silky-soft embrace. He'd fill her right up and fuck them both to paradise.

"Are you on the pill, Sellie?" He kept finger-fucking her.

"Yes. Oh please, yes!"

Hearing her beg him to take her bareback made his dick swell to the point of pain. There was nothing he wanted more, to come in her and give her his seed.

He pulled his finger out of her pussy, moved up to her clit and teased it to hardness. When her breathing was ragged and her legs started to tremble, he turned her over and rolled on top of her. He swirled the head of his cock through her juices. Her breathing hitched, and he knew she was waiting for that to-die-for sensation of him entering her body.

He didn't, even though he had to grit his teeth to stop himself from burying his cock inside her wet pussy.

"Beg for me, Sellie," he panted. "Beg for my cock."

Her eyes flew open, insecurity blooming in them. Kyle moved the slick tip over her engorged clit. *So intimate, so erotic.* She moaned. Loud.

"Beg. I want to hear you beg for my cock." His voice was thick with lust and his vision blurred.

He continued to move the head of his cock over her clit, pushing and teasing. Distracting her. She tilted her hips, trying to get him inside her.

Slap!

She yelped. He'd hit her breast. As she stared at him in shock and disbelief, her pussy clenched. Kyle read it in her eyes and it triggered a need that shook him. He slapped her breast again. Her whimper made his cock throb, and when her chest arched in a plea for more, it required all his control to not ram himself to the hilt into her cunt.

He slapped her other breast and she wailed.

"Beg. For. My. Cock." He put enough power in his voice to get through to her, and she complied.

"Please, give me your cock," she begged as she pushed her chest up for more. "Pleeease!"

He let out a low growl and rewarded her with another slap, loving the intense expression of need on her face as she took the pain.

"Please, Master!"

He fisted his cock and pushed inside until he was right up against her cervix. He held still, enjoying the feel of her rippling cunt around him, hungry for more. She attempted to move underneath him. More begging came from her lips.

"You are still tender. I'm being careful, sub," he grunted.

"Not gentle. Lion, please! Hard. All!" She was almost sobbing. He couldn't resist any longer. The sight of her dazed, begging eyes and her heaving swollen breasts robbed him of his last shred of restraint. His mind blanked, he let his own need take over and he gave her his full length. A shrill cry broke from her.

She wrapped her legs around his hips and he took her hard and deep.

"You feel so good," he panted. He bent his head, took a nipple into his mouth and sucked hard. Even though she whimpered, her pussy clamped down on his cock like a tight, wet fist. A groan welled up in his throat and he kept hammering into her. They reached the top of the cliff at the same time. Her body shocked underneath him, her cunt tugging and squeezing his cock. His balls exploded and pushed up his cum, the sensation exhilarating. He let out a guttural growl as he shot his semen inside her for the first time. A glorious feeling of possessiveness came over him that stirred up another fire in his core. Surprised but pleased, he took her a second time with short, fast thrusts. Before long, he came, and the intensity of the orgasm shook him. Sheer ecstasy blew his mind as he fucked the last spasms out of his body.

* * * *

She lay sprawled out over him, her head in the hollow of Kyle's shoulder. Before they had collapsed, he had rolled them over to take his weight off her. A happy sigh came from her—she was nice and warm, and right where she wanted to be.

After a while she pushed herself up a bit, opened her eyes and smiled at him.

"You've shaved," she mumbled, and let her fingers caress his smooth jawline.

He nodded. "Last night after you'd passed out. I showered and shaved. After I'd put you under the covers. And after I'd cleaned your pussy."

Sellie blushed. He had washed her…there? And she hadn't even woken up?

Kyle grinned.

"Girl, you'd gone out like a light." His voice deepened. "You were so beautiful. Like you are now. Your after-orgasm face is bedazzling."

He pulled her head down for a long, sweet kiss. When he released her lips, her stomach growled. He grinned.

"Time for some breakfast!" Kyle rolled her off him and they both got up.

She watched as he grabbed clean boxers and jeans and put them on which brought to mind that she had nothing to wear. She wasn't quite sure what to do and she decided to stay put. He was about to walk out of the bedroom when he seemed to realize she hadn't moved. Kyle crossed the room, brushed a strand of hair from her face and stroked her cheek.

"I like my sub naked, but I'll get you a shirt. This time."

He browsed through the closet, took out a black shirt and handed it to her.

"Thank you," she said, grateful she'd have a bit more than her siren outfit to wear.

Note to self, don't leave home without normal clothes!

She slipped the shirt over her head and pulled it down. Her eyes met Kyle's and she sucked in a breath when she saw the hunger in his eyes.

"You're damned stunning, no matter what you wear," he muttered.

Sellie didn't understand what he meant until he turned her around so she faced a full-length mirror. Sellie took in the redhead staring back at her, breasts emphasized by the deep vee of the lace-up collar, legs a mile long underneath the way-too-short shirt that had difficulty covering her pussy. The back was a little longer and reached over her behind. Her green eyes held the lazy look of a woman who'd had a good seeing-to and was up for more.

She swallowed and met his eyes in the mirror. He reached around her, cupped her breasts and rubbed his thumbs over her nipples.

"You're like a sex goddess," he said, sounding hoarse. "But right now we need food."

He let go of her breasts and pressed a kiss on her cheek.

She moved her hands up to the lace of the V-neck, wanting to tie it up so she'd feel a little less exposed. Kyle pushed her hands aside.

"Leave it." He grabbed her hand and took her to the kitchen.

Soon eggs were sizzling in a pan, crispy toast filled the toast rack and croissants were turning a deep golden brown in the oven. Sellie set the table while Kyle filled glasses with orange juice and brewed fresh coffee.

When all was ready, they sat down and hungrily ate the eggs and toast. After that, she grabbed a warm croissant, buttered it and put strawberry jam on it. She sank her teeth into it and let out a content sigh as she chewed.

"Man, that is good!" She licked the sticky jam from her lips.

Kyle grinned when she went for another croissant. Her face flushed. She scooped up a strawberry and enjoyed the flash of lust in his eyes as she suggestively put it in her mouth, her lips briefly pouting around the red fruit.

She peered at him from under her lashes, pricked the fork into

"A woman who doesn't count calories is a woman after my own heart!" he said with a smile. He got himself the last of the eggs. "I think I'm going to need these."

Knowing eggs allegedly helped sperm count and another strawberry and held it in front of his mouth.

"I think you should eat some." Her voice was husky.

"Why is that?"

"Strawberries make sperm taste sweeter!"

He gave her a lazy smile.

"I'll have Marie make a large strawberry field in the garden. Fresh stock. Anything to please my woman." He took the strawberry off the fork with his teeth and chewed.

"I like chocolate." Kyle got up and walked around her. Softly he stroked over her hair toward her collarbones and slid underneath the shirt. Shivers ran down her spine when his fingers grazed over the swell of her breasts and her hard nipples, then he firmly cupped them both. She mewled softly in the back of her throat and dropped her head against his hard abdomen.

"Chocolate syrup," he said softly, his hands kneading. "Beautiful chocolate patterns over your breasts, a drop on your nipples."

Sellie's breathing got a little faster.

"Over your stomach, toward your pussy." He moved his hand down, fingers tickling over her belly, circling around her navel, inching closer and closer to her mound, all the while mumbling sexy things in her ear.

"My tongue will follow the chocolate lines until it finds your needy clit." His voice had deepened. His finger reached her clit and pressed. Her hips jerked and a moan escaped from her. He teased her, circled around her hardening clit, pushed against the sides and occasionally brushed over it. Her brain turned to mush. Her world narrowed down to the throbbing need between her legs and her swollen breast in his hard hand. His touch and voice hypnotized her.

"Drops of wax splattering on your belly…heat and pleasure as I go closer and closer to your pussy, dropping wax. Drip. Drip. Drip," he mumbled. "Your clit aching, waiting for it, a hot splash falling down… You'll feel the warmth right before it hits you…then…hot wax on your clit, fire shooting through your pussy, and you'll come… screaming my name."

"Oooh yes!" she moaned, pushing her hips against his finger.

"You want that, Sellie?" he asked huskily.

"Yes! God yes!" she panted, then the words sank in and she realized what he was talking about.

"Wait. No! Wax?"

She almost jumped off the chair, but the hands on her breast and pussy held her immobile.

"Wax play is really quite hot," he said, his tone making clear that he was enjoying the play on words.

"Are you insane?" Sellie was really shocked.

"No, love, seriously kinky, that's all," he answered.

"No wax play!" She turned her head and glared at him. He smiled and planted a kiss on the lips she had firmly pressed together.

"Right now I think we need more coffee," he said and pulled his hands out from underneath her shirt.

Sellie wasn't sure whether to be glad or annoyed. Her pussy was still pulsing and wet. The thought of hot wax...on her clit of all places! She glared at his back. All muscles. Damn him for being so sexy. And damn him for putting that arousing thought in her mind. Hot wax. *No way!* Nevertheless, her vagina clenched at the thought.

Kyle put two coffees on the table then walked to the cupboards again. Her eyes were glued to his body. His naked chest, the rippling muscles, his narrow hips. He was just too damned perfect.

Kyle turned around, holding a candelabra and candle. Her insides quivered. Did she want it so badly that she was hallucinating? She blinked. *Nope, no hallucination.*

He held her with his intent eyes, put the candelabra on the table and pushed the candle into place. He reached into his pocket and dug up a metal lighter. She heard its *clink* when he flicked it open and let his thumb strike the wheel. Without breaking eye contact, he lit the candle. The flame was reflected in his eyes, vying with the fire that was already burning in them.

Sellie swallowed hard. Suddenly she wanted to feel hot wax on her body. She tried to keep the desire from showing up in her gaze, but she read in his eyes that he'd already seen it. Confusion set in the second she realized she'd allow him to do this for real, and she knew he saw that too.

He closed the lighter's top with a flick of his wrist, walked to her, pulled her out of the chair and drew her into his arms. Her body was trembling.

"Kyle... how much... How far will I let you go?" A mere whisper, a cry for support, his strength. She clung to him as if he was a buoy.

He simply held her close, stroking her hair and back.

"I really don't want that, the wax, and…and now… I think I do." She was so confused.

"I know, baby, I know," he mumbled over the top of her head. "That's why we will have to talk. Soon."

* * * *

They walked through the gardens, hand in hand. Kyle knew it would be easier to talk when not sitting across a table, staring at each other. Walking would also help to keep it more lighthearted than having her sit on his lap. And the gardens were stunning, so why not enjoy that as they discussed what had gone down between them and their budding relationship?

He sensed she was edgy and eager to discuss it, so he didn't put it off by talking about flowers or other chitchat. He got straight to the point and asked her how she felt about the night before in the club.

"I think… I want to…explore. More." Her voice was soft and held the same odd mixture of certainty and insecurity that had spread over her face.

Kyle stopped her and cupped her face in both hands.

"I'd like that too, but we'll tread carefully," he said. "All this is new to you, so we are not going to rush into anything. We'll discuss upfront what we'll do during a scene until we know better what we both like and need."

"Okay. Sounds like a plan," she said with a glint in her eyes.

Kyle chuckled. "You suddenly seem to be a lot more comfortable."

He pulled her into his arms and splayed his fingers over her naked ass and squeezed to make her aware of how scantily dressed she was. She blushed accordingly and he grinned.

"That's better. I like to see my sub a little shy and awkward, and getting aroused by it." He pulled her against his hard body, held her head in one hand and kissed her. She opened her lips for him and he explored her mouth softly and slowly, taking his time to savor the kiss.

Finally he pulled back and smiled at her.

"You know, I want you to think about what you want to experience," he said. "I want you to tell me how you'd want the next scene to go, what you'd want to do."

Sellie looked at him with horror.

"Me? But why? Aren't you supposed to-to…" she stammered, very awkward about it all. "And how on earth am I supposed to do that anyway?"

"Read a few more books. Talk to Rebecca. Do an internet search," Kyle answered. "You're a smart woman, you can work it out. See what turns you on and what you'd like to try."

She stared at him in disbelief and shock. Then her innate fiery personality kicked into gear.

"I am so not going to do that. I simply will not!" After she'd almost spat the words out, she turned around and stomped toward the mansion, unaware of how darned sexy she was in the shirt.

Sellie had barely gotten into the kitchen when a strong hand curled around her upper arm twirled her so she faced him. Another hand pulled her head back by her hair and she found herself looking into Kyle's strong eyes. There was no doubt in her mind he wasn't happy with her behavior and she swallowed.

"Kyle, I—"

"I want it by Friday," Kyle interrupted. "And it better be good."

"Yes, Sir," she whispered.

"Good." He let go of her hair and arm. "Now go and have a shower while I make more cappuccino."

Sellie left the kitchen without hesitating, and it wasn't until she was washing her hair that she realized he had ordered her around. That she had *let* him order her around. And had obeyed like a meek puppy.

"Asshole! Bastard Master!" she cursed under her breath.

Chapter Thirteen

Over the following days, Sellie kept thinking about their next scene and what she had to come up with for that. Like Kyle had suggested, she read another book and lots of things online, only to find it didn't help her one bit. She tried to imagine what it would be like to be tied up, to have certain things used on her body or put inside her. All it did was confuse her, because she wasn't quite sure what it would be like. How it would make her feel.

Apart from that, she knew that coming up with things to do would give him quite the insight in her mind. All of her most intimate, private, secret fantasies and thoughts. The kind of stuff she wouldn't easily share with anyone. Some not even with herself. She tried to come up with things that were rather neutral, that wouldn't give away too much about her deepest, darkest desires, only to find that was impossible.

And there were so many variables concerning the scene that she didn't know, like how long was it going to be? Was he really going to do everything she'd come up with or take them as options to choose from? Were they going to do the scene in the club or in private? She didn't have the answers to any of those questions.

When she got to work on Wednesday, she was in a foul mood. It didn't help her painting, and after an hour she decided it would be best to take a break. Maybe it'd be better to take the day off. The week even. She was quite sure she could paint again after Friday, after the scene. As it was, her mind and nerves were all over the place. Knowing the object of her troubles was in the office on the other side of the building didn't help. So close, yet so far away.

Kyle walked into the kitchenette while she was frothing milk for her cappuccino.

"Morning!" he greeted her. "I'd like one too please."

"I can't. I don't know how to do it," Sellie blurted.

Kyle raised an eyebrow.

"Seems to me you're doing fine," he said, a dry undertone to his voice.

"I wasn't talking about the coffee, asshole!"

"Neither was I." He gave her his most charming smile.

Sellie was tongue-tied for a second. A split second. Then her bad mood took over.

"You call this fine? I'm a mess, I'm tired, confused and upset. I can't even paint and…"

He shut her up with a kiss, soft and sweet, but when she moaned and pushed her body against his, he took complete possession of her mouth. He moved his hands over her back, squeezed her ass, and when the proof of his excitement pressed against her belly, she moaned again.

Both their breathing was ragged when he let go of her lips.

"I hate you," she whispered.

"No, you don't," he whispered back. "And you can do it. Stop worrying so much, girl."

"Yes, but—" she started.

"No buts. You can do it. Period," he interrupted. "I'm flexible, I can work with whatever you come up with. There's no need to be awkward or shy. I've seen every inch of your body."

Yes, but I don't want you to know every inch of my mind too!

His gaze pierced hers and a corner of his mouth turned up. Sellie's cheeks got hot. *Is he reading my mind?*

Kyle drew her into his arms and held her.

"You can do it, sweetie. Breathe, relax," he mumbled into her hair.

Oddly enough, she did relax for the first time in days. Having his arms around her, the warmth of his body against hers, his presence, made her feel so much better. Calmer and grounded. She stood there in the circle of his arms, basking.

After a few minutes he let go of her.

"I've got to go back to work now. I suggest you do the same," he said, tapped the tip of her nose and walked back to his office.

Around three in the afternoon, Sellie decided to call it a day. The painting was going well. It would take another two sessions to do some finishing touches, then it would be done. She sighed. She'd miss working here, miss the short and sweet—and always unpredictable— intermezzos with Kyle. And the girl talk with Rebecca.

Speak of the devil. Rebecca walked in when Sellie had just finished cleaning up for the day.

"Care for a drink?" Rebecca asked.

"Yes, I'd love to," Sellie said.

A little later, they were enjoying drinks at Ernesto's. When Rebecca asked how she and Kyle were doing, Sellie grimaced.

"We're fine. Thing is, he told me to come up with a scene," she said. "And I'm stuck. I haven't a clue."

Rebecca laughed.

"You poor thing! You've only been at it for a short while and he's already got you bending over backward. No pun intended," Rebecca said with a smile.

"Yeah, yeah. Thanks for your moral support!" Sellie said, grinning. She took another sip of her drink.

"You know, I could do with your help here."

Rebecca giggled. "Are you sure about that? I excel at getting in shit!"

"I'll take my chances!"

"Okay. More drinks, then I'll tell you what you can do," Rebecca said with a sparkle in her eyes. "It'll be fun!"

Two hours later, they left Ernesto's and Sellie had a big smile on her face. Rebecca's plan was great. It made her life easy and put the ball back in Kyle's court.

"Piece of cake! Let him sort it out!" she mumbled.

Chapter Fourteen

The club was buzzing with life—music, banter, the husky sounds of excitement and the scent of sex.

It went unnoticed by Sellie who was sitting at the bar, clutching a glass with whatever Kyle had ordered her. As he sat next to her, he was talking about whatnot. She tried to hold up her end of the conversation in spite of the jitters low in her belly. The thought of having to discuss the scene they were going to do, and what she had come up with for that, put her on edge. Somehow Kyle managed to distract her and after about half an hour she was totally relaxed and had let down her guard. She secretly hoped, prayed, he had simply forgotten about it all.

"So what do you have in mind for tonight, sweetie?"

Sellie almost dropped her drink.

"Geezzz, talk about going for the jugular!" She scowled at him.

A slow smile pulled at his lips as he looked at her. The power in his eyes seared through her, made her feel like a little mouse. Trapped. Cornered. Something inside her wanted to run for the hills, but another part that wanted to stay kept her in place.

"Stop doing that!" She had wanted to snap, sound strong, yet it came out as a plea.

The corner of his mouth turned up a bit more, and that did nothing to make her feel any better.

Breathe, Sellie, breathe! But how could she when he took her breath away? And her willpower? Where the hell had her backbone gone?

She needed to break the eye contact so she could tap into her resolve again. Provided it was still there. She wasn't too sure. Somehow she managed to tear her eyes away from his. Her hand trembled as she picked up her drink and knocked it back in one go. All the while, she sensed his gaze on her. It seemed to penetrate her very essence. She found she couldn't not look at him. As if he had the power to reel her in by an invisible cord, her head turned back to face him. She wasn't able to stop it. Her breath caught when the blue fire in his eyes seared her.

"Okay," she whispered. "I can do this. I'm a grown woman, dammit!"

"I was thinking... You put out fifteen items that you'd like to use and I will sort them in order of yes, maybe, no, no way! Then you decide which ones you want to use," Sellie said, stumbling over her own words.

Kyle's eyes sparkled with...something. She was unable to fathom what it was, but her gut instinct told her it wasn't going to be good. For her. Had she come up with something stupid? She wished she hadn't knocked back that drink now—her brain wasn't processing as fast as it normally did. Or was it being affected by him?

Before she could give it any more thought, he said, "Excellent idea!"

Sellie let out a breath, and relief washed through her. Until he spoke again.

"Let's alter it a little bit though."

Mild tension settled in her shoulders. *Now what?*

"I'll put things I like to use out on a table, you sort them to your liking. You'll pick ten you want to try and I'll use those ten items."

She tried to think of something that was off about this, but drew a blank. Ten items sounded doable to her, so she nodded.

"Deal!"

The glint in his eyes told her she'd just put her foot in something, but she couldn't work out what it was. Her heart rate went through the roof.

Kyle flashed a smile, picked up his bag and guided her through the club toward a scene area. Walking past other people doing scenes didn't help to put her at ease. There was a man being tortured by a Domme, a woman's nipples stretched to a point she hadn't thought to be anatomically possible, someone's ass red and welted from being caned.

Then they got to the area Kyle had in mind and he positioned her in front of a large rolling table. He glanced at her — she knew he did that to assess her. The man never seemed to miss a thing and she couldn't hide being uncomfortable. Then he went on with his business and she figured he'd decided she was fine. She watched him as he put his bag on the table with a loud thud and rummaged through it.

Nerves made Sellie shift her weight from one foot to the other as he began to put items out on the table.

A blindfold. She almost let out a sigh of relief.

I can live with that. See, I can do this!

A soft, fluffy glove.

Sure, what could be bad about that?

Her shoulder muscles started to relax. This wasn't too bad. She was going to be fine!

Then he put a butt plug on the table and her eyes widened in shock.

No freaking way!

Nipple clamps.

Maybe. Possibly. Much better than that...that...butt thing!

Next Kyle put some weird-looking thing on the table. She hadn't a clue what it was.

Hmm, I'm not going to choose that!

A ball gag.

Don't want that.

A flogger.

Looks okay. Yes.

Some kind of wheel with a handle?

What the hell? I think not.

A whip.

A whip? You have got to be kidding me. NO! She glowered at Kyle and he smiled.

Rope.

Sure.

Sellie was curious to see what else he was going to put on the table, but Kyle put his bag aside and gestured for her to start sorting. She stared at him, dumbfounded.

"Can't you count? That's only ten items!" she said, sarcasm dripping from her voice.

"Indeed."

"We agreed that I'd choose ten things. There's nothing to choose when there's only ten items!"

Kyle sighed an exaggerated sigh. "Sweetheart, you agreed to picking ten items and sorting them to your liking."

Her jaw dropped when she realized he was right. "That's not fair! You know full well this is not what I'd had in mind!" Her voice rose as she spoke and anger bubbled up inside her.

Kyle leaned forward, his lips almost touching hers.

"I never said I'd be fair," he whispered, his low voice almost a caress. She was too upset to be soothed by it.

"You...you asshole! You tricked me!"

People around them were turning their heads as she started to rant.

"Sellie, you best show a little respect." His smooth voice was sharp enough to cut and it shut her up mid-sentence. A tremor went through her as her eyes met his. The full force of his dominance washed through her, his displeasure with her clear in his gaze. Her anger turned to shame, then shock as he picked up the ball gag and walked toward her.

"Let's try out the first item." How could such soft-spoken words sound so threatening? Her mouth went dry.

His gait seemed to emphasize his power, instilling fear. And lust. Her body reacted to it, and even though she stepped back to get away from him, her nipples hardened and her pussy got wet. Then her back touched a wall and she started to plead.

"Please, Kyle. Sir. I-I didn't m-mean to be rude," she stammered.

Kyle loomed over her, dangling the ball gag in front of her face.

"I believe you were quite sincere when you called me asshole. And bastard. And the rest of it," he said. "Open your mouth, Sellie."

"Please, Kyle. Master. I'm sorry!" To her surprise, she found her regret was real. Her eyes brimmed with tears.

His gaze softened but she sensed he was not going to give in to her plea.

"Let's make sure you aren't going to spew out more profanities. Open up!" A clear command and she could do nothing but comply. She lowered her gaze and opened her mouth. Kyle put the gag into place and fastened it with sure fingers.

"Let me see," he said.

He gave her the time she needed to obey. She knew he'd wanted to see her with a gag from the moment he'd laid eyes on her. That didn't mean she had to like it, though. Having the ball gag in her mouth was humiliating and made her want to hide. At the same time, she wanted to please him and look up at him. When she did, he groaned. His reaction helped ease the sense of humiliation but she couldn't stop a few tears from rolling down her cheeks. He brushed them away with his thumbs and he smiled at her.

"Are you ready, sweetie?"

Sellie nodded and he pressed a kiss to the top of her head before guiding her back to the table.

She started sorting the remaining nine items in order of her liking. As she was working, her mouth filled up with spit. It shocked her to learn how fast that happened. She tried to swallow, but that wasn't easy with that wretched thing in her mouth. It was tempting to glower at him, but that would mean raising her head. With spit running out of her mouth. Not what she wanted him to see. Too awkward. Humiliating. Infuriating. *I hate you, you bastard!*

Thank goodness he didn't laugh or chuckle, even though she was certain he knew what was going through her head. She wasn't quite sure what she'd have done if he had chuckled. That would've been too much for her to handle. She'd guessed she'd break out in tears. Her eyes were prickling as it was and she was glad when she finished sorting the items on the table.

"Well done, love," he said.

Sellie nodded and waited, keeping her gaze lowered. Then he was with her, drew her into his strong arms and pulled her against his chest. He didn't speak, just held her close, stroked her hair, comforting. Warmth flooded her and she clung to him. She hadn't even realized how much she had needed his strength and reassurance. Everything inside her relaxed and she melted against him. Right now the ball gag didn't bother her so much. All that mattered was being with him, being close, reveling in the strength of the bond between them. Joy replaced the depressing feeling that she'd gotten in her stomach, and when he let go of her, she was all right. She dared glance at him and he smiled. A jolt ran through her as she saw the love in his eyes.

"Ready, sweetie?"

She nodded.

"Good!"

She watched him as he lowered chains, wondering what he was going to do.

* * * *

She was floating. Kyle had pulled her arms up in a vee with chains and had buckled the ankle cuffs to rings in the floor. In spite of the chains, she was sure she was flying. Her brain had long since gotten fuzzy and her legs felt like spaghetti.

He had blindfolded her, then started to work her up with whatever. It wasn't possible for her to see what item he was using. At first she'd tried to work it out. Soft things, hard, spiky, warm, cool. He had sensitized her skin, overwhelmed her senses, until her entire body was tingling, burning and aching with need. Her breasts were swollen, both from his torture and from arousal, and her pussy was throbbing inside and out.

He removed the ball gag.

"I like hearing your sexy moans a hell of a lot more than muffled sounds," he said, his voice hoarse.

Something spiky touched the skin of her bottom, and she figured that had to be the wheel she had seen earlier. He ran it over her bum, taking his time as if to make sure he didn't skip an inch. The feeling was odd, but turned her on nonetheless, and she almost wished her ass was bigger. The thought made her giggle.

When it stopped, her entire rear end seemed to be burning. Then the spiky wheel was put on her breast.

She sucked in air as he trailed it over the upper and undercurve, and back up. The tiny stings were painful and arousing. The wheel crept up toward her nipple. Closer and closer, not deviating, a straight line. Her heart was hammering in her chest. It stopped just short of her nip and she let out a sigh — whether from relief or disappointment, she didn't know. Then it moved, a spike pressed down hard on her nipple and she yelped. Pain shot out from her tortured peak and raced over her nerves straight to her clit, which spasmed with joy. Before the pain had even subsided, the wheel was rolled to her other breast and rolled over the upper curve. He teased her, ran it over her breast, went close to the nipple.

Her breathing was shallow, her heart rate through the roof. The wheel moved away from her bud, and she relaxed. Just as she unclenched her fists, he ran it over her nipple. A white-hot flash of pain blanked her mind and shook her body. A wail came from her and she jerked on the chains. She needed something to counter the sharp pain.

"Pleease!"

She almost sobbed when he put a finger on her clit. The sting from her nipples was overwhelming still—it wouldn't take much for her to come. As she bucked her hips in an unspoken plea, he began to move his finger, slid it around her clit, over the hood, up against the bundle of nerves, and it swelled against his finger. Heat flowed through her in waves, up and out. It turned into a fire, its flames licking across her nerves, searing her skin. The pain from her nipples added to the sensations and she whined. *So close!* Everything inside her coiled tight. Time seemed to come to a halt as she hovered over the precipice. One more slide over her nub pushed her over. The inferno in her core flared out of control, her clit pulsed and she cried out as sizzling hot waves shook her body. A starburst of light and color behind her eyes blew her mind. Sheer ecstasy flooded her. He drew out every shock until she was spent, hanging heavy on the chains.

When she regained her senses, she was in his lap, wrapped in a soft blanket, his arms around her. She glanced up, still fuzzy. Warmth flooded her as their gazes met. The gleam in his blue eyes opened her heart, the feeling so euphoric it almost made her cry.

I love you so, so much!

Chapter Fifteen

Sellie drove past the diner, searching for a place to park. It was late in the afternoon and she fancied a cup of coffee and a bagel.

She found a parking spot opposite the diner – it had to be her lucky day. After gathering her things, she was about to get out of the car when she saw Rebecca and a woman go into the diner. It was obvious the woman and Rebecca were friends. Sellie smiled, always up for meeting new people. Maybe the three of them could have some nice girl talk.

Then she saw a tall blond man inside the diner. *Kyle!* Her heart skipped a beat and she got butterflies in her stomach. Her smile froze on her face when she saw the woman walk up to Kyle to give him a hug. Sellie's heart skipped another beat when Kyle put his arms around her, hugging her as well. An intimate hug. The kind of hug that revealed the two of them were close and knew each other well. It looked much like a lover's embrace.

Sellie's heart was racing now. Exactly how close were they? And how well did they know each other?

A pang of jealousy shot through her when she saw the two laughing together. And it got even worse when Rebecca joined in. Rebecca, her friend, knew Kyle was close with another woman?

Sellie's throat seemed swollen as she choked up. She put her foot back into the car, slammed the door shut and threw her handbag onto the passenger seat. The sheer force with which she'd done that made it tumble to the floor, and the contents fell out. A sob welled up in her throat and tears pooled in her eyes as she looked at her makeup, cell phone, bankcards and whatnot, spread out over the floor. Her lipstick rolled back and forth, back and forth, as if to taunt her.

Tears rolled over her face now, and in between sobs, she cursed. Everything and everyone was against her. Her best friend, Kyle — the asshole — that…that woman. Even her handbag seemed in on the conspiracy.

"Breathe, girl, breathe! Stop being irrational," she mumbled. Kyle liked her — he couldn't be two-faced. *Or could he?*

She glanced over at the diner again and saw them sitting at a table, Kyle across from the woman. The way Kyle and the woman smiled at each other made her stomach turn and twist into a knot. Rebecca was nowhere to be seen. Had she left the two lovebirds?

Sellie had seen enough. With the back of her hand, she wiped the tears from her eyes, started the car and almost rammed into the car parked behind her. She cursed out loud, shifted to drive and accelerated. Someone honked and hit the brakes and only just avoided hitting her car.

Her hands began to shake when she realized she hadn't even checked to see if there was another car coming up. Forcing herself to focus, she sped off and decided to go to her parents' log cabin in the woods.

She didn't bother to go home first — she was too upset, and not thinking straight. Not yet. All she knew was that she had to get out of there, out of town, and be on her own for a bit to sort out her emotions. She had the clarity of mind to stop along the way to pick up groceries. Before she went on, she checked her phone and saw that Kyle had phoned her. Six times. And Rebecca.

For a minute she considered phoning Kyle, wanting to talk to him and to hear his explanation. Then the vision of him and that woman — that bitch — hugging and laughing together clouded her brain.

Sod him! He'd betrayed her. As had Rebecca. She switched off her phone and put it in her handbag.

Her emotions were all over the place while she drove to the log cabin. Thank goodness there was little traffic as her mind wasn't on driving. An hour later she arrived at the cabin, and she sat in the car for a while.

What was she doing? Why did she go here, running away like a child instead of facing the situation head-on and talking to Kyle? Would she be chasing after him if she phoned him or went back into town to see him?

She'd trusted Kyle one hundred percent. Had she been so wrong in her judgement of him? Was he even able to cheat on her, considering the depth of their connection?

Sellie let out a tired sigh. This wasn't going to help. Her mind went around in circles. She reached for her purse and shopping bag and got out of the car. A short while later, she'd put the groceries in the cupboards and fridge, and made herself a fresh brew. She sat down on the deck, sipping the hot liquid, not knowing what to do next. She was confused, upset, angry and shocked that she could feel this way. She had never been the jealous type. Not really. Her self-esteem and self-confidence were quite solid. But now... Why did Kyle have this effect on her? What was so different from the other men she'd been with in the past?

It dawned on her that she'd never gone as deep with anyone else as she'd gone with Kyle. Never had she exposed herself, bared her very soul, to a man like she'd done with him.

Was she jealous now because she'd been his submissive? No, she still was his sub. Or was she? The thought of him not wanting her as his submissive anymore made the knot in her stomach even worse.

"How wonderful! The beauty of BDSM. You've got to love it!" she mumbled to herself, then grinned as she heard the sarcasm drip off the words.

Aren't you supposed to become stronger because of it? More whole. Happy and complete.

"And look at me now. A total, utter mess," she whispered, and tears pooled in her eyes again.

* * * *

Kyle looked out of the window when he heard a car honk long and loud, and his jaw dropped as it almost rammed another car. Not any other car. Sellie's car.

His shoulders stiffened and terror crossed his face as he watched the near accident which involved the woman he loved. For a few seconds everything appeared to move in slow motion—both cars hitting the brakes, a mere hair's breadth in between, Sellie's panicked expression as she glanced over her shoulder, the brief eye contact with him as she turned back. Things went back to normal when she accelerated and sped off, leaving him shell-shocked.

"Kyle? Kyle!"

He blinked and stared at Olivia, who sat opposite him, then at Rebecca, who'd come back from the restroom.

"What's going on?" she asked.

He tried to concentrate, but the pain and emptiness he'd seen in Sellie's eyes during that split second was imprinted in his mind. His insides had turned into a knot. Something was very wrong.

"A woman leaving the parking lot almost caused an accident," Olivia told Rebecca.

"Sellie," Kyle mumbled as he rubbed his chin.

"Sellie? Oh God! Is she all right?" Rebecca frowned with concern.

"Yes," Olivia replied. "Who's this Sellie?"

"Someone I better ring right away. Ladies, excuse me." Kyle gave them a polite smile, went outside, got out his cell and phoned Sellie.

No answer. He cursed out loud. She'd been okay when he had talked to her earlier, so it must have been something that had happened right here and now. He went over events in his mind—Sellie across the street from the diner where he was with Olivia. Rewinding the events like a movie, he recalled hugging Olivia. She was nothing more than a friend, but Sellie didn't know that, and granted, Olivia had been a bit over-enthusiastic.

"Fuck it!"

He was certain the woman had gotten all kinds of ideas in her head. Bad ideas. He'd have to deal with it, sooner rather than later, before things escalated, but he wasn't looking forward to it. Her fiery personality was what had attracted him to her, but now that he'd have to convince her there was no other woman, it was more than likely her innate temper would be an obstacle as opposed to something he could toy with.

His gaze unfocused and he ground his jaw as he went over his options. From the corner of his eye, he noticed an elderly lady who gave him a sidelong glance, stopped then crossed the street. Kyle forced himself to smile at her, but instead of smiling back, she scurried away.

"Marvelous," he muttered, pocketed his cell and went back into the diner.

Both women were unsettled, Rebecca more so than Olivia. A line had formed between her eyebrows and she was chewing on her bottom lip. Hope bloomed on her face when he approached their table.

"And?" she asked.

"I'm scaring old ladies now," he said, deadpan.

"What?" Olivia frowned.

"Oh hell," he grumbled, and gave them an account of what had happened, which didn't take long. He didn't have a five-minute story to tell. "I'll leave you girls to it. I'm going to try to get hold of Sellie."

* * * *

Two days had gone by and Kyle was going up the wall. He had given up on phoning her, as it was clear her cell had been switched off. For two goddamned days. What was he to do? He'd had his fair share of trouble in life, but in general he always had it together. Never before had he been out of his depth like this, and for the first time in decades he didn't know how to cope.

Rebecca had tried to calm him down, had talked to him and advised him to give it a bit of time. Her husband, Cal, had come over, hoping to sort the situation, but the dark-haired man wasn't cut out for coaching. Patience wasn't his virtue, unless it came to his sub.

"I could deck him!" Cal grumbled to no one in particular. "Maybe that will shut him up for five minutes. And if I hit him good, fifteen!"

"What are friends for?" Kyle replied, sounding tired and sour. He took a deep breath. "Any other suggestions?"

"Phone McGregor. Ask his help," Cal said. "And do us all a favor, do it now!"

It annoyed Kyle to hear their sighs of relief when he got out his cell and he treated them to his darkest look. Then he called Ian McGregor, another club master and a police detective in day-to-day life.

"Ian, I need your help. On the double," Kyle snapped when Ian answered.

"Good afternoon to you too, Kyle," Ian replied. "What seems to be the problem?"

"It's an emergency. Someone's missing," Kyle said, impatience clear in his voice.

"Ah. Well, then you best come over to the station, like everybody else does," came Ian's advice.

"McGregor! I haven't the time for this!"

He waited as Ian drew in a breath, knowing full well that the man didn't like to be snapped at. No Master did.

"I'm sorry, Ian, I'm just…" Kyle didn't finish his sentence. Even he heard the desperation in his own voice. Now Ian got straight to the point.

"Who's missing?" he asked.

"A sub," Kyle growled.

Ian chuckled.

"Right. Well, the club is large, but not that large," Ian replied. "Are you sure she's not hanging on an Andrew's cross somewhere?"

"Not fucking funny, Ian!" Kyle shouted in the phone. "My sub has disappeared!"

"How the hell can you lose your sub? What happened?" Ian demanded, dead serious now.

A few minutes later, Kyle had told the whole story, and Ian asked for Sellie's name, address and other data on the girl.

"I'll get back to you. Give me half an hour. An hour max," Ian said, and hung up.

He kept his word and phoned Kyle half an hour later.

"Her parents have a log cabin in the woods. Could be she went there," Ian told him. "You want me to come with?"

Relief washed through Kyle.

"No. I'll go over there right now. I'll keep you posted," Kyle replied, glad he was able do something. "Oh, and, Ian, thank you. I owe you one."

Chapter Sixteen

Sellie grimaced.

"Girl, you look like shit," she told her reflection in the mirror. Her skin was pale, her eyes dull, her hair had lost its shine and she had bags under her eyes from lack of sleep. Not only was she dead tired, she looked it as well.

She'd been working hard for the last two days. Staying busy kept her from wallowing in misery. And at least she was able to sleep a little when she was exhausted. First, she had cleaned the house. Then she'd checked out the garden.

Her mother was a passionate gardener and her loving touch showed in the pruned shrubs and lush flowering plants that surrounded a well-cared-for lawn. Her parents hadn't been there for a few weeks and the grass had been rather high when Sellie had arrived. She didn't mind. Mowing the lawn had turned out to be a nice distraction from her sorrow. After that, she'd tended to plants that required attention, and within a day the garden was in pristine order again. Her mom would be thrilled.

With all the chores done, her mind began to churn again. What on earth was she supposed to do? Kick him to the curb? She wasn't sure if she could. Yet, if he wasn't trustworthy, she'd be better off without him, no matter how much ending their relationship hurt. She went back and forth between talking and making up with him, and breaking up. Of course she couldn't stay here forever. Hiding wasn't the solution. People would be worried about her, maybe even the cheating asshole. Apart from that, there was her work to think of. Being a freelance painter, time off equaled no income. She did okay, but she couldn't afford to lose out on work and pay.

She decided to take one more day, two max, then she'd have to go back and face reality. And let people know she was fine, although fine was relative. Her heart had been ripped out of her chest and she hadn't slept well, nor eaten a decent meal in the last couple of days. The thought of food alone made her sick.

"One more day," she mumbled. "Then I'll pack up, go back. And switch on my phone."

Would he have left messages or would he have given up after a few calls?

"How much do I mean to you? Do you really care?" Her heart was racing in her chest. What if he hadn't made a serious attempt to get in touch? That'd hurt like hell. Worse than seeing him with that woman.

She shook her head, realizing she had to do something lest she'd go mental. *The firing range!*

Her dad liked to come out here for peace and quiet, and to shoot, and had made a range at the back of the premises. Shooting would help her to let off steam. She seemed to have inherited her father's skills, although she wasn't as good a shot as he was. But she did enjoy it, and as it was she needed it to focus her mind and to think about something other than Kyle. And that woman.

She collected everything she'd need and crossed the yard to go to the shooting range.

The guns and ammo were out on the wooden table that was placed in front of the two firing ranges — one for handguns, the other for rifles. Her dad had built retaining mounds behind the target lines of both.

The handgun was first. She picked up a mag and started filling it, pushing the bullets into place with her thumb. When she was done, she put on the headset to protect her ears and walked to the line from which she wanted to shoot. The six aluminum targets that were next to each other on the stand wouldn't be hard to hit. She positioned her feet, wiggled her butt a bit to get comfortable, raised her arms, took aim and pulled the trigger. Her arms flew up.

"Damn. Focus, Sellie!" she cursed.

The gun didn't have a lot of recoil, but she'd still have to pay attention to what she was doing. She drew in a deep breath, aimed again, fired and hit all the targets one by one. She hummed, walked to the stand, turned up the targets and continued until the mag was empty. At the table, she refilled it and shot and hit the targets again and again until she got a little bored with it.

Time to get the rifle out. A nice rifle with a scope, built to not have too much recoil so it could be used without much strain. She thought of the one her dad preferred — bigger, stronger and with a much longer range. If only she could shoot that. But no way was she able to handle a rifle like that. Its recoil would rip her shoulder apart.

After she'd sat down at the table, the rifle supported by a tripod, she adjusted the scope, aimed, pulled the trigger. And missed the target. A displeased grumble escaped her lips. She could do better than that.

She inhaled, rolled her shoulders, then focused on the target.

"I'm going to hit you, bastard!" she mumbled.

Kyle almost laughed out loud as he heard her words. He'd arrived minutes earlier and relief had washed through him when he'd seen her car. That relief was short-lived as his heart almost stopped when he heard a gun being fired at the back of the cabin. He ran around the building, regretting not carrying a gun himself, and stopped dead in his tracks when he saw Sellie. His Sellie, out there in the sun, sparks flying off her red hair. With a rifle. He couldn't help but chuckle as he stood there, waiting for his heart rate to go down and the knot in his stomach to uncoil.

A loud bang echoed through the woods when she pulled the trigger. This time she hit the target. She yanked off the headphones and cheered.

"Well done, siren!"

He didn't miss the tremor that shook her when he spoke. He hoped it was due to the same mixture of emotions that affected him — relief, happiness and lust.

A smile pulled at his lips when she jumped up and turned around, her cheeks pink, chest heaving, eyes wide. The way her nipples strained against her T-shirt told him two things — she wasn't wearing a bra, and she was as pleased to see him as he was to see her.

Within seconds he was hard as granite. And pissed off. The little vixen who had given him so much grief was out here having fun while he'd gone mental with worry. Hours of anger and frustration funneled into a high-pressure jet that needed release. Crazy, wild sex would do the trick. His cock throbbed and he clenched his jaw as he fought the urge to take her down and fuck her brains out. Damned if he didn't want to mark her as his own and make clear he wasn't a man who'd put up with this kind of crap from his woman.

He managed some control and began to walk toward her. As he stalked closer, her nostrils flared, her soft whine alluring as hell, and he lost the inner battle for control. The craving was too strong.

"Kyle..." she started.

"Not now!"

"Y-yes, but..." Sellie stammered.

"Not. Now!"

Panic and passion flickered in her eyes, neither giving way to the other, rousing his sinful thoughts further. He growled when she stepped back, bumped into the table, put her ass on the top, swung her legs over it and faced him again. He held her with his gaze as he veered around the table. For a moment she stood as if nailed to the ground, then she spun on her heels and made a run for the woods. Kyle allowed her a few seconds' head start. A false sense of freedom would heighten the fun they were going to have. He counted to six and chased after her. Although she was fast, she hadn't gotten far yet and his long legs crossed the few meters with ease. Adrenaline rushed through his veins as he grabbed her forearm and swirled her around. The sheer velocity took them both down and he yanked her on top of him to absorb the shock of the fall himself, grunted as he did so, then they rolled over once more, to end with her underneath him.

Kyle blinked at the sense of déjà vu, having his cock where it craved to be and — like a few weeks back — not able to do what he wanted to do with it. The impact of the fall had sobered him enough to realize that talking had first priority, not indulging, but his raging hard-on disagreed with him. He shook his head, trying rid himself of the vision of going balls-deep inside her cunt.

"We have got to stop meeting this way," he panted.

"Please, Kyle!"

Her husky words shot straight to his loins, making his cock jerk.

"We have to talk."

How was he supposed to when his blood had left his brain and was pulsing in his core?

The plea in her eyes and the invitation of her lips robbed him of his control. There were limits to a man's willpower, and being on top of his hot and willing woman proved too much, even for him. He bent his head, claimed her mouth and swept in, hungry to taste her, all of her. Kissing was good, for starters. The open-mouthed mating drove him wild and he thrust his hips forward, pressing his erection against her crotch, getting himself a mewl. Driven by instinct, he pushed himself up, grabbed hold of her T-shirt and ripped it apart. A low groan welled up in his throat as he cupped her breasts, kneaded, then replaced his hands with his lips and sucked a nipple into his mouth, loving how it hardened under the torture. He pulled harder, her cry of want urging him on to her other breast. Sellie bucked and writhed beneath him as he sucked on one bud while rolling the other between his fingers.

"Yes, oh yes!"

Unable to wait any longer, Kyle let go of her nipples, leaving them swollen and red. He unzipped her jeans, yanked them down with her thong and put her on all fours. With the jeans around her thighs, he couldn't spread her legs very far, but when she arched her back, her pussy glistened in the sunlight. His mind blanked, and his cock and balls ached. He undid his fly, fisted his cock and put the tip against her inviting, wet cunt. One day he'd make gentle love to her. Today was not that day. With one thrust he buried himself inside her, making them both groan. Desire swept over him. He took her hard, encouraged by her whimpers and pleas. Her pussy convulsed around him and clamped down on him, driving him insane. He bent over and reached for her breasts that swayed back and forth each time he pounded into her.

"Oh damn, yes!" she moaned.

As he tugged at her nipples, her cunt clenched like a wet fist and he almost roared out in sheer delight. How he'd craved this, to take control and fuck her like rough and merciless. It was a visceral need that emanated from fear of having lost the woman he loved. Through his haze, he sensed the same desperation in her that he'd had in his gut. With each thrust he fucked it out of them both. Each slick slide of his cock in her cunt eased the pain and stirred up a cleansing fire of love.

"More, I need more, Kyle," she whimpered.

Not stopping his rhythm, Kyle leaned over, pulled her nipple, and the sudden wetness and tightening of her pussy told him she was about to come. It stirred up the heat in his loins into a blazing inferno that filled his being until nothing else mattered other than the throbbing of his cock. His balls tightened, drew up further, aching with the need to push up his cum. He shifted to short, fast thrusts and put his fingers on her clit to rub it. She exploded at the touch, and her sucking cunt took him with her over the edge. Her cries of passion mingled with his low roar as his cum shot up his shaft and out of the tip in mind-blowing spurts. Over and over, he rode the waves of utter ecstasy until the fire in his core died down to a simmering glow.

* * * *

They were cuddled up together on the sofa in front of the hearth, sipping hot chocolate with rum.

After their intermezzo in the yard hours earlier, Kyle had put her in an Adirondack chair on the deck. He had gone back to collect the weapons and ammo, made sure they weren't loaded anymore, and put them indoors.

The happy smile on her face as he walked back out on the deck tugged at his heartstrings. He reached out his hand, pulled her out of the chair.

A corner of his mouth curved up when he saw twigs and leaves in her hair. She struck him as a wood fairy. A sated wood fairy. Gorgeous and sinful.

"You need a shower, girl," he mumbled. "Come on."

Plucking all the dirt out of her long hair was quite the task, but he didn't mind. When they were both clean, he wrapped her in a large towel, dried himself off and put the towel around his hips.

Now they had both settled, cuddled up, being comfortably uncomfortable. They needed to talk. Kyle spoke up at the same time she did, and they both laughed, which lightened the mood.

"You start," Sellie said. Her expression revealed she was not certain she was ready to hear what he was going to say. He touched her cheek.

"Do you remember me telling you I tried a vanilla relationship a while ago?" Kyle asked.

When she nodded, he continued. "She is a friend of Rebecca, Olivia. I suspect you saw her in the diner the other day and saw us hugging. But you know, Sellie, there's nothing between us anymore. We are only friends."

Kyle observed her closely, trying to read what was going through her head and her heart. It was painfully obvious that she was confused, in two minds. Hope and pain alternated with each other in her expression. He could tell she wanted to believe him, but still wasn't sure.

"It looked like you were very…close friends." Her voice sounded rough.

Kyle put his hand under her chin and lifted her face. She kept her eyes lowered. He understood she didn't want him to read her, but if they were to get through this, they both had to be completely open and honest. Hiding wasn't an option. And he needed her to trust him, even if that meant she had to take a leap of faith.

"Look at me, Sellie." Nothing more than a whisper from his lips, soft and sweet. She complied.

Kyle smiled at her.

"Woman, can't you see I'm only interested in you?" he asked. "You could say Olivia is a good friend, in a way. There are no ill feelings between us, but we aren't in touch either."

Tears filled her eyes and her expression changed, telling him his words and honesty were starting to sink in. In spite of that, he sensed that her pain hadn't subsided yet. She sat there, stiff as a plank. His heart ached for her, but she had to work this part out herself before he drew her into his arms to comfort her further.

"Kyle, I feel so stupid," she whispered. "I don't like feeling this way. Why is this happening to me? I really don't want to!"

She sagged against Kyle's chest and started crying.

He simply held her, made soothing sounds and let her get it out of her system. After a while she calmed down and her breathing told him she was starting to doze off. *The woman must be spent.* So was he. Yes, they needed to talk some more about it all, but it'd have to wait.

"Come, babe, time to sleep," he whispered into her hair.

"Goodnight," she mumbled against his chest.

Kyle grinned.

"I was thinking in bed, girl. Move your ass!"

"Don't want to move," she slurred.

"God, you're a pain," he muttered. "I want to get comfortable too, woman."

A giggle.

"Then carry me, Master."

Kyle cursed under his breath as he got hard. He had to be in deep shit if a simple "Master" from her sweet lips aroused him that fast. Visions of making love to a sleepy siren went through his head, making him throb.

"Get up, Sellie. Now." The command had the desired effect and she did as she was told.

"You woke me up!" She glared at him.

Before he had the chance to tell her that glaring didn't please him, her towel came undone and slid down her body. That did please him. A lot. Kyle groaned when he saw her breasts, her smooth skin, the delicious curves of her hips and legs. He fought the urge to unzip, pull her onto his lap and have her ride him. Damn, she'd look divine on him, her red hair and skin lit up by the light of the fire in the hearth, breasts bouncing as she moved up and down.

The way the light flickered over her body as she stood there made his mouth water, his heart race and his cock ache with need.

"Bedroom. Go. I'll be right there." There was an unintentional snap to his voice, but he was about to lose control.

Sellie blinked her eyes and started to bend over to pick up the towel.

Kyle stopped her, ran his fingers over her cheek and smiled.

"Don't, sweetie. Nothing is wrong. I just need a minute to…"

Get my brain working instead of my raging hard-on.

He cleared his throat and finished his sentence. "Put out the fire."

He almost laughed, as that was exactly what he needed to do.

Sellie gave him a lazy smile and pressed a soft kiss on his lips before heading toward the bedroom. Kyle hauled in a breath when she walked off. It was going to be a long, long night.

He waited another hour before he went to bed, time he spent staring at the glowing embers in the hearth. When he was sure he was tired enough to sleep, he got up and walked into the bedroom. Sellie was fast asleep. He smiled. Her red hair was fanned out over her pillow, her lips full and a bit pouty. She was downright gorgeous. She looked so sweet and innocent, yet sexy as sin.

Best he'd think of something else or he'd get horny as hell again. He didn't fancy spending another hour with the dying fire in the living room to gain control over his dick. He undressed, slipped into bed beside her and dozed off within a few minutes.

* * * *

Kyle was asleep, having a very sexy dream that he enjoyed so much that his dick was standing up like a flagpole. He groaned, dreaming of a hot redhead on top of him, her creamy breasts bouncing and swaying as she rode him. Her wet pussy slick around his cock, clamping down on him, hot and tight.

He stirred in his sleep and another groan came from his lips. It was so goddamned good, his core was on fire. Waves of pleasure ran from his crotch through his ass, his legs, his stomach. He felt himself engorge as the dream-siren rode him harder, wilder. Insane sensations washed through his entire body, getting more intense the more her wet cunt tugged and sucked. He stirred a bit—it was too good to lie still and too good to be a dream.

Please, let it be real or I'll come all over the sheets like a teenage boy.

Kyle opened his eyes.

It was real all right, the sight goddamned hot. His gaze roamed over her body, taking in her breasts, her hard and swollen nipples, her rolling hips. The image made his cock jerk inside her and he thrust his hips up when she moved down, hitting her deep and hard. Tongues of fire seared through him.

"Damned best wet dream I've ever had." His voice sounded hoarse with lust.

Then his mind blanked — all he registered, as if from a distance, were her husky moans and sounds. His balls pulled up more and muscles started to spasm in a to-die-for dance of pleasure. His cock, back, legs and ass all joined the party. It felt so good — this party wasn't going to last long but it sure as hell would end in mind-boggling fireworks.

Sellie touched her clit and started to move almost out of control. His cock enlarged further and started to throb in anticipation of what was to come. The pressure in his balls kept building up, almost uncomfortable, yet so erotic.

Then she came, her vagina muscles contracting and sucking. He couldn't hold back anymore. Didn't want to either. His cock expanded and his semen rose from his balls, through his shaft, centimeter by centimeter. It shot out of the head of his cock, wave after glorious wave, and indescribable, mind-shattering sensations cascaded through him, leaving him feeling masculine and vulnerable as he gave her all he had to give.

Sellie collapsed on his heaving chest, her hair soft and tickling. His muscles started to relax, his mind still blank. Ripples of pleasure kept washing through his body, his heartbeat pounding in his ears. He wrapped an arm around her, sated. He sensed she was drifting off, and before long he fell asleep as well, with a smile on his face and his woman sprawled out on top of him.

Chapter Seventeen

Another two days had gone by. Sellie had appreciated Kyle's help with cleaning the cabin. After that, he'd gone with her to her place for the remainder of the day. They had talked a bit more, made dinner together and had a great time, and great sex, before he had gone home.

While she didn't like to see him go, she was doing much better. She was in good spirits, and even though her work kept her busy for the rest of the week, she was looking forward to club night.

Friday night arrived and she was a bit nervous. When they'd parted a few days earlier things had been good, but what if he behaved differently now? What if he had thought about it all and had decided she was a drama queen? Maybe he wouldn't want her anymore. After all, no man wanted a high-maintenance woman in his life. She was no relationship expert, but she knew that much.

On top of her concerns, she'd had a bad dream last night and had woken up crying. In her dream, Kyle and Olivia had been hugging and kissing, and it had been very intimate and passionate.

Right now she needed some reassurance that things were okay between them. That would mean telling him about her concerns and nightmare, and she wasn't sure about doing that. It seemed to scream 'drama queen' again.

Now there he was, relaxed, smiling at her, happy to see her, and she was a nervous wreck.

He drew her into his arms and she melted against him. Sellie looked up at him, offering her lips. Kyle kissed her. A slow, hot kiss that made her legs wobble. Her soft mewl mingled with his groan, and when she wrapped her arms around his neck, he took her deeper and plunged in. His unbridled passion made the blood roar in her ears, and her tongue tangled with his in a wildly exciting dance. He cupped her breast and kneaded. Another moan came from her and she pushed her hips against him, needing to feel him. Her breast seemed to swell in his hand and her pussy dampened. He found her nipple and tugged, gently at first, harder when a shudder went through her body. Her bud tingled and hurt at the same time. Her clit received each tiny message of pain and pleasure, and little shocks ran through it.

Kyle let go of her lips and bit her earlobe, pressed kisses down the side of her neck and nipped the curve. She arched her chest to push her breast more firmly in his hand and she couldn't help but moan. Heat rose from her core when he moved his hips and pushed his rock-hard dick against her. She hoped to God he would continue, even though they didn't have time.

"I'd love to go on, baby, but then it'll be a quickie," he said, sounding throaty. "I need more than that, and so do you."

Sellie nodded. He was right. A quickie wouldn't suffice. He let go of her breast and held her close, giving them both time to calm down.

"We're going to have a lot of fun tonight," he mumbled into her hair.

Sellie glanced at him and smiled.

"I think I better get dressed then," she said, and walked off toward the bedroom. She sensed his gaze on her behind, and in the doorway, she looked over her shoulder to give him a saucy look. "No peeking!"

Kyle grinned.

"No promises, baby. I love watching a woman getting dressed."

She blew him a kiss and closed the door behind her. She undressed and got the latex dress she wanted to wear out of her bag. Kyle's words came to mind as she slipped into it.

'I love watching a woman getting dressed.' A woman. Not her, but a woman. As in any woman? Would he have meant any woman? Her stomach got into a mild knot.

She told herself to stop it, but the harder she tried to do that, the more her brain kept repeating the words, like a broken record.

Not much later, she walked out of the bedroom, praying Kyle wouldn't notice she was upset. She smiled at him, but her shoulders were tight, and somehow the muscles in her face had a mind of their own too. Even she knew her smile looked fake.

"Are you all right, sweetie?" he asked, and tilted his head as he took her in.

"Yes, I'm fine, thank you," Sellie said with another smile.

Her heart was racing. Fooling a Master like Kyle wasn't easy, if it could be done at all. The man had years of experience with submissives and was used to paying close attention to them in and out of scenes. He sure as hell could tell when someone was lying, and she knew he disliked it when a woman put a smile on her face to pretend everything was all right when it was not. Kyle was all for honesty. So was she, but right this minute she found it impossible to do.

His keen eyes were on her still, and the gleam in them told her that it didn't elude him that her muscles tightened a bit more under his scrutinizing gaze.

She hoped to God he wasn't going to press the matter. Before either could speak, his phone rang. *Saved by the bell.*

"I'm sorry, I have to take this," he said. "A work thing. Why don't you go to the club? I'll join you there in a minute."

Relief washed through her when he brushed his knuckles over her cheek and he walked toward his office. At least she was off the hook for now.

The relief was short-lived as she realized she had to go into the club on her own. The thought didn't appeal to her. Sellie sighed. *So much for a great evening.* Maybe it was for the best if she went home.

She mentally kicked herself in the butt. There were plenty of people in the club that she knew. Kyle would be there soon as well. Nothing was wrong. She had to stop fussing.

A few minutes later she sat at the bar with a mint julep, feeling alone. She was almost glad when an attractive man in a suit walked up to her. *A man in a suit has to be pretty safe, right?* A few minutes she concluded that looks were deceiving indeed. The man was dominant in a very unpleasant way, making her feel incredibly uncomfortable.

"It's nice meeting you, but I'm waiting for my Master." She blurted, realizing it wasn't very smooth but it did the trick. He mumbled an excuse and walked away. She took a deep breath, glad to be in a decent club with good rules, and protection if need be. All members knew their membership would be revoked on the spot if they harassed other people. People's safety and sense of security were of the utmost importance to Kyle, and he made damned sure members were informed about that.

Then a Domme and a male sub came over to her. Sellie started to get awkward again. This entire world and its people were still a bit strange to her, and she had never talked to a Domme before. Fingers crossed the woman wasn't interested in her as a sub.

She relaxed when the woman asked about the mural she had made in the dungeon. Sellie was pleasantly surprised to find out people knew she had painted it.

The Domme, Kayla, asked her how she'd gotten inspiration for it and soon they were having a wonderful conversation.

"Well, I think I have to attend to my love now," Kayla said after a while, and smiled at her sub, her love for him clear in her eyes. She looked at Sellie again. "Can I give you my card? I am interested in your work. I have a room that could do with a mural. I'd like you to come over to have a look at it."

Sellie accepted the card and promised to phone her. She smiled as the Domme walked off with her sub in tow.

Her eyes drifted toward the clock on the wall near the bar. Half an hour had gone by and Kyle still wasn't there. Sure, she'd had an interesting conversation with Kayla, and the promise of more work was great, but she was getting more and more restless nonetheless.

Where are you?

Another Dom came over to talk to her. There was something about him that made Sellie dislike him right of the bat. Unfortunately he was rather tenacious, and it took all of her strength not to snap at him and tell him off. She was about to wave over a nearby Dungeon Master when the man gave up, and with an almost angry look, turned around and stalked off.

The place was starting to get on her nerves now. Under different circumstances, she didn't have a problem with holding man off in a polite yet playful way. But somehow that skill seemed to have abandoned her tonight.

Her gaze swerved through the room, hoping to see someone she knew. Nada. Just a lot of people that by now were fully engaged in all kinds of BDSM activities. The typical sounds of the club that she normally found exciting and arousing now only made her feel out of place. There she was, all dressed up in a tight and sexy latex dress, but without her Master. Not involved in the scene, not involved in a scene, and not even sure she wanted to anymore either.

Sellie decided to leave. She'd wait in Kyle's private quarters then make up her mind about staying or going home. As quick as her high heels allowed, she made her way toward the exit. When a hand curved around her upper arm, she almost slapped the person that had grabbed hold of her.

"Easy, girl!" Cal's deep voice reverberated in her ears. His dark eyes assessed her and Sellie stood as though glued to the floor. *Damn, that man has strong eyes!* It was as if he could see right through her and read her mind and thoughts. *Talk about intimidating.* She wanted to lower her eyes but found it impossible. His powerful eyes didn't allow her.

"What's going on, Sellie?"

"N-nothing. Sir," she stammered.

"Girl, I don't know what I dislike more. Someone else's sub wanting to slap me in the face or having her lie to me!"

Sellie's legs turned to mush, and not in a good way. Rebecca had to be a glutton for punishment to have married this man. No way would she want to be scared out of her wits all day, every day, by her husband!

She swallowed hard and tried to find her strength again. And her vocal cords.

"I'm... I'm sorry, Sir. I didn't mean to. Please don't hurt me!" She was shocked to hear how pathetic she sounded. What had happened to her? She used to be a strong woman, spirited, confident. *What the hell has this place done to me?*

When she saw something that resembled sympathy in Master Cal's eyes, she was close to crying.

"Wow, little lady. Calm down. Take a breath. That's it. And again," Cal said, his voice soft and soothing. "Good girl!"

He put his arm around her waist and ushered her toward the bar.

His care and the strength of his arm made her feel a bit better. Seeing Rebecca waiting at the bar helped a lot too. It helped Sellie to tap into her usual strength.

"I don't want to sit at the bar again," she said, a bit defiant.

"Sit." The soft-spoken command shattered what little strength she had found and she hurried to put her behind on a barstool, her eyes lowered and her hands in her lap.

Cal checked what she had been drinking and ordered another mint julep.

"I'm not sure Master Kyle would approve of me having my second drink now," she whispered and lifted her gaze.

"I think your Master would be pleased that I'm taking care of you in his absence, and right now I think you need it," Cal said. "Drink."

Sellie did what she was told. She didn't dare defy this man, and she very much doubted anyone dared do so.

"Sellie, what's going on?" Rebecca asked.

The concern and warmth in her friend's eyes opened her up and she blurted out what had happened.

"Don't you think Kyle would much rather be here with you than on the phone dealing with work on his night off?" Cal asked, a bit sarcastic. It was obvious women and their logic were sometimes beyond him.

Sellie blinked. She had been so absorbed in feeling sorry for herself that she hadn't even thought about how Kyle would feel.

"I... I think so," she said, and a sense of guilt came over her.

"I know so," Cal said.

"But still..." Sellie objected, like a dog with a bone, not willing to let go.

Cal raised an eyebrow. Sellie glanced at Rebecca for support.

"But still what?"

"Well, if he truly cared he wouldn't have let me go in here on my own now, would he?" Her voice sounded shrill now.

"I think it means he trusts that you can take care of yourself," Rebecca said. "You've been here before. You've met some people. Sellie, why are you so insecure?"

Sellie cast a quick look at Cal, not comfortable talking with him around, even though she needed to talk to someone about the turmoil inside her head and heart.

Cal sighed.

"All right. Off you go. I'll entertain myself with a whiskey," he said with a slight smile.

Rebecca beamed and kissed him.

"Thank you! You are the best husband and Master!"

"Yeah, yeah, go, woman." Cal's grumble contradicted the love that shone in his eyes.

"I won't be long, Master." She was eager to spend time with her husband and Master, and desire rushed through her veins.

"I'm sorry for spoiling your evening," Sellie said with a hint of guilt.

"Stop fussing now." Rebecca gave her a stern look. "We're going to talk, and since I'm missing out on a really good flogging, you better tell me everything!"

Not much later, Rebecca knew all that had gone down, and she realized Sellie was making a mountain out of a molehill. She also understood that her friend hadn't found her feet yet after what she'd seen with Olivia and Kyle. But even her reaction to that event, disappearing for days on end, had been over the top.

Rebecca had always known Sellie to be strong and confident, and the way she was behaving of late was unusual for her. There had to be more to it. Right now, in the club during a play-night, was not exactly the best of moments to delve deep into emotional issues. But Sellie sure as hell shouldn't be doing any scenes when she was this upset and emotionally unstable.

For a minute, Rebecca was in doubt what to do next. Kyle could walk into the dungeon any moment now, expecting to find his sub waiting for him. He'd want an explanation as to why she wasn't there. This wasn't something to spring on him out of the blue, nor was it her place to do so. This was between Sellie and Kyle and they had to sort it out. Apart from that, her own Master was expecting her back soon. But leaving her friend hanging like this wasn't an option either. *Decision, decisions.* Rebecca drew in a breath.

"Sellie, I want to talk to you about all this, because I think there's a lot more going on," she said. "But we haven't got the time for that now. The best thing you can do now is to talk to Kyle. Tell him you're not in the right mood. You really shouldn't be doing anything tonight, you know. Way too tricky when your emotions are all over the place."

Sellie nodded.

"You're right. I know," she sighed. "But I don't want to let Kyle down. He was so looking forward to this evening."

"As were you," Rebecca said. "Sometimes things just work out differently. I doubt Kyle will think you let him down when you're being honest. He knows scening isn't the smart thing to do when either one is upset. He'll understand. And then maybe the two of you can talk."

"Thank you, Rebecca," Sellie said with a smile. "You truly are a great friend!"

"You're welcome," Rebecca replied, glad Sellie was smiling a genuine smile now. "Let's go back inside before we both have ourselves a pissed-off Master!"

* * * *

As soon as they entered the dungeon, Sellie spotted Kyle at the bar. He flashed her a smile and her heart jumped for joy to see him happy. He met her halfway and drew her against him. She wrapped her arms around him and closed her eyes, breathing in his scent, basking in his warm embrace.

"Hi, sweetie! I'm so sorry it took longer than I thought," he mumbled into her hair.

Sellie could tell he was sorry for having left her to her own devices for that long. And there she was, fussing and being difficult about it all.

She smiled and offered him her lips, which he took. When he pulled back, her head was spinning and her knees were weak. *To hell with talking. It could wait.* Things seemed good between them — why spoil it?

"I've heard you already had two drinks," Kyle said. "You can have some water while I finish my whiskey. After that it's play time!"

Her insides melted when she saw the heat and desire in his eyes.

"Yes, Sir!"

Even as Kyle's gaze turned her spine to mush, she sensed that Rebecca was staring at her. Sellie avoided making eye contact and relief flowed through her when Cal guided his wife into the dungeon to play. She'd deal with Rebecca later if need be. For now, she was glad that Kyle hadn't noticed anything. Nothing much ever escaped his attention, but he'd had his back turned to them as he was ordering their drinks. He gave Sellie her spring water and she took a grateful sip.

He didn't speak. She wasn't sure what to say, and it began to make her a bit nervous. Somehow his fingers caught her attention. She loved his hands. Strong and masculine. The way he moved his fingers to turn the whiskey glass in his hand was almost sensuous. Languid, caressing the glass with his fingertips, yet his grip was firm so the glass wouldn't slip from his hand. How she craved to have his hands, and his fingers, on her. In her. Touching and teasing, pinching and probing. When the amber liquid was swirling, he brought the glass to his lips. As he drank from his whiskey, his gaze caught hers. Her heart skipped a beat when his blue eyes darkened with desire. They'd been together long enough for her to recognize that glint in his eyes when he was thinking of something kinky. He put his glass down and lowered his gaze to her breasts. Heat welled up in her core and her nipples bunched tight against the latex dress.

His voice was low and hoarse when he spoke up. "I'm going to wrap you up like a present."

"Oh?" Not much more than a whisper. Visions of being wrapped in cling film, unable to move her arms or legs, filled her mind, and a strong sense of not wanting that. Her stomach knotted, but the thought of not pleasing him as a sub was also daunting. *How am I going to deal with this?*

Kyle brushed his knuckles over her cheek and said, "Ropes around your breasts."

She let out a sigh and her stomach relaxed. Her pulse quickened when he drew his fingers down over the exposed flesh of her neck and upper chest. He continued over the latex, toward her nipples that puckered tight in sweet expectation of his touch.

"I want your tits swollen, taut."

He ran his fingernail over her nip and her clit spasmed in response.

"Look at me." Soft spoken, throaty with arousal.

She complied, glancing up to meet his gaze. The intensity of the eye contact was breathtaking and increased the pulsing between her legs. He held her with his gaze and put his hands around the base of her breasts. Then, as if to demonstrate what he wanted to do, he squeezed. Sellie gasped. The sensation was odd. A little painful, yet pleasant and in a strange way liberating. The pressure got harder and she sucked in a breath. She would've objected if it wasn't for the sheer possessiveness in his eyes. She drank it in, needing it as much as she needed air to breathe.

"Please…" Her tongue refused to work as a deep urge to submit flooded her. She begged him with her eyes.

A slight smile pulled at his lips as he understood her unspoken plea.

"Don't worry, baby, you'll get what you want, and anything else that pleases me."

He downed the remainder of his whiskey, grabbed her hand and guided her into the dungeon. The mild throbbing of her breasts from his firm grip sent heated messages to her lower body and her arousal turned up a notch. When they got to a scene area, he twirled her around, pulled her against his chest and conquered her mouth. She mewled as he swept in, exploring, teasing, stroking. Then he intensified the kiss, and lust spiraled up from her core when he forced her to open her mouth further. He was controlling her, dominating her with his lips and tongue, demanding that she surrender to him. There was no point in resisting. He was too powerful, his confidence overwhelming. Wrapping her arms around his neck was all she could do to steady herself as she trembled under the hot onslaught. As she let him take what he wanted, she writhed against him. The pressure from his hard-on stirred up the fire in her core and she moaned. At last he tore his mouth away from hers, leaving her panting and overheated.

He rubbed the pad of his thumb over her lower lip.

"I love your swollen lips," he mumbled. "They'd look lovely around my cock."

Sellie's face warmed and she averted her gaze. He laughed.

"Your shyness is so charming," he mumbled. Then he continued, all Dom again. "I want to play with your tits. Unzip."

Her head flew up in shock.

"What? No. Why do I have..." she objected.

"Now!"

His command reverberated through her and her fingers obeyed before her mind could even process what she was doing.

For a second she fumbled with the zipper, then pulled it down. Why was this so awkward? Humiliating even. He had seen her undress before, but it had never intimidated her like it did now. Amazing how different things were in the club. She glanced at him, hoping he'd grow impatient and do it himself. Instead, he raised an eyebrow as if to ask what her problem was. She let out a demonstrative huff, decided it was best to get it over with and pulled the zipper down over her breasts. They came free and she stood there, expecting him to reach out. Nothing. Seconds went by without a touch or word and she grew uneasy. In the end she dared to look at him. He hadn't moved at all—his gaze was still on her.

"Sir?" she asked with a slight tremble in her voice.

"I said *unzip*, girl, not bare your tits." He spoke soft and slow, as if addressing a child.

Sellie blinked, not sure she'd understood him right.

"Unzip, as in, lose the dress."

Oh, how she wanted to scream at him. *Isn't it enough that my boobs are hanging out? Of course it isn't enough. Why settle for uncomfortable when you can have bloody awkward!*

Her hand was shaking when she pulled the zipper farther down, exposing more of her flesh. Her belly button came into view, and she swallowed before continuing over her mound. A second later the dress opened fully, leaving her front naked, except for a miniscule golden G-string.

The corners of his mouth curved up when he saw it.

"I like how you always come up with surprises."

He stepped in, slid the dress down her arms and let it drop to the floor. Without wasting any more time, he began to work her up—squeezing her breasts and ass, toying with her nipples, playing with her clit until it was throbbing against his finger. Her knees were wobbly, her leg muscles quivered and heat flared up from her core. Soon her breasts were full and swollen, and he got ropes out. It didn't take him long to create a corset around her upper body. She was almost disappointed when he kept it short, leaving her belly exposed. She loved the graze of rope on her bare skin and she'd have liked more of it. In spite of that, she let out a happy sigh when he finished the last knot. The ropes pulled the skin of her breasts taut, the increasing pressure on them arousing. Again, that odd sense of liberation flowed through her. Her nipples tingled and her pussy was soaking wet. A soft moan of need fled her lips.

"Time for you to lie down," he mumbled, led her to a bondage table and helped her get on. With swift movements he fastened her to it with leather straps over her upper body. Before she could even think about protesting, he'd parted her legs, put cuffs around her ankles and attached them to the table.

Now her brain kicked into gear. She was in two minds. Part of her loved this helplessness and for him to have full control over her. Another part was a little scared. She hadn't a clue what he was going to do. All he had said was *'ropes around your breasts.'* He had done the ropes, and now she was on her back, immobilized, with her pussy exposed for his use. The thought gave her a little jolt. It sounded so wrong. So hot. The heat in her core turned up a notch and she got even wetter.

She caught his gaze and her heart did a somersault as the fire in his eyes bored into her, searing her flesh.

"Oh yes, you are ready." His voice had gone low and little hoarse.

She hadn't a clue what she was ready for, but the promise alone was so arousing that her nipples hardened to the point of pain. She was close to not even caring what he was going to do, as long as he did it.

Yet when he turned to the table to grab an item from it, she watched with mild concern to see what he picked up. A vibrator. It whirred to life and he ran it over her breasts, teasing her with it. He traced it over her nipples and tiny but strong currents of pleasure shot out from them and connected with her clit, which responded in sync with tiny jolts of joy.

He moved the vibrator down over her belly, in a straight line toward the junction between her legs. Her breathing got faster and she tilted her hips in sweet anticipation as he got closer and closer. Her mind blanked and her clit pulsed. Then he held still, the buzzing tip right above her nub. Vibrations ran through her pubic bone, stimulating her clit, but it wasn't enough. A keening protest slipped from her. He ignored her and kept the vibrator in place, bent his head and his lips closed on her nipple. Now she whimpered, attempting to raise her chest, but the straps didn't allow her much space to move.

"Oh, please!" she panted as he circled her areola with his tongue and lapped over the taut peak. His teasing drove her wild. Not enough stimulation on her clit, not enough on her nipple either. Then he pulled her bud into his mouth and she moaned out loud as pain zinged from her nip and made a beeline for her clit. Shocks of pleasure shot through it. Instinct made her open her legs further, a desperate unspoken plea to be touched there. She tried to push her lower body off the table, hoping the vibrator would move. Right that moment, he let go of her nipple and moved the vibrating toy to her upper legs. The buzzing sensation on her thighs was very enjoyable, but she required it elsewhere. Her pussy was pulsing inside and out, her clit aching.

Kyle switched off the vibrator, trailed it up over her thigh to her pussy and circled her inner labia with it. He lifted his head, he gave her a lazy smile, moved the toy to her entrance and pushed it inside. Her cunt clamped down on it.

"Please!" Her voice trembled with need.

He didn't reply, just held her with his gaze, his eyes now half-lidded with a gleam of passion in them. She swallowed, wanting to shy away from the raw desire, but the intensity of the contact had her transfixed. Her pussy convulsed around the vibrator and heat spiraled up from her core. How she wished he'd switch it on. It was plain he was enjoying her ordeal. All of it—her arousal, the straps, the ropes. For a brief moment, it infuriated her that he loved to see her helpless and exposed like this. She almost wanted to swear, but the urge ebbed away as fast as it had risen. Every shred of resistance melted. She blinked and looked at him in wonder, not understanding how her anger slipped through her fingers like loose sand. Then something inside her shifted, softened, and she surrendered to his will and his desire. She knew he'd seen it too when his eyes flashed with dominance. Her clit spasmed in response and a shiver ran down her spine.

The *please* she now whispered sounded nothing like the ones from before. Those had been demanding—now she was truly asking. Begging.

He traced the backs of his fingers over her belly and placed a kiss there. Without turning around, he reached for something on the rolling table. He had a bottle in his hands, squirted some of its contents in his palms and began to rub it over her breasts. It was smooth, and she realized it was oil. The slide of his hands over her flesh was erotic, and by the time he was done her skin was tingling all over. As he turned to put the bottle away, she let her body sink into the padding of the bondage table. All her muscles were relaxed and her mind was at ease and unfocused as she watched his back. She smiled when he faced her again, holding a burning candle. The smile froze on her face and she sucked in a breath. The memory of their conversation about wax play came to mind, as did the way it had turned her on. She knew she'd let him do it, just as she knew she wanted it. For him and for herself. A thrill coursed through her at the thought of hot wax on her body, but at the same time, it scared her. Needing his strength, she sought his gaze. The calm in his eyes and the confidence that exuded from him erased all doubt and fear. Instead, a sense of excitement and curiosity came over her. The corners of his mouth curved up, telling her he was pleased with what he saw, then the vibrator whirred to life. The unexpected sensation shook her and a surprised "Oh" came her lips. As her pussy clenched with pleasure, the first droplet of wax landed on the swell of her breast. Its heat seared her and she gasped. When it cooled, her shoulders relaxed, but he tipped the candle and another droplet hit her breast. Again she gasped. Bead after hot bead landed on one breast, then the other. She parted her lips to allow her harsh pants to escape. At some point, the vibrator was turned up and the fiery stings merged with the pleasure between her legs. She cursed the straps that stopped her from moving. Her brain was fuzzy, her eyes half closed as she surrendered to the cravings of her flesh and the sensations that tortured her body. As the hot stings circled closer and closer to her nipples, her heart rate went up. Then a bead of hot wax splatted on her left nip and another fiery sting hit her right one. She shrieked and her eyes flew open, expecting to see him holding two candles, yet seeing only one.

"Ice," he said with a devilish smile as he had a cup in one hand and a candle in the other. He tipped both, and she watched a bead of wax fall down, as if in slow motion. It hit her nipple, followed by a drop of ice water. She arched her neck and whined. The overwhelming sting raced across her nerves to her throbbing clit. How could ice feel so hot? She didn't get time to think as he continued — wax, ice, wax, ice. Her breasts seemed to be on fire, and her nipples ached and sent heated messages of pain and pleasure to her core. Her pussy was having a ball with the vibrator, and her clit pounded. Continuous mewls and moans seeped through her haze, adding to her excitement, and she realized they were her own. The sensations were so arousing, and she was floating in her happy place. Her entire body was on fire, the hot wax now on her belly and mound. It seemed to increase the vibrations in her pussy. An inexplicable wave of excitement began to rise from her center as more hot splashes seared her skin, lower now, landing on her labia. *Oh God, not on my...*

A hot bead splatted on her clit and a shrill cry broke from her, and as drops of ice water hit her throbbing nub, she came. Exhilarating ecstasy flooded her, wave after glorious wave. She felt like melting and exploding at the same time, out of control, swept away by the complete release.

After what seemed like an eternity, her orgasm turned to rippling pleasure and the occasional shudder, and she became aware of something touching her skin. She wondered what it was and opened her eyes. Her vision was blurry and she tried to focus on Kyle. He glanced at her and smiled.

"Hi, sweetie," he mumbled, then continued to scrape the wax off her body with the blade of a knife.

"What ary' doing?" she slurred.

"Cleaning you up, baby," he said.

She tried to get her brain to work, but failed at it. Her tongue refused to cooperate as well, so she relaxed and let him do what he was doing. Realizing he was using a knife on her was weird. And it felt odd too. Nothing like the hot wax, but her skin was so sensitive now. She drifted back to her happy place and moaned. As he continued, a new fire ignited between her legs and she got wet and needy. Then his mouth was on her.

"Oooh yess!"

She tilted her hips as he licked through her slit, moved up to her nub and lapped over it again and again.

"Oh God, more!"

He stroked and sucked her nub, and before long she was in a state of delirious need. Everything in her core coiled tighter as she neared the sweet precipice of orgasm. He slid two fingers into her now soaking wet cunt and thrust them in and out. A few more strokes with the point of his tongue and she plunged over the edge. She cried out as orgasm trembled through her body—the force of it blew her away. Sizzling hot waves of fire kept rolling up and out from her center. A starburst of joy filled her, mind, body and soul, making her float in a state of sheer, utter bliss as he sucked every shock out of her.

* * * *

Hours later, Sellie woke when the early morning sun peeked through the window of the master bedroom, a ray of light caressing her face.

She sensed Kyle next to her in bed and a smile lit up her face. With her eyes still closed, she stretched her muscles. Her body still ached a bit here and there from last night's play.

And hadn't it been a great night! By the time they'd gone to Kyle's private quarters she'd been happy and sated. She was sure that whatever problems they'd had were gone and that there was no need to talk and drag it all up again. They were fine.

Sellie cuddled up against Kyle. In his sleep, he wrapped his arm around her. She yawned and fell asleep again with a smile around her lips.

Chapter Eighteen

Serenity was coming to life again. Saturday nights were always busy.

Peta, a submissive, was at the reception desk with Melissa, another sub. They were checking in visitors and handing out tokens for alcoholic beverages.

She looked at Melissa's ruddy face and knew her own face looked the same. Not only because they were busy, but mostly because of the cheeky comments some of the Doms and Masters made. Her heartrate went up when Master Rafe approached the reception and she quickly lowered her gaze.

"Don't they look lovely tonight!" Master Rafe said with lust in his voice.

Peta looked at him, about to thank him for his compliment, only to find that his eyes were glued to her bulging breasts.

Peta's face burned now. She fancied Master Rafe and breast play. As did he. They had never played together yet, but she wouldn't mind. Not at all. The man was ruggedly handsome and had an aura of power about him that made her wet just looking at him.

Right now, she was tongue-tied, though. And his eyes were still on her heaving chest.

"Come look for me when you finish up here, sweetling," Master Rafe said. "If you want, of course."

Then he sauntered toward the club doors and disappeared inside.

"Peta, tokens!" Melissa nudged her and gestured that another Master was waiting for her to do her job.

"I'm sorry, Sir," Peta hastened to say, and handed the man in front of the desk his tokens for tonight.

From the corner of her eyes, she saw Master Kyle approach with his gorgeous redhead submissive on his arm.

"Peta, a moment, please," Kyle started.

Peta's heart was racing in her chest. Had she done something wrong? And why was the redhead glaring at her?

She walked toward Master Kyle.

"Sir?"

"When the doors close tonight, I want you to go and find Master Rafe," Master Kyle said.

"But, Sir —" Peta objected.

"No buts, girl," Kyle interrupted. "I've seen how you wanted him for a long time. Keeping yourself from playing with Doms who'll give you what you need won't get you anywhere."

Peta couldn't hold herself under his strong gaze and lowered her eyes.

"Master Rafe can give you what you need. I know it, you know it, he knows it," Kyle continued. "Tonight you're going to make yourself happy. And him. Understood?"

"Yes, Master Kyle," Peta whispered. It was awkward to be commanded by Master Kyle to scene with Master Rafe. But she knew — sensed — that Master Kyle cared and was only looking out for her, making sure she'd get what she craved. And yes, she'd waited far too long, trying to satisfy herself with Doms whose interests didn't match hers, mostly less strict Doms. She needed a strong hand and a powerful man whose desires and needs equaled hers. That was scary, but maybe if she dared go there, she'd go home fulfilled for a change.

It was reassuring that Master Kyle cared about her and wanted to help her to step over that threshold.

"I'll make sure someone else comes to help Melissa finish up so you can leave early," Kyle said.

Peta smiled at him, grateful.

"Thank you, Master Kyle!" She was beaming.

"Good! I trust you'll have a good time, Peta." Kyle grinned a chuckle. "Master Rafe won't let you down."

Heat crept up Peta's face. She had watched Master Rafe scene a number of times and his submissives always had mind-blowing orgasms. Knowing that tonight she'd be that lucky girl sent a jolt through her lower body.

Again she thanked Master Kyle, and before walking away, her eyes met the redhead's.

Her glare was so intense that it sent shivers down Peta's spine. Peta hurried back to the reception desk and got caught up in work. Soon she'd forgotten the redhead's angry gaze. All she could think of were Master Rafe's dark eyes, full of promise.

* * * *

Sellie's stomach was in a knot as she sipped from her drink.

Why did that damned girl have to look at Kyle like that? All flushed and heated. Lowering her eyes as if she was his submissive.

The way she'd smiled at Kyle, her Kyle, flashing her eyelashes, all smiles and sweetness! How she flaunted those huge melons.

Damn, she would have loved to slap that adoring smile off the woman's face!

Sellie took another sip of her drink and tried to forget all about it. Kyle was here, with her. They were going to scene tonight. She was going to sleep with him in his bed tonight. Not that girl. There was no reason to be upset. None whatsoever.

She hauled in air and glanced at Kyle. He smiled at her, put an arm around her waist and kissed her lips.

"You look delicious tonight, babe!"

Sellie fluttered her lashes and flashed a sexy smile at him.

"You're not too bad yourself, handsome!"

Kyle groaned deep in his throat.

"When you look at me that way, I want to put my hands all over you." The desire in his voice made her quiver and the hunger in his eyes melted her insides.

Her breathing sped up as she tried to hold herself under his piercing gaze. His lips curved up, telling her he knew.

She let out a soft sigh of relief when turned his attention to her breasts. Pushed up by her corset, they almost popped out when she sucked in air.

Kyle looked up as he ran a finger over the swell, teasing and tickling.

The fire in his eyes had an amazing effect on her pussy. The femme fatale act she'd attempted to pull off only seconds ago fell apart and she felt naked under his scrutiny. Naked and vulnerable. All she wanted was to melt against him, to offer herself to him, mind, body, and soul. A soft mewl came from her.

"Problems, love?" he asked as his finger inched closer to a nipple that was only just hidden by her corset.

Her areolae puckered and both her nipples presented themselves in their full glory, pressing against the fabric.

He pressed a soft kiss on her lips.

"I want to be closer, babe," he said, sounding a bit hoarse.

He pulled her of the barstool and ushered her to the dance floor with his hand on her ass.

A number of other couples were dancing, their attire depending on whether they were submissive or dominant. Kyle twirled her around and pulled her against him, and as she was about to complain that he was holding her too tight, he took her mouth. He didn't waste time teasing her to open up. His lips and tongue could be every bit as dominant as the rest of him. Sellie had no choice but to surrender to the delicious, firm pressure of his mouth. Kyle swept in, plundering, taking, demanding a reply.

His hands were all over her body, stroking, caressing, kneading. He knew how and where to touch her to get her aroused.

Soon Sellie's legs were like jelly and she clung to him. He released her lips and nibbled her neck, nipped her earlobe and swirled his tongue inside her ear. A husky moan welled up in her throat. She moved her head to allow him easier access to her oh-so-sensitive neck and ear. Her lower body seemed to have a mind of its own and she writhed against him, enjoying the pressure of his erection against her. She needed to feel his excitement, had to know that he wanted her.

Shivers of pleasure ran up and down her spine as he worked her up. A tiny part of her felt awkward about the public fondling, but the biggest part of her didn't give a rip. Until Kyle mumbled, "I love your sexy behind!"

Sellie moved her hips against him, then realized she felt the warmth of his hands on her skin. He had pulled up her skirt to bare her ass.

She stiffened in his arms and started to pull the skirt back down.

"Leave it." His soft-spoken command made her quiver.

How could he sound so goddamned dominant and strong without even raising his voice? She looked up at him, not sure whether to glower or beg.

"So fucking sexy," Kyle whispered.

Sellie stood there, not certain what to do or say. The overwhelming power that oozed out of him enveloped her, and it screamed sex. Wild, passionate sex. Her pussy clenched in response to the mating call of her man and Master—who right this very hot minute looked like he was about to take her on the spot. More predator than man. King of the Jungle, a Lion, ready to spring into action if his prey so much as moved a finger. She was his prey, and it scared the hell out of her. Yet, she wanted it. So, so much. Her body loved it. Her breasts were aching for his touch and her clit was sending nonstop fiery messages through her lower body.

The moment seemed to last forever, but only seconds had gone by. Then Kyle hauled in a deep breath, turned her around and pulled her back against him.

"I think it's time to find ourselves a playroom," he mumbled into her hair. He fiddled with her corset, opening the first two hooks.

Sellie glanced down to see what he was doing. Her breasts almost spilled out now—she could see her nipples.

"Kyle..." she started.

"Ssshhh. No complaining. I like it. A lot." His voice sounded hoarse.

He tugged at her nipples and she arched her chest to counter the sweet pain that seared straight to her core.

A longing mewl escaped her.

"I know, baby," he muttered. He moved his hand down over her belly, toward the hotspot between her legs and cupped her pussy. Next he slid his index finger from her entrance to her clit, ran over it and held the tip of his finger on the hood.

Shocks shot through her body. The soft pressure of his finger so close to her aching nub was annoying, and delicious.

"If you need to use the bathroom, do it now, Sellie," Kyle whispered. "I intend to keep you busy for quite some time."

She drew in a breath to stabilize herself before she was even able to think about walking to the restrooms. Again, she started to pull down her skirt.

"No."

Sellie shook her head in disbelief. The restrooms were on the other side of the club. Did he think she was going to walk over there with her breasts hanging out and her ass exposed? One look into his eyes told her that not only was he thinking that, he was demanding it.

"But…" she tried.

"No."

The steel in his voice when he spoke that one word had her nailed to the floor. The dominance in his eyes didn't help much either.

"You can go like this and relieve yourself or scene without." *Does he have to sound so ruthless?"* I do not recommend the latter. I promise you'll find it quite uncomfortable."

Kyle crossed his arms over his chest, giving her time to think. And she did think. She'd had two drinks and a bottle of water — she needed a bathroom break.

"Sweetheart, you should be happy that your Master thinks of your comfort," Kyle said, a hint of amusement flickering in his eyes.

She doubted that whatever he had in mind for tonight had anything to do with her being comfortable.

She glowered, turned around and stomped off to the restroom.

* * * *

The restrooms were every bit as posh as the rest of the club. Spacious, huge mirrors, piles of clean towels, various liquid soaps, disinfectant, feminine freshness wipes and a few bottles of perfume.

Sellie avoided looking in the mirrors when she entered the room and went into a stall to do her thing. When she was done, she pulled down her skirt. *Force of habit.* She pulled it back up again, cursing under her breath. As she exited the stall, a few other submissives entered the restroom.

Sellie fought the urge to go back into the stall to hide herself and her nakedness until the other women had gone.

They didn't bat an eye, though, and she let out a sigh of relief. Of course they wouldn't be shocked. This was a BDSM club. People walked around half-naked for fun. Compared to some others she was still overdressed, even with her ass bared and most of her breasts exposed. She'd seen a woman walking around in nothing but ropes. The woman had looked very proud, showing off her tightly bound breasts. No shame or awkwardness about being naked except for some rope.

Sellie had gotten used to seeing such things — some of it even aroused her. In spite of that she was certain she'd never be comfortable walking around half-naked herself.

She washed her hands and couldn't help but look in the mirror. Her cheeks turned red. Dammit, she looked way too exposed. She couldn't quite think of the right word. Yet what she saw reflected was hot. It turned her on. If it had that effect on her, it had to have the same effect on Kyle. That realization made her feel sexy and her entire vibe changed. She could see the transformation in the mirror. The insecure, angry woman had gone and now a femme fatale was looking back at her. A smile lit up her face.

"That's more like it! You look good, girl!" one of the submissives said. "I'm Kate, this is Ruth."

"Hi, I'm Sellie. And thanks. It's just... I wonder if I'll ever get used to this," Sellie replied.

Kate laughed.

"If your Dom is any good, you never will. He'll think of something else again and again to keep you on your toes." she said, still smiling.

Sellie chewed on her lower lip.

"I see your point. Kyle is quite good at that."

"Kyle? You mean Master Kyle?" Kate's eyes twinkled. "Girl, you better get used to never getting used to anything."

Ruth joined the conversation.

"Oh, the things I've seen Master Kyle do. Damn!" she said, a dreamy look in her eyes. "There isn't a sub who wouldn't want—"

"Ruth!" Kate interrupted.

Sellie's self-confidence crumbled. Now she had visions of Kyle scening with other subs. And of course he had a past. She wouldn't hold that against him. Everyone had a past, including her. But that tended to be a past with lovers, not submissives. Somehow that seemed different. Hearing Ruth say that all subs wanted to scene with him didn't do much for her confidence levels either. Most of the women that frequented the club were experienced and knew how to please a Dom. And a Master like Kyle.

She swallowed. Could she live up to that and be good enough for Kyle? Doubt crept into her system and a quick glance in the mirror told her it showed in her eyes.

Kate saw it too and she cursed out loud. She grabbed Sellie's upper arms and shook her.

"Look at me, girl." Her voice was every bit as strong as a Dom's could be. "You're going to be all right. You hear me?"

Sellie looked at her, drinking in the strength she saw in the other woman's gaze.

"But what if I can't please him?" she whispered.

"You already please him or he wouldn't be with you," Kate said.

Ruth nodded her agreement.

"I'm so sorry for upsetting you. Master always says I talk too much," she said, giving her a rueful smile. "I get to wear his gag a lot."

Sellie couldn't help but laugh.

"There you are. Give us a hug!" Kate said. They hugged for a minute and Sellie did feel a lot better.

After thanking Kate for her help, and wishing both her and Ruth a great evening, she walked out of the restroom. She started to make her way to where she'd last been with Kyle while swaying her hips, a smile on her face.

Until she saw Kyle with Peta. He laughed out loud at something Peta had said.

The green monster of jealousy woke up at the speed of light and coursed through her veins. Every cell of her body seemed to burn and shake as they absorbed the poisonous energy. Then it flooded her brain, reducing her from a rational woman into an emotional bundle of pain.

Her brain screamed and her heart pounded in her chest. She had to leave, get out of there before she lost it altogether.

Sellie turned around, had the clarity of thought to get her bag and car keys and left the building as fast as she could.

Somehow she managed to pull down her skirt, but didn't bother with the corset. Her fingers were trembling too much.

It took forever for her to unlock the car door. She couldn't get the key into the lock right away and tears of frustration ran over her face. At long last she succeeded and got into the car.

Before she collapsed into a heap of misery, she hauled in a deep breath and wiped the tears from her cheeks with the back of her hand.

She screamed when the door was opened and strong hands yanked her out of the car. Kyle. A very unhappy Kyle. A very angry Kyle.

"What the hell are you doing?"

Her lips moved, but her tongue refused to work. She couldn't think of anything to say anyway. Her mind wasn't working. She wasn't sure it ever would again. And now he was angry with her as well.

Couldn't she get anything right? Why wasn't she able to please him? Fear of losing him mixed with the hurt and jealousy that ran through her. An ugly mix, too much to handle.

The only thing that went through her head was *I can't please him. Can't please him.*

A sob welled up in her throat and her muscles gave in.

Kyle cursed, swung her up in his arms and carried her back indoors. He handed her car keys to the doorman.

"Please take care of her car and bring in her bags."

Kyle continued walking, straight to his private quarters.

Something was very, very wrong, but he hadn't a clue what. How the hell could he have missed something being so wrong that would upset her this much?

He'd find out later. Right now, he needed to take care of her. Clean her up, calm her down, get something warm inside her. Soup would be good.

And they had to talk. First things first, though — a warm shower was what she needed. He undressed her, took off his own clothes and got into the shower with her.

She clung to him. He tried to make out the words she mumbled.

Her *"Can't please you"* shocked him.

* * * *

Now, more than an hour later, Kyle was staring at the ceiling. Sellie was asleep in his arms. After the shower and soup, she had seemed to feel a bit better, and he'd decided to ask some questions. He had to find out what had happened to trigger such a strong emotional reaction. Before he knew it, he'd had a raging woman on his hands. The things she'd thrown at him had him off-kilter. He'd gotten accused of flirting with other submissives, wanting to play with others, subs who could please him. Then she had started crying and had asked him what he needed her to do so she'd please him.

He didn't understand it at all. What the hell had gotten into her? She had yelled about Peta, Olivia and something that Ruth had said. Then she'd gone on about not being good enough for him and that he'd be better off finding someone else, only to contradict that statement by bawling her eyes out the next minute because she didn't want to lose him.

His male brain had fried, unable to follow how she jumped from one thing to the next, going from anger to despair and back. It had taken all his strength to not lose his own temper. He wanted to help her, find solutions, but he couldn't do that when she was all over the place. No matter how much he wanted to, he didn't get her train of thought.

In the end, they'd both been exhausted. He'd taken her to bed and managed to reassure her enough so that she'd sleep.

But he couldn't. And he failed to understand it. They were a perfect match—physically, mentally, emotionally. He had been happy as a lark to have found the woman of his dreams, someone who complemented him both as a man and as a Master. Now there was a spanner in the works. A major spanner.

Kyle drew in a deep breath. He needed rest. There was nothing he could do right now to solve things. He visualized the problems as clouds in the sky above him—not affecting him, not demanding his attention this very minute, just floating by.

After a while his eyelids grew heavy and he drifted off into a deep sleep.

Chapter Nineteen

"Sub-jealousy. Oh joy!" Kyle exclaimed.

He had contacted the other Masters to talk to them about the situation with Sellie. It was too serious for him not to ask their advice. To be honest, he was out of his depth and needed their help.

They'd gathered at the mansion to discuss the matter over drinks. Without preamble, Kyle had gotten the point. After he'd told them what had gone down, and how strong Sellie's reaction had been, they all agreed that indeed she was suffering from sub-jealousy.

The group had fallen silent for a while.

"Crying shame," Cal said as he rubbed the stubble on his chin. "She's such a bright girl, and to go through something so intense, something that could turn real bad and nasty."

The others concurred and expressed their concern.

As it turned out, most of the Masters were familiar with the concept of sub-jealousy, but few had ever come across it. Luke and Rafe were the only ones who'd ever had to deal with it in person.

"Tricky business," Luke muttered. "By the time I realized what was going on, it was too late."

"Yeah, you've got to catch it in the very early stages," Rafe said. "It happened to me and my sub Lisa when I involved a second submissive in a scene. She wanted it as much as I did. We had gone over all the details. But it proved to be too much for her."

"How did you handle the situation?" Kyle asked.

"It took time. A lot of time." Rafe thought about it for a bit. "I managed to make clear that I cared an awful lot about her. It did help that I stopped the scene the minute I noticed something was wrong. Knowing that her well-being mattered more to me than the scene — or the other submissive — helped Lisa to get over it. When we parted a year later she was fine."

Kyle absorbed all the information, happy and relieved he could talk with the other Masters about sub-jealousy, what it entailed and how one could go about it to at least stopping it from progressing and escalating.

"Most Doms and Masters are possessive and protective, but subs can be protective as well. And territorial," Cal pitched in.

"You've been there too?" Kyle was shocked.

"To be honest, I'm not sure. It's been a while." Cal's forehead furrowed. "She was jealous all right, but within borders of normalcy, if there is such a thing. I did read up about it though."

Kyle gestured to urge him on and poured himself another whiskey as he listened.

"If a sub gets triggered the wrong way, she can become insecure." Cal's gaze met his when he continued. "She can come to think she cannot please her Dom, which adds to her insecurity."

A pause, and Kyle raised an eyebrow. "And?"

"Oh com' on, man. You know the drill." Cal looked none too pleased.

Kyle slammed his hand on the table.

"Tell me!" he growled. Cal's gaze met his, level but with discernable anger in it nonetheless. He raked his fingers through his mane and sighed. "I'm sorry. Please continue. My brain is fried. I must have more information."

Without breaking the eye contact, Cal knocked back his drink and went on.

"A sub who feels she cannot please her Master is a sub robbed of a deep, core need. It'll strip her bare from her identity and can cause tremendous pain. Once convinced that she indeed cannot please her Master, jealousy will kick in. Even serious depression can occur. Reversing the entire process can be difficult, if not impossible."

"Fucking hell," Kyle muttered, and his shoulders sagged. They all sat in grave silence for a while until Rafe got up to pour refills.

"I knew all that," Kyle said as he swirled the whiskey in his glass. "Through the years I've seen and heard it all, but let me tell you, when it happens to someone you care about..."

His voice trailed off. *What if she never recovers from this?*

The sheer thought of not having Sellie in his life anymore was gut-wrenching. He took a deep breath, straightened his shoulders and allowed his gaze to go over his friends.

"If anyone has more tips, I'm all ears. I'm aware there's no manual for this. I'll have to ad-lib it." His voice was soft but steady.

All the Masters nodded.

"You have our support all the way," Rafe said.

After his friends had gone home, Kyle sat in front of the hearth. The crackling fire warmed his flesh but couldn't dispel the coldness in his heart. He put his elbows on his thighs and rested his chin on his hands. As he stared at the dancing flames, he allowed his thoughts, hopes and worries to roam free through his head.

Worries, as he wasn't sure their relationship would be strong enough to survive this. Concern, as he suspected her sub-jealousy would increase if they split up over it, and spill over into her normal life. He'd do his damnedest to keep that from happening—he just wasn't sure he could.

Then there was hope she'd make it. A lot came down to her inner strength as a woman. If she was able to tap into that and bounce back, they had something to build on.

"I sure as hell will do all I can to help her with that," he told a flame that was licking at the woodblock in the hearth. For a second the flame flared up as if in agreement, and Kyle shook his head.

"Damned whiskey!" Yet he grinned as he watched the flame continue to do what it did, burning and gnawing at the chunk of oak with its heat. The way it moved, never faltering, as if it knew in the end it would defeat the wood, undeterred by the fact it itself would die at the exact moment it had won the battle. Kyle pondered the thought that fire wasn't able to burn slower, nor decide to stop. It could do nothing but eat its way through the wood fibers, then fade away into nothingness. It had no choice—it could only do what fire did. Not so different from him. He didn't have much of a choice either. Losing Sellie was not an option. His shoulder muscles loosened and at long last the cold in his heart melted, whether from the flames or the whiskey he did not know. He sat back in his chair, slid down and rested his head. A smile spread across his face as things began to click in his mind. He'd spend quality time with Sellie, but not too much. Making her dependent on him wasn't smart. All he wanted was for her to sense in every cell in her being that he wanted her and only her. That she could trust him.

He'd spend time with her in private and public. Take her out on dates, go dancing, have romantic dinners, go to the movies. Time for them both to close that gap again, to find and build trust.

"And mild public scening," he mumbled. He considered no scening at all, but figured she might take that as rejection. "No, I don't want her to think she can't please me."

Mild scening would be good. Nothing too over the top until things between them had been restored.

Kyle sighed. It would be quite a ride. It'd take a while and eat up a lot of his time and energy.

"But she's worth it!"

Nevertheless, he was a busy man who worked long hours, and he had the club to run as well. He didn't have a lot of spare time as it was.

Plenty of practical reasons to hope it wouldn't take her too long to get back on track. Then there was the other reason he hoped she'd bounce back fast. He missed her. He missed the Sellie he had come to know.

"Dammit, I want you back, girl. I love you!"

Chapter Twenty

Sellie pushed the doorbell and twirled a lock of hair around her forefinger as she waited. Soft footsteps approached on the other side of the front door and she hoped Rebecca would open, not Master Cal. The last thing she needed was that intimidating man looming over her when she was nervous as hell.

The door swung open and she couldn't help but sigh in relief when her friend stood in the doorway.

"I need help," was all she had to say. Rebecca grabbed her hand and guided her to the living room. Sellie's vision swam with tears, and when her friend wrapped her arms around her, she couldn't hold them back anymore. Being a little taller than Rebecca, she found herself staring over her shoulder, straight into Master Cal's eyes, and a sudden shyness flooded her. She broke free from Rebecca's embrace and fumbled with her purse as she forced back a sob.

Cal peered from his wife to Sellie and back, walked to a cupboard and strolled back with a large box of tissues. After he'd put it on the table he left the room with a "Ladies."

Rebecca smiled when Sellie's mouth fell open.

"Wow!" Sellie mumbled as the door closed behind Cal. "He's just…"

"Great," Rebecca finished, her eyes sparkling with love. "He may be strict, but he does know when to make himself scarce."

Sellie dropped down on the couch and sat in silence for a moment before glancing at her friend.

"You were told about me and Kyle, right?" When Rebecca confirmed, she continued. "I'm a bit at a loss. I cannot expect Kyle to do all the work. I want to do something myself too."

Rebecca didn't speak, and Sellie lowered her gaze and sighed. She shifted on the couch and rubbed her hands over her jeans-covered thighs. Then she pressed her lips together, swallowed against the lump in her throat and looked up.

"I don't think I can do this alone," she whispered. "I need someone to help me, but…"

"But you don't want it to be me?" Rebecca asked, her voice soft and warm.

Sellie nodded.

"It's…it's not that I don't trust you," she hastened to say. "But this is so intimate."

Rebecca leaned forward and patted Sellie's knee.

"Hun, it's fine, I'm not offended," she said. "I think it's a smart choice even. And it's good you want to get some help with this. I agree, this is too much to handle on your own."

A knock on the door interrupted the conversation.

"Can I come in?" Cal's voice asked.

A giggle bubbled up in Rebecca's throat.

"He's not into crying women and tissues," she whispered, and raised her voice when she continued. "Yes, love, it's safe."

Sellie sat in silence when Cal peered around the corner, a sheepish expression on his face as he first glanced at her and Rebecca, then at the untouched box of tissues and back at his wife.

"I thought you girls could do with a drink." He walked in with a tray of drinks and snacks and put it on the coffee table.

A smile tugged at Sellie's lips, and she gritted her teeth as she tried to keep her shoulders from shaking. She kept her gaze lowered when Cal walked out of the room, and when the door closed behind him, she burst out in laughter.

"I never knew tears and tissues could reduce the scariest of Masters into a scurrying—"

"Shhhhh!" Rebecca interrupted, and her gaze darted to the door. "The man's hearing is astounding, as is the new whip he bought last week. My ass doesn't like it at all. Please shut up!"

"I'm sorry." Sellie hiccupped, yanking a tissue out of the box on the table to wipe away her tears. "Gosh, I am in better spirits now."

"My butt won't be if you continue." Rebecca grimaced.

"That bad, huh?"

"You have no idea!"

Sellie grinned when her friend's eyes gleamed.

"You cheeky girl, you love that whip."

Rebecca laughed now.

"Hush! He doesn't have to know." She kept her voice low and fidgeted in her chair as if she'd just been whipped. Her cheeks flushed. "The darned thing hurts like hell, but gosh, does it make me fly!"

"Hmm." Sellie fell quiet, overwhelmed by a sudden longing for her Master.

"Coffee's getting cold," Rebecca said, and gestured at the cups.

They took a moment to drink.

"I so want what you got," Sellie whispered in between sips.

"You will. I'll give you Diana's calling card." Rebecca put down her drink and got up to get the card from her purse. "Here you are. She's a great coach. You can trust her."

Reminded of her problem, Sellie slumped on the couch, fighting the tears that were pricking. She sniffed and accepted the tissues that her friend handed her.

"I-I t-think I need a cuddle," she stammered, and started to cry.

Rebecca jumped up, sat next to her, pulled her close, and Sellie bawled her eyes out on her friend's shoulder.

Chapter Twenty-One

While her coach Diana was typing on her laptop, Sellie looked around the room. It was flooded with light that came through a large window. Two comfortable seats were placed off the center with a low wooden table in between. The white walls were decorated with paintings that were colorful and neutral, but too abstract for her taste. As she drank from her coffee, she studied them and found she couldn't quite make out whether the vague figures were supposed to be horses or people. She wrinkled her nose.

"Intrigued?" Diana asked with a smile.

"Intrigued and annoyed," Sellie blurted, and her cheeks got warm. "I'm sorry."

Diana laughed.

"Don't worry. I chose them for a reason." The coach put her laptop on the table. "Back to you. You're suffering from abandonment anxiety."

Sellie nodded and sat back in her chair, waiting for the woman to continue.

"Regurgitating old traumas doesn't always lead to healing," Diana explained. "If nothing else, it keeps the problem alive. I prefer a more positive approach."

"Meaning what?" Sellie asked with eagerness in her voice.

"We are going to work on self-esteem and inner strength," the coach said. "And replacing old beliefs that are relevant to the issue. You are motivated and strong-willed. I have no doubt we can work through it."

Those last words almost made Sellie laugh as they reminded her of what Kyle had told her. Not when they were talking about her problems, but when she had refused to sit at his feet. The things he had done to her to make her obey still made her insides quiver. The man sure as heck knew how to push her buttons. She shook her head and focused on Diana.

"You will get there, as long as you come to our sessions and do your homework."

"Wow, the last time I had homework, I was a skinny teen with pigtails." Sellie grinned.

"Good to see you're positive about it. You'll get a lot of it!"

Diana told her what she'd have to do and Sellie's head was spinning by the time she went home. All she remembered was having to keep a journal. Thank goodness her coach had printed the assignments for her.

As the weeks went by, she made progress. She wasn't as naïve as to think she was there yet, but things were improving for sure. Her stress levels had gone down, she was more relaxed and found it easier to focus on her work instead of fretting about her relationship. Diana had noticed it as well.

"I'm impressed," she said during the last session. "I think we can turn it up a notch."

They discussed the new assignments, and when they were done, Sellie put the printed sheets in her purse, said her goodbye and walked out. On her way home, she stopped at the baker's to get some fresh bagels and a chocolate muffin that was too delicious to resist.

Back home, she tossed her car keys onto the coffee table, and she'd just sat down to go through her homework when the doorbell rang. Rebecca greeted her when she opened the front door.

"Got time for a drink?"

"Of course! Come in. I'll make a fresh pot of tea." Sellie smiled. "To be honest, I can do with some distraction."

They settled outdoors with tea and cake, enveloped by the scent of the many roses that surrounded the patio. Honeysuckle grew on an arbor over the single path that wound its way to the back of the garden. A chime tingled its sweetness, buzzing bumblebees visited the abundance of flowers, and water spouted from a Buddha statue and disappeared in the pebbles that surrounded it.

Rebecca's jaw dropped. "This is gorgeous. And so are you."

"Thanks. It's small, but it has what I need." Sellie sat back with a contented sigh. "I love to sit here and recharge the batteries."

"I may want to come here to recharge mine every now and then," Rebecca replied.

As Sellie poured out tea and cut cake, Rebecca asked, "Now, tell me how you are doing. I'm dying to hear how things are working out with Diana."

Sellie tilted her head and laughed. "Nosy parker."

"Guilty as charged." Rebecca grinned, rested her elbows on the table and gave her a quasi-Dom-look. "Tell me."

"Yes, Sir!"

In between drinking tea and nibbling cake, she told Rebecca everything.

"I have to do visualizations. Easy for me, since I often meditate," she said, put another piece of cake in her mouth and chewed. "First they were about fun things, about me and Kyle at home. I enjoyed envisioning us cooking, dining, making love, having kinky sex."

Her cheeks got warm when her friend lifted an eyebrow, a smile tugging at her lips.

"Kinky sex, huh. Not bad!" Rebecca laughed out loud now and Sellie couldn't help but join in. When they quieted, she continued her story.

"Imagining going out together in public wasn't a problem either. Not even when I had other women enter the scene in my mind." Sellie fell silent and stared at her tea as she turned the cup around in her palm with her fingers.

Rebecca reached out over the table to stroke her cheek, her voice soft when she said, "We don't have to talk about it if you don't want to."

Sellie's eyes were watery when she glanced up. "Thank you. I don't mind. I'll have to get over it."

A sigh escaped her, and she took her time to pour more tea and spoon a lot of sugar into it.

"Sellie…"

"It's okay. I do use sugar sometimes, you know," Sellie mumbled with a half-hearted smile. "It got difficult when I visualized being in the club with Kyle, and with other subs around. I lost it. Diana forbade me to go there. For now. Said we'd work toward that."

An understanding nod from Rebecca urged her on.

"I have to journal about how it makes me feel when I get in a frenzy. Have you any idea what it does to your body to be so off-kilter and so scared?" Sellie choked, a few tears rolled over her cheeks and she blinked to clear her vision. Before she could dig up a tissue from her pocket, Rebecca handed her one and she dried her eyes and blew her nose.

"I get sick to the stomach just thinking about being around other subs with Kyle," she whispered. "Even now, my heart rate is through the roof and my shoulders are tense. It's horrible!" She swallowed against the lump in her throat.

"That's why Diana won't let you go there yet," Rebecca explained. "The idea is to get you to tolerate situations without getting upset. That takes time. Baby steps. Breathe now, girl, let it go."

"Gosh, is that coach or Mistress Rebecca speaking?" Sellie couldn't help but laugh.

"Neither, it's friend Rebecca," Rebecca replied. "The similarity is remarkable at times though, isn't it?"

"Not half!"

They both giggled, the mood lightened, and Sellie got up to get a bottle of wine.

"I need something stronger," she said, filling two glasses and handing Rebecca one. "Come on, let's stroll through the garden. I have to stretch my legs."

They walked down the path, smelled roses and honeysuckle, and Sellie gently patted a bumblebee that had landed on the arbor.

"Are you crazy?" Rebecca exclaimed. "I didn't know you could do that."

Sellie laughed.

"Bumblebees are really quite okay."

When they got to Buddha, Sellie dropped to her knees and let the water flow over her hand. Caught up in the sensation, her eyes closed and her lips parted, the soft hum that escaped her almost a moan.

"I bet you're a sucker for sensory play," Rebecca said, amusement in her voice.

"Beats the hell out of a whip." Sellie's eyes flickered with pleasure. "Pun intended."

Rebecca rubbed her ass and pretended to wince. "Has Kyle ever used a whip on you?"

Sellie shivered at the thought. "Hell, no! I'm not into whips."

She jumped to her feet and gazed at the droplets that ran from her fingers, then dried her hand on her jeans and started strolling back to the patio.

"I love water. Which reminds me... Diana made me think of a happy meditation. I have to do that to finish my homework on a high vibe."

"And yours has to do with water?" Rebecca asked, intrigued.

"Uhhuh. And I'm not allowed to have Kyle in it. Diana said that was too easy," Sellie explained. "She doesn't want me to come to depend on him to feel good and stable. I have to be able to find that place on my own. And I did!"

Her friend gestured for her to go on.

Sellie lowered her voice in an attempt to imitate Master Cal's. "Impatient sub!"

"Forget about it, girl. No one can do a Master Cal." Rebecca's eyes went glossy, then she gave a slight shake of her head before she continued. "Now, about that water meditation."

"I visualize myself as a beautiful mermaid, swimming in the ocean." Sellie relaxed. "The wonderful sensation of being free and happy and alive. I love it!"

Rebecca's gaze warmed. "You'll get there, girl. I'm sure of it."

The assurance did Sellie good. She was proud of herself as it was, but the support from her best friend meant a lot.

"Thanks. I still have a ways to go, but I'm getting the hang of it. And I sure as heck will get there."

A calm certainty settled inside her as she poured out more wine and raised her glass.

"To my success!"

"Bottoms up."

Chapter Twenty-Two

Even though it was a regular working day, Kyle had decided to take the afternoon off so he could spend quality time with Sellie.

She'd arrived early as they'd planned to cook and dine together, and have the entire evening to themselves.

It did him good to have her around. The woman seemed to fill his home with light. As they were prepping their meal, she was singing and dancing. A silly grin was plastered on his face, and he couldn't help but cast her sidelong glances, even as he was cutting meat. She made him happy. He put down the knife, about to sprinkle salt on the steaks, when she flitted past him and slapped his ass. Hard. He jerked upright, his hand with the saltshaker in midair, the smile frozen on his face. Her soft gasp reached him over the ticking of the clock and the bubbling of the boiling sauce on the cooker. He blinked, not certain what to do or say. No woman had ever dared do that. Then his sense of humor got the better of him and he burst out laughing. He spun around, her shoulder muscles relaxed, and her mouth curved into a smile. Until he stopped laughing as suddenly as he had started and bored his gaze into hers, the vibe between them laden all of a sudden. She swallowed and got as red as the bell pepper she'd been slicing.

"I'm sorry," she whispered, fumbling with her apron.

"You will be," he promised, and dabbed the tip of her nose with ketchup. "Now stir that sauce before it burns."

"Yes, Sir."

Her automatic reaction made him chuckle and he hummed as he continued sprinkling salt and pepper on the meat.

It didn't take her long to find her balance again. It never did. Soon she was back to singing, and he to smiling. Nonetheless, he did pay heed whenever she came near in case she slapped his ass again. Once he would tolerate. Twice, not so much. She did nothing of the kind, although she did flutter around him for no apparent reason while giving him saucy glances. Knowing he was being toyed with, he snorted a laugh. He could appreciate a bit of playfulness, yet he almost jerked when she rubbed his buttocks as she brushed past him.

"You're playing with fire, girl," he mumbled under his breath, not bothering to look up.

Her husky giggle started a warm glow in his core that lasted all the way through dinner. He made sure he kept her on her toes with fleeting touches and well-timed words. The pink that colored her cheeks clashed with her ginger hair, and he thought it the most adorable thing he'd ever seen. He couldn't take his eyes off her.

After dinner, Kyle got the hearth going in the living room and they cuddled up on the sofa, rosy from the wine they'd been drinking. His arm was around her shoulders, her head resting against his.

He closed his eyes, basking in the moment, thrilled that Sellie was doing so well and how wonderful it was to be with her. The thing he had come to sense in his gut had gone. Before she'd started therapy, it had been as if he had some kind of energetic hook inside him, and it hadn't been pleasant.

A contented sigh fled his lips as she caressed his forearm, and he was about to doze off when she whispered, "Is it okay if I go into the club?"

His eyes flew open, his heart skipped a beat and his dick stirred to life. He had to clear his throat before he was able to answer.

"Yes, of course," he replied, attempting to be casual, yet his voice was a bit hoarse.

He got himself a kiss and she was off, leaving him there. For a moment he sat perplexed, his limbs heavy as if he had turned into a clay puppet. At the same time, his cock grew harder by the second and moved up in his pants.

"Brilliant," he grumbled as he recalled how they'd only done things in private since her breakdown. A few times he'd brought up playing in the club but even the suggestion had upset her. And now she wanted to go in there. On her own.

Kyle heard a door open and close, and he knew she was in there. Right now. While he was here on the sofa in the living room. Just him and the full power of his dominant needs. With a raging hard-on.

As the doors closed behind her, Sellie took a deep breath.

She needed a bit of time. Time to allow herself to get a feel of the place, and to become aware of what it did to her body to be in there.

She closed her eyes. Her legs were trembling. A bit.

"You can do this! You can!" she whispered to encourage herself.

The smell of the dungeon was familiar. A smile lit her face as she let all the different scents and the vibe envelop her.

She took another deep breath and opened her eyes. The room was dark—not pitch black, but dark nonetheless. The only light came in through the stained-glass windows high up on the walls. Pale moonlight that could have been eerie as it cast long, dark shadows and revealed nothing more than the shapes of BDSM equipment. It didn't scare her. She wasn't afraid of the dark and never had been. If nothing else, the contrast of light and dark in the room woke up the artist in her. A sudden inspiration to paint came over her. A sensation that clashed with what the scents in the room triggered—deep, urgent, wanton desires.

Sellie closed her eyes again, her entire body trembling now. Not from anxiety, but with need. She hadn't known what to expect, but the overwhelming desire to be in here came as a shock.

She made her way toward the light switches and the club was bathed in soft light. Her gaze went through the large space, lingering on some equipment. She moved toward the bar, letting her hand slide over the polished wood as she walked past. Further inside she went, past scene areas, touching equipment, ropes, chains and cool leather.

The Andrew's cross appeal to her and she touched the dark wood. It was so smooth. She'd never been tied to an Andrew's cross and she wondered what it would be like on her bare skin.

A longing sigh escaped her lips. Her breathing had sped up and her heart was thumping in her chest.

Maybe she ought to get Kyle. Would that be too soon? She wasn't sure. But they could talk about it.

Sellie turned around and a shiver ran up her spine when she saw Kyle. He was leaning against the doorjamb, legs crossed at the ankles. Considering the bulge in his trousers, he was pleased with what he saw.

Sellie swallowed. Hard. *This is like déjà-vu. That seems to happen a lot.*

He was standing the exact same way as he'd done when they had first gone into the dungeon together. The difference being that back then he had appeared casual, and now he looked hungry. Even more so, he looked starved. And very ready to storm across the room to plunder.

Kyle fought for control. He had entered the club, careful to not make a sound as he didn't want to disturb her. He'd thought he'd do better being in here with her than out there on his own. *Big mistake!* To watch her as she was touching, sensing, taking it all in, was almost too much to bear. It created a turmoil in his head, heart and groin. And stirred up a longing so strong it knocked his socks off.

He recalled being in the exact same position months ago, when they'd first gone into the dungeon. The desire that had coursed through his veins then had been strong, but nothing compared to the mind-boggling craving that flooded him now. Knowing how she reacted to his touch, her taste and the softness of her skin added a new tier to his emotions.

He was aching now, and not just his cock, his heart just the same.

As her hands stroked over equipment, he had visions of her on it. Tied up, bent over, legs spread, her pussy open and available to him. Her chest heaving, nipples taut as he tugged at them. He could almost hear her soft mewls and whines of need.

He suppressed a growl and hauled in air, forcing the kinky images out of his mind.

It was too soon for such things. She wasn't ready.

In the end he managed to get some sense of control, only to come close to losing it again when she ran her hands over the Andrew's cross.

Then she spun around, and when their gazes met, he saw the desire in her eyes. Her need seemed to fill the entire club like a sweet perfume. A groan welled up in his throat as his entire being reacted to it.

"If you don't want this yet, tell me now." His voice sounded raw.

Fuck if he knew how to get out of there if she said *no*. He wasn't even sure he was able to walk. His heart was pounding in his chest as he waited for her reply.

Her *Please!* needed no further explanation.

An overwhelming aura of power radiated from him, as if he had flicked a switch. The sudden change shocked her, scared and aroused her. Her pussy clenched and a soft mewl fled her lips.

Kyle pushed himself off the doorjamb and stalked toward her, holding her with his eyes and the pure raw lust that shone in them.

Closer and closer he got, his dominance almost palpable now. Paralyzing her.

She hated it when he was in full dominant mode, yet she loved it and wanted it. That intense feeling of being overpowered, overruled, not in control, was aggravating and it made her want to resist and fight back. Knowing that she'd lose no matter what — realizing she wanted to lose — made it even worse.

Why are you so goddamned strong? She should have gone for a more yielding Dom.

Sellie fought to hold herself under his strong gaze. She so wanted to avert her eyes, to hide from the power in his, but he didn't let her.

I hate you!

"No you don't."

Had she said that out loud? *Oh damn.*

Then he was upon her, tall and handsome, taking her breath away. Her head was spinning and her knees wobbled.

"I don't want this," she whispered.

"Yes you do!"

A gasp fled her when Kyle fisted his hand in her locks, arched her face up and took her mouth. He pushed his tongue past her lips. No teasing or gentleness — he was a man on a mission, out to conquer and claim. It blew her mind to be handled as if he owned her, and a pulsing heat surged through her. As she began to writhe against him, he tightened the grip on her hair and curved his other hand around her throat. Not tight, but the impact was strong enough to trigger her instant surrender to his will, allowing him to take whatever he wanted. He groaned, kissing her deeper, demanding even more. Her knees were about to give in when he swept her up in his arms and carried her away to the dance floor.

"I'm going to fuck you here," he whispered against her flesh. "After you've begged me to allow you to come."

The promise made goosebumps rise on her skin. He set her down and Sellie was glad he steadied her before letting go. Her legs wobbled, her brain was hazy and she couldn't even see straight. Her entire body was aching for him, yearning for his touch, his kiss, and in the end, getting him inside her. Her clit spasmed at the thought.

She blinked, attempting to focus on Kyle instead of the aching need between her thighs. Their eyes met and a slow smile lifted the corners of his mouth.

"So feminine." His voice was low and soft as a caress.

Ever so gently, he brushed the backs of his fingers over her cheekbones, slid to her lips and traced his forefinger over them. It tickled and she mewled as he went farther, over her chin, her throat, inching toward the curve of her breasts. Her heart was pounding as he stroked her collarbones, now using both hands. The butterfly touches moved down, slipped underneath her dress, over the swell of her breasts, getting closer and closer to her nipples, which tingled in sweet anticipation. Her breath hitched. Just a bit more and he'd...

Sellie shrieked when he ripped her dress to bits. Buttons flew through the air and tinkled when they hit the floor. The ruined fabric pooled around her ankles.

Her eyes widened with shock. Before she was able to find her bearings, he tore off her bra and G-string.

"I don't want—" she started.

"I don't care," he interrupted.

The hungry way he stared at her sent shivers up and down her spine. Instant heat pooled in her lower body and her pussy clenched. She wondered how being intimidated could turn her on so much, and make her feel cherished and loved at the same time.

The thought eluded her when he wrapped an arm around her, lowered his head and closed his mouth over one nipple. Sheer delight shot through her as he lapped and sucked, then moved to lavish his attention upon her other bud. It puckered tight beneath his tongue as he circled around the tip, licked over the crest and sucked hard.

"Oh yes!" she moaned and tangled her fingers in his hair. As if encouraged by her husky sounds and plucking fingers, he used his teeth and nipped. A whine broke from her as sweet pain drew a fiery trail across her nerves, straight to her pussy where it turned to hot pleasure. A jolt went through her clit as it received the messages of desire. Again he bit, a little harder, the sting intense, and she clutched at his golden mane as she tried to breathe through it. Her head was buzzing when he let go, leaving her nipple throbbing and aching, yet she found she wanted more, and she keened a protest when he abandoned her breasts. A soft chuckle was his only reply. He reached out to caress her body, not leaving an inch untouched. His lips followed his hands wherever he could, and little mewls sounded from her as he stroked over her stomach and the gentle curve of her belly, circling his thumbs around her navel and dipping his tongue in its shallow depth. Farther he went, approaching her mound. He slid his hands over her hips to her ass, splayed his fingers over her buttocks and yanked her toward him. His mouth kept moving, his warm breath now wafting over her labia. Her clit throbbed as he went lower and lower. Her heart hammered in her chest, then his tongue slid between her pussy lips and rubbed over her nub.

"Oooohh!" Her hips jerked as a wave of heat flooded upward and out at that oh-so-delicious first lick over her clit. Again and again he lapped over it with slow strokes. "Please, more!" she begged, and tugged at his hair, lost in a haze of need. He continued at his leisure until the fire in her lower body was near unbearable. The strokes got harder and faster, each one sending shocks through her pussy. Before long, her leg muscles began to quiver and her world narrowed down to his tongue on her clit and the raging inferno in her core. She was so close, the pulsing of her nub a constant burn, an ache almost, and the pressure that was building inside her coiled into a tight ball. For a moment she hovered over the point of no return, caught in a throbbing void of nothingness, waiting for that last delicious touch to send her over the edge of release. The next stroke of his tongue was long and firm and her world exploded.

"Yess! Ooohyess!"

She surrendered to the heat as she was free falling into space, her body spasming with joy. She pushed herself against his mouth, riding his tongue as he kept moving it over her clit, demanding every shock out of her. The waves became gentle ripples, the fire a wonderful glow that warmed her body from the inside out. Her muscles began to relax and a content hum fled her lips that turned into a soft protest when he licked over her still sensitive nub. Attempting to focus, she glanced down, straight into his eyes, their piercing blue darkened with lust.

"I like how you come. You can do it again," he said. The husky timbre of his voice aroused her and a little jolt ran through her clit. She chose to ignore it.

"I cannot."

Slap!

Sellie yelped—her left thigh was stinging and instinct made her rub the aching spot he had hit with his hand.

"Leave it!"

For a brief moment she thought of objecting, but the glint in his eyes stifled the words in her throat. He held her pinned with his gaze, and she trembled under the power in it, yet her pussy clenched and her nipples hardened.

"That's my girl," he mumbled, and she sighed in relief when he released her, only to moan when he lapped over her nub. One soft stroke, then nothing but his warm breath over her pussy. Disbelief filled her when she found she wanted more, even though she'd come just minutes ago. She bucked her hips, hoping he'd pleasure her.

Slap!

"No!" she whined. Pain shot from her aching right thigh, straight to her longing pussy.

"Yes," he mumbled, and hit her thigh again, then put his lips around her clit and sucked. He had been gentle the first time, but now he was forceful, demanding her body to react. He was taking, which gave her so much pleasure. How she needed this! It blew her mind, and her arousal peaked from zero to full blast in a split second. Her nipples tingled, her breasts were swollen, and her pussy was soaking wet.

He took her labia between his fingers and opened her up.

"Oh God, yes!"

"Not God, honey, your Master."

His tongue pushed against the sides of her now exposed clit, went over the hood, toward her entrance, slid over her inner labia and back up. Her leg muscles trembled when he licked right up against her nub over and over, faster and faster.

"Oh yess!"

The heat in her core coiled tighter and tighter as orgasm was building up. Delicious waves rose, getting her closer to the point of climax. She lost her momentum when he pulled back. A sense of loss filled her and she keened a protest as the promise of release slipped away. Then he pushed a finger inside her, moved it in and out, crooked it and rubbed her G-spot. The sensations were wonderful, yet so different from his wet tongue on her clit that it took her some time to ease into it.

"I love your cunt," he muttered, his voice hoarse.

Another finger, and he thrust deep, brushing her nub with his thumb each time he pushed inside her. Enough to keep the fire going, not enough to make her come. Not nearly enough. Her pussy clamped down on his fingers as if to try to suck him in farther, and to get him to move faster. She tilted her hips, desperate for more pressure on her clit, then she circled on the fingers that pumped inside her.

"More. Please!" she begged.

Slap!

A wail broke from her as he hit the same spot he'd slapped earlier, the sting harsh, but soothed by the thrusting in her cunt. Another slap, a bit lower down, another moan as the sting shot straight to her clit and poked up the heat in her lower body. The next slap landed on her thigh, and she pushed herself deeper on his fingers. She wanted this so very much.

"That's it, baby, ride my hand like a slut," he whispered.

Encouraged by his words, she gyrated her hips and fucked his fingers while he nipped her flesh and slapped her thighs. Her mind blanked—all that mattered was the increasing heat between her legs. As she neared orgasm, he slowed down, only to work her up again. After her third almost-orgasm, she couldn't stop a continual whimper of need. Her body was on a constant high that remained even when he slid his fingers from her pulsing pussy. Sheer joy flowed through her as he was all over her with his hands and mouth. She had given up trying to follow what he was doing. It was impossible. He alternated slapping her ass and thighs, then kissed them, nipped, slapped and caressed. Alternating pain and pleasure, soft and hard. Tender and rough.

Just as she thought she was going to collapse in a bundle of ecstasy, his command cut through her haze like a knife through butter.

"Kneel."

Sellie complied, grateful for the solid support of the floor.

"Stay here, I'll be right back." His soft voice floated to her and he brushed his fingers over her cheek.

She nodded, content to sit there, enveloped in a haze of unrelenting need.

As Kyle walked off, she blinked a few times, trying to emerge from her trance but failing at it. She watched as he got to a nearby scene area, wheeled a piece of equipment to the dance floor where she was sat and placed it right in the middle. He smiled at her, which concerned her, as did that thing beside him. She wasn't all that familiar with the names of BDSM equipment, but she was a smart woman and she could work out how it was to be used. It had a narrow, padded top and padded leg and arm supports on either side. Leather restraints, steel rings. She was quite sure it was a spanking horse. No matter the name, she decided she didn't like it. Her enthusiasm got even less when he patted the top and said, "It's a spanking horse. Hop on, love."

Sellie stared at him, wondering if he'd lost his marbles.

"I most definitely will not!" Little droplets flew as she spat out the words and cast him a vile look meant to ward him off. His smile didn't falter.

"You will," he said, as casual as if they were discussing what to have for dinner. His certainty that she'd obey infuriated her. Even more so, because deep down she knew she would. At some point. The annoying smile and the amused flicker in his eyes told her he was aware of that too. That didn't make her any more inclined to climb on the spanking horse. She wasn't going to 'roll over and play sub' whenever he pulled her strings. The problem with that was that, as her lover and Master, he was familiar with her sassy behavior, and her qualms and quibbles wouldn't bother him in the slightest. If nothing else, she suspected he'd count on her resisting him, enjoying the game of winning her over. There was no doubt in her mind that he'd be victorious, and maybe that should've killed the desire—instead, her insides melted at the thought of him toying with her until she gave up and surrendered. However awkward it was to have her limits pushed, she craved it nonetheless.

Her gaze went to the spanking horse. Getting on that thing meant her private parts would be on display, available for his use and pleasure. With each second that went by, her reluctance grew, as did embarrassment about the idea of him staring at her exposed pussy and her rear end.

She pressed her lips together.

"I don't want..." she began.

"I don't care."

She tried to withstand his unwavering gaze, but she was no match for his power. A tremor shook her as she breathed it in, absorbing it, needing it and allowing it to gnaw away at her defenses. She scrambled to her feet, still not sure whether she was okay with this. The urge to resist him — and her own needs — was warring with her desire to submit. How she wanted to please him, and to be pleased by doing so. But not on a spanking horse. If only he'd chosen an Andrew's Cross or a spiderweb. Hell, she would have settled for a tree in the garden. Anything but that horrible thing.

She lowered her gaze and her cheeks got warm.

"Kyle, Sir..." she whispered. "Please, help me out?"

"Always!"

Sellie shrieked when he swung her up in his arms, walked to the spanking horse and put her on it. Before her brain could process what was going on, he had her tied up.

"You...you...bastard!" Sellie yanked at the restraints. "I asked for help, you asshole!"

Kyle slapped her butt and she yelped.

"Stop the swearing or I'll spank you till the cows come home."

The warning in his voice shook her.

"I'm sorry," she whispered.

"Apology accepted," he said and pressed a kiss on her back, followed by caresses that helped her to get used to the position.

"How...how is this helping me?" she dared ask.

"Baby, you were too awkward to get on it yourself," Kyle replied. "I removed that obstacle for you."

"Oh."

"You may thank me." The amusement in his voice didn't hide the serious undertone.

"Thank you? For putting me in this god-awful position on this torture device?" she spat out.

Kyle chuckled.

"You seem to need a lot of encouragement tonight."
Smack!
Sellie cried out when he hit her ass.
"Thank you!" she hastened to say.
"Not very convincing, girl. I think you can do better."
Sellie's mind was racing. He'd had a good point. Climbing on this thing had been too daunting for her, so in that sense he had indeed helped her out. Admitting to that wasn't easy, yet more appealing than the thought of him walloping her ass. Although the idea turned her on.
Something inside her relaxed.
"Thank you," she whispered, meaning it this time.
He hummed.
"You're welcome," he replied, then knelt in front of her to look her in the eye. "The next part is up to you."
"Next part?" Her voice trembled. The glint in his eyes worried her.
Kyle nodded and smiled, which did nothing to make reassure her.
"Yes. I was looking forward to playing with a willing sub," he said. "I haven't seen that yet—now I'd like to hear it."
Sellie blinked and she silently cursed him for being so damned demanding. He had her on this bench thing with her pussy exposed and her breasts hanging down. It was humiliating. Wasn't that enough? Now she had to tell him she wanted this? Did he have to make her life even more difficult?
Please gag me!
She almost laughed at the thought of asking to be gagged, which up until now she'd considered the worst thing ever.

"Hear what?" she whispered, quite sure she didn't want to know.

"You telling me how much you like to be up here, exposed for my pleasure," he said.

Her eyes flared wide.

"Telling me how you love having your pussy spread open, eager and ready for me," he continued. "Willing and eager for anything I want to do to you."

Heat crept up her face to the roots of her hair.

"I-I c-can't," she stammered.

"Not to worry. I'm not the worst of Masters. I'll give you some time to think about it." Kyle smiled. "I'll get myself a drink and sit here with you as you make up your mind."

He sauntered toward the bar, and in the quiet of the dungeon Sellie heard him pour something into a glass.

She couldn't believe it. Here she was, naked on this thing, ready and available for him, and he walked off to get a drink? Granted, she hadn't been all that willing, but she was on display regardless, exposed for him to take her any which way he wanted. And he didn't?

In spite of her frustration, she didn't dare swear out loud. She knew he had been quite serious about a spanking if she did. Considering his muscles, he wouldn't tire fast. She couldn't do that to her ass.

Which brought her to her more urgent dilemma, as she was certain she'd get the same thorough spanking if she didn't give him what he'd asked for in his oh-so-polite tone of voice.

That meant she had to choose between her ass and her pride. She wasn't quite sure which of the two she valued more.

Kyle came back, sipping his drink. She glanced at him when he stopped next to the spanking horse. It was crystal clear that he liked what he saw and that he was happy to be doing this scene with her. A shiver spiraled up her spine. It filled her with joy that she pleased him. She loved being in here with him, if only she hadn't forgotten how embarrassing it could be.

He walked around her and ran his fingers up her leg, circling his thumb, zigging and zagging over her tender inner thigh. Inching closer and closer to her pussy. Need flared up and sweet anticipation made her leg muscles quiver. Her breathing got shallow as she waited for it, and she bit back a curse when he skipped over her clit. He moved down her other leg, away from her nub, his touch arousing nonetheless.

Erotic circles moved up again, higher and higher. Soft fingers tracing over her inner thigh. Shivers ran through her and a mewl fled her lips. The fleeting caresses came closer to her pussy, melting her insides. *Almost there, one more inch.* Her pussy was pulsing and Sellie dug her fingernails in the padding of the armrest, hoping, waiting, aching for his touch. Disappointment washed through her when he slid down her thigh again.

"You bastard!"

Smack!

Sellie's shriek echoed through the room. A sob welled up in her throat. So much for her pride, and her ass for that matter. It burned as if someone had started a bonfire on it. She breathed through it with her eyes closed and her lips pressed together. All the while he stroked her back, and in spite of the stinging, she was grateful for that. Knowing he was there for her, beside her, was as soothing as the tender touch. Yet she wondered how he was able to be this gentle after that harsh slap.

Then the pain wore off and she sagged on the spanking horse.

Kyle walked to a chair in front of her and sat down. "You got ten minutes," he said.

Her gaze lifted and found his. Her disbelief met his resolve. Kyle smiled at her as he sipped from his drink.

Sellie came close to glaring at him, and she quickly lowered her head to stare at the floor. No way was she going to rile him up again tonight.

Her mind started churning. *Now what?* It was clear he expected her to tell him that she wanted to be on this bench. Even more so, she had to tell him in detail just how much she wanted that. She'd hoped he had forgotten about it.

Her options were rather limited. Ass or pride. Her ass was still aching. She wasn't looking forward to more of that. She knew outsmarting him would never work, nor could she get up and leave.

Joy or pain. Why is that such a difficult choice?

She peered through her lashes at Kyle, who seemed to enjoy his drink, and judging by the tell-tale smirk on his face, he loved her dilemma and the view as much as the amber whiskey in his glass.

Then he raised his arm with a theatrical movement, glanced at his watch and flashed her a smile.

Sellie yanked at the restraints. Nothing budged. An utter waste of energy. He had her cornered, trapped. It was only a matter of time before something had to give. If not the restraints or his resolve, then all that remained was her stubborn pride. Her gaze met his and the entire world seemed to narrow down to his eyes and the strength in them. Her breath hitched and her heart pounded in her ears. Then her resistance collapsed like a brick wall that got hit by a battering ram.

"Please," she whispered.

Kyle tilted his head, waiting for her to continue.

She tried to find the words, even though her brain had turned to mush.

"P-please, I-I want to be here. On here. F-for you," she stammered. "Oh damn. I can't remember. Can't think."

She begged him with her eyes to understand.

"I want to please you," she whispered.

Kyle got out of the chair, sat on his haunches in front of her, caressed her cheeks and smiled.

"You are. And you will!"

He kissed her, stood and disappeared from her view.

Soon her skin tingled all over, her nipples were aching, her pussy was throbbing and incredibly wet. She couldn't see what he was doing or what he was using. She could only take what he gave her. Her whimpers and moans were almost continuous, and she couldn't care less. She was on fire. He put clamps on her nipples, her labia, and one on her clit. The teeth of the wretched things had a serious bite and made all her sensitive bits throb.

"Too much!" she whimpered.

"Just right."

Of course it was just right. He was always right. *Dammit.* It turned her on beyond belief.

He put more clamps on her labia.

How many of these things does he have? Normal people would buy one, maybe two of them. But not Kyle. No, her greedy master had to collect the whole set. *Oh, joy!*

A cold blob landed on her anus, making her shiver. Something touched that sensitive spot, was circled around the rim and pushed inside her ass. Nerves woke up, sending fiery messages straight to her clit, which twanged in response.

Sellie moaned and arched her back. The heat in her core was out of control. Her body felt like an over-sensitized, overstimulated bundle of nerves.

"Pleease!" Her voice sounded throaty.

Just when she thought she couldn't take much more, the thing in her ass began to vibrate. She gasped as hot waves of desire shot from her rear end straight to her pounding clit. Her vision blurred when Kyle thrust two fingers inside her pussy and bent them, stimulating her G-spot.

"Ooooh, yes! Pleeease!"

Her mind blanked and her body took over, surrendering to the exhilarating pleasure that stormed her senses. Instinct had her moving her hips in rhythm with his fingers. The rubbing and pressing inside her cunt, the vibrations in her ass, the bite from the clamps on her clit and nipples — it was too much.

"Yesss, ooooh yesss!" A husky cry broke from her. All her muscles tensed when she reached the peak of inexplicable joy. Then the hot pressure in her center exploded. Flames shot up and out, licking at her flesh. Ecstasy flooded her as she thrashed and shook, riding wave after glorious wave, until she sagged on the spanking horse, floating on a fluffy and warm after-orgasm cloud.

While she was recovering from her orgasm, he removed the labia clamps and gently put a small vibrator inside her pussy. He switched both the anal and vaginal vibrators on and walked around. He unzipped, fisted his cock and waited for her to look up.

"Suck me."

Sellie put her lips around him and he groaned. She ran her tongue up over his length and swirled it around the tip.

Kyle let her play for a bit, but he wasn't in the mood for lengthy teasing. Right now he was the one who needed more. He fisted his hand in her hair and pushed himself inside her mouth. Her lips closed around his shaft, and when he touched the back of her throat she flattened her tongue so she wouldn't gag. He moved his hips, taking her mouth as fast and as deep as she could handle. The to-die-for feel and view of her lips around his cock made him swell even more. He would need release very soon. He wasn't going to last long in her hot, wet mouth.

For a split second he considered coming, but decided against it. *Not this time.* From the way she moved and sucked, he could tell she was enjoying what she was doing and was every bit as turned on as he. The vibrators in her pussy and ass, and his hard cock in her mouth, had gotten her all excited again. However much he liked it, the thought of thrusting inside her tight, slick cunt appealed to him more. It would allow him to let go whereas now he had to hold back so as not to hurt her.

Kyle pulled back and released her hair. Sellie keened a protest.

"Another time, I want to fuck you." His voice was hoarse with lust.

He walked around her, removed the vibrator from her pussy and placed the head of his cock against her entrance.

"Oh, yes! Please!" Sellie moved her hips.

"You'll get me, baby. Every inch of me," he groaned, and pushed inside. A sensuous whine broke from her when he gave her his full length. He held still and bent over. He reached for her breasts, inched his fingers toward her nipples and removed the clamps.

The moment her wail of pain bounced off the walls, he started hammering into her. Her vagina walls clamped down on him like a vice. He growled. His balls drew up, aching, heavy, feeling too full. Knowing he wouldn't last long, he picked up the vibrator he'd removed from her pussy and put it against her clit.

Her vagina was hot and wet around his cock, sucking and tugging. Shocks of pleasure coursed through his body and he groaned in delight, then he angled himself in a different position to aim for her sweet spot, hitting it hard.

It was all she needed to fly over the precipice. She screamed his name as orgasm took her head off. Her hot, wet cunt convulsing around his cock made him swell more, and he got even harder. His mind blanked and he gripped her hips. He needed but a few more thrusts, then his balls pushed his semen up through his shaft, the feeling so intense that his vision blurred. It went up and up until hot spurts shot out of the tip again and again, leaving him empty and completely sated.

Chapter Twenty-Three

Sellie woke up and stretched her body like a lazy cat. She took another few minutes to snooze.

A month had gone by since the scene on the dance floor. It had been a great month. Things between her and Kyle kept improving. She kept improving. Their intimate play on the spanking horse had helped to rebuild the trust between them. Their bond had strengthened because of that one scene.

Soon after that night, she'd found that she could tolerate the thought of being in the club with him. Diana, her coach, had been very pleased. She had encouraged Sellie to put it to the test.

'If you feel any anxiety, use your coping techniques,' she had said. *'If it doesn't work, do not go there yet. Don't push yourself too far. Make sure you communicate with Kyle. If need be, you can phone me anytime.'*

Tonight would be that night. Sellie was both excited and nervous about it. The excitement was prevalent though. If she was honest, she was looking forward to it. She wanted to go and enjoy a play night. Not just for herself, but for Kyle as well. It was more than obvious to her that he missed being at the club.

Since her breakdown that dreadful night, he had spent less time in the dungeon. Sellie had encouraged him to go, even though the thought of him in there, surrounded by willing submissives, had made her jittery. But she couldn't expect his world to revolve around her problems. As owner, he had to be present, show interest and interact with the club members. And with the other Masters. Kyle needed that as much as they did. How could he be King if he couldn't be in his jungle?

Kyle wasn't aware she wanted to go.

She picked up her cell to send him a message. Her fingers were trembling.

Before she changed her mind, she typed the message and, after a few seconds of hesitation, pressed 'send'. Then she switched off her cell. She didn't want to know what he'd reply. First she wanted to go to Shine in the Dark, the BDSM shop in town. On her first night in the club in what seemed like forever, she wanted to look her best.

A short while later, she parked her car in front of the shop and walked inside.

"Good afternoon, can I help you?" Carl, the shop owner, came up to her.

"No, yes. I don't know," Sellie said. "I'm looking for something special, but I'm not sure what."

Carl looked her over and hummed.

"How about leather? I think I got just the thing for you."

Sellie thought about it. She'd never had anything leather. So far she'd gone for latex dresses and skirts. Leather would make for a nice change. She nodded her approval.

"Surprise me!" she said with a smile.

Carl ushered her toward the dressing rooms and kept walking back and forth with garments.

First Sellie tried on a soft leather skirt. It was so short that she wouldn't even be able to sit in it without showing her underwear. However impractical that'd be, the thought turned her on. The skirt had lace-up splits over each thigh. It made her legs appear even longer.

Now she had to find a top to go with it. She rummaged through the items Carl had brought in, and her eye caught a gorgeous red sequin corset. It was tight and made her breasts bulge.

Great! Love it! Tonight she was going overboard.

She stepped out of the dressing room to look in the king-size mirror on the wall.

Carl whistled.

"Girl, you look great!" he said. "And I got just the boots to go with that."

He asked her shoe size, stalked away and came back a minute later with red lace-up thigh boots.

"Wow! I like them!" Sellie said as she admired the shiny boots. They'd go really well with the red sequin corset and black skirt. A bold combination.

She wanted to try them on, but then she'd need to sit down, which was awkward as she didn't want Carl staring at her crotch. Thank goodness Carl was discreet and turned around as she struggled to get the high-heeled boots on. When she was done, Carl lent her a hand to get up from the stool and guided her toward the mirror.

Sellie was speechless. The outfit was great. She looked good. Hot and sexy.

"I love it!" she said, impressed.

As she twirled around in front of the mirror, she saw something from the corner of her eye and she turned to see what it was. An elderly couple stood in front of the shop window, the man staring straight at her. His eyes almost popped out of their sockets when he took her in. Then the woman on his arm saw what her husband was drooling over and yanked him away from the shop.

Sellie glanced at Carl and they both burst out laughing.

"What can I say?" he hiccupped. "You sure as hell look the part, girl!"

Suddenly she got a bit shy, prancing around in a revealing outfit in the middle of a shop. Her cheeks got warm and she mumbled a 'thank you'.

"I am going to take this outfit," she said, smiling again. "Oh, do you have a red sequin thong to go with it?"

Not much later she left the shop. *The outfit cost a bomb, but heck, was it worth it!*

* * * *

Kyle was pacing back and forth through his living room. He was in two minds about tonight. Part of him wanted to join the fun in the club, but part of him didn't.

He had attended club nights by himself only to find it wasn't the same without Sellie. Somehow it didn't seem right. He missed her there. His woman. His sub. Being in the dungeon on his own made him want her more. King of the Jungle all right, but a Master without his sub.

The nights he didn't go, he missed it. Missed his friends, the hustle and bustle, the vibe of the club. The nights he did go, he wasn't his usual self because she wasn't by his side. Whatever he did, he was losing out on something.

His phone buzzed.

"Now what?" he muttered.

He picked up his cell. A text. From Sellie.

You, me, tonight, dungeon, ten p.m. Don't be late!

He got hard on the spot. Rock-hard.

A smile grew on his face and he chuckled. Not asking him, but telling him what to do. *Cheeky girl!*

His phone buzzed again.

Please don't be late. Master

Kyle grinned, in much better spirits.

"Good catch, subbie," he mumbled to himself.

For a minute he pondered not replying. The idea of letting her stew for the rest of the day, wondering why he hadn't acknowledged her invite, was tempting. But that sort of teasing could be too much for her still and trash her budding confidence.

He picked up his cell and typed a message.

I'll be there. Prep for full body inspection.

She wouldn't have the foggiest what that meant. Neither did he. But it would be fun — he'd make sure of that. He pocketed his phone and decided to take the rest of the afternoon off. Time to go through his toys, although they probably wouldn't get to scening. He wasn't counting on it, but whatever would happen, he was okay about it. He was more than happy to just be with her in the club on a playnight. Nevertheless, if the vibe was good, he wanted to be ready.

Kyle put on his favorite rock music, turned up the volume, walked to the bedroom and got out his bags. As he sang along with the music, he started going through his colorful collection of dildos, vibrators, ropes and other pleasurable things. The anticipation of what was to come made his core glow.

The bag-to-go filled up with interesting items. Cuffs, flogger, blindfold, paddles. He considered a whip, then decided against it. The ball gag was a go. Knowing how much she disliked it, he couldn't help but grin.

As he rummaged through his bag, he felt cool steel against his fingers. He took out the item, looked at it, and a smile pulled at his lips.

"Oh yes, tonight is going to be great!" he mumbled.

When he was finished in the bedroom, he went to the club's reception desk and booked a playroom that had the equipment for what he had in mind. Thinking of the scene turned up the heat in his groin. An enjoyable sensation.

He told himself not to get carried away. He had to bear in mind that it might not happen yet.

Nevertheless, he had a semi hard-on for the rest of the afternoon. The day seemed to last forever, as if time itself wanted to taunt him. He never had a problem focusing on things he wanted to do, but no matter what he tried, it didn't work. His mind kept going back to Sellie and the scene he hoped to do that night.

Half an hour before the club would open, he had a quick shower and put on his favorite leathers and a black shirt. He grabbed his toy bag and left his private quarters.

* * * *

Kyle was waiting in the reception area and checked his watch for the umpteenth time. He couldn't believe how impatient he was. A little nervous even, like some newbie Dom getting ready for his first scene ever.

At long last, she walked in. Ten sharp.

Her gaze found his and he gave her a wicked smile. A charming red colored her cheeks. Kyle didn't miss the hint of insecurity that bloomed in her eyes. He reached out and she flew in his arms. When he hugged her tight, she sighed and melted against him. His heart was pounding in his chest as he breathed in her vibe, the softness of her body, her scent. He was thrilled to have her with him, here in the club, willing to spend the evening with him. He mumbled sweet nothings in her ear and got himself a soft mewl.

After a while she glanced up at him, a vulnerable expression on her face. For a few seconds he thought that maybe it would be too much, too early for her to be here. Then she smiled, and confidence and willpower flashed in her eyes.

"I can do this, Kyle," she said, her voice soft but stable.

He couldn't help but smile back. She was vulnerable all right, but ready nonetheless.

"I believe you are," he said, and caressed her face. "Let's go in, love."

Sellie nodded and walked off to the dressing rooms to put her coat and bag in a locker.

Kyle's jaw dropped when she came back out. She stood still for a minute, allowing him to take her in, and he did. Head to toe. Her chest was heaving, her breasts bulging above the shimmering red corset. The leather skirt hugged her hips and was so short it barely covered her pussy. He wondered what he'd find underneath.

Bare flesh? His gaze roamed farther down over shiny red thigh boots. They made her legs look a mile long.

He swallowed. She was hot as hell. Slutty, yet classy. A lethal combination. Things began to stir in his groin. He feasted his eyes when she pushed herself off the wall and sashayed toward him. She stopped in front of him, leaving a few inches between them. A groan welled up in his throat when she glanced up and fluttered her eyelashes at him. He yanked her against his body, one hand on her ass, one on her head, and took her mouth. As she opened her lips, he swept in. He fisted his hand in her hair to hold her still, loving the moan that broke from her. He took her deeper, tangling and dueling with her tongue, licking over her lips, nibbling them then plunging in again. She writhed in his arms, rubbed her lower body over his erection and pushed her breasts against his chest. Her soft sounds of arousal had liquid fire coursing through his veins.

Just when he was about to slip a hand between her legs to check if she was wearing any underwear, he heard someone call his name.

He let go of Sellie's lips and turned his head to see who had the audacity to disturb him.

Master Ian.

"What?" Kyle snapped.

Ian gave him one of his typical cynical smiles.

"We all like the show," Ian said in his typical dry tone. "But you may want to take it inside."

Kyle glanced over Ian's shoulder and saw that they'd gotten quite the audience. His tunnel vision shattered on the spot and he cursed under his breath.

"Club rules," Ian continued. "No play outside the dungeon. I wonder who made those rules?" He tilted his head, pretending to think. "Ah, I remember now. It was you!"

"Piss off, asshole," Kyle grumbled. He wrapped an arm around Sellie's waist and walked her toward the club.

Inside, they sat at the bar, sipping drinks, exchanging flirty glances, chitchatting. Easing into the scene.

From the corner of his eyes, Kyle saw that the other Masters — his friends — were close by, eager to greet the two of them, but nevertheless giving him and Sellie some time to settle. He saw Ian was stopping others from approaching him, he guessed they were people who wanted to ask him questions about the club or techniques. Whatever it was, it was nothing Ian or any of the other Masters couldn't handle, but he knew he'd have to get off his ass soon to mingle, talk to members, and stroll through the club. He wanted that too, with her by his side. He just hoped she was truly ready for it all.

Then her hand was on his and she gave him a warm smile.

"It's okay, Kyle. I'm fine," she said.

He chuckled. Master Kyle, owner of Serenity, reassured by his sub. *That will be the day.*

"Thank you, dear," he said, giving her a sweet smile.

Sellie's heart skipped a beat when his smile disappeared as fast as it had come up. His blue eyes were now cold as steel, boring into hers. The power in his gaze was too much to bear, and she averted her eyes. The unexpected change in him had her off-kilter.

She glanced up through her lashes and saw him grab a cushion from a pile. It was thrown on the floor in front of her.

"Kneel."

The cutting edge in his voice made her wince, and she complied as fast as she could with her high heels. Wanting to please him, she sat up straight, her thighs apart, her head a little lowered. Then she saw her skirt had ridden up and her crotch was exposed. Her bare crotch. This was not what she'd had in mind when she'd decided against wearing the thong. *Goddammit!* She grabbed the hem of the skirt, knowing it was going to be futile — the wretched thing was too short — but she lived in hope.

"Leave it."

Sellie swallowed, wanting — needing — to cover her private parts, but she daren't rile him up when he was this direct. If there was a buildup, she could fence him off. For a bit at least. But she was lost whenever he went for the jugular. She let go of the skirt.

"Good girl," he said, stroked through her hair, then started talking to someone.

Good girl? Did he have any idea how much she disliked being called a good girl? She could never quite work out if it was meant lovingly or not. It always sounded condescending to her. As if she was a puppy.

Kyle left her to her own devices and was chatting with God knew who. No way was she going to glance up and find out. It was far too embarrassing to look people in the eye while she was sitting there with her pussy exposed. In the bar area at that. This was a far cry from how she'd envisioned her first night at the club. She'd thought they'd have a drink, talk to people, saunter through the dungeon. Watch scenes together while he had his arm around her, and seeing and feeling how proud he was to have his sub with him again. And here she was, on her knees on the floor.

Staring at his boots. With her pussy exposed. And being ignored by him.

Then, as if he could read her mind, he cupped her face, his warm touch pulling her out of her misery. Happiness flowed through her. He wasn't ignoring her! She leaned into his hand and rubbed her cheek over it, both because she loved the sensation and to let him know she appreciated his token of care.

Her gaze rose and her heart did a triple somersault when she met his. Kyle's face didn't show anything, but his eyes held a peculiar mix of raw masculine power, dominance and love. It pooled in her lower body and started a glow that spread upward through her belly. Her nipples tightened into hard peaks and her pussy dampened. His gaze was so strong, intimidating and arousing at the same time, that a sudden shyness came over her and heat rolled into her cheeks.

His lips curved into a smile, then his eyes released her. She let out a sigh. That had been intense. Would she ever get used to these mercurial changes from ease and love to shy and awkward? She doubted it. *And isn't that part of the game?*

After that moment of visual intimacy, he kept caressing her or let his hand rest on her shoulder. Although she was on the floor, she relaxed. His presence and energy were like a warm embrace, even when he wasn't touching her. The bond that connected them was strong and ran deep, and it was all she needed to feel safe and loved. She waited for him to be ready. What for, she didn't know, nor did it matter.

"Get up, love."

Sellie blinked. Her mind had drifted. Kyle reached out and helped her get up. Now that she had stood up, her feet tingled with pins and needles. She shook her legs to get rid of the uncomfortable sensation.

"You've done well, girl. I'm proud of you," Kyle said, and brushed a kiss across her lips. His gaze dropped to her still bared crotch, and heat crept over Sellie's face again. He pulled the skirt down over her ass.

"Better?"

She nodded and gave him an appreciative smile.

"Thank you," she whispered.

"You're welcome. Enjoy it while you can!"

Her smile froze on her face. What was he thinking of? It was obviously going to be a scene, but what? She had hoped he'd want to play—then again, just spending the night in the club together would've been great too. He had mentioned a full-body inspection. Whatever the hell that meant.

Her thoughts got interrupted when he gave her a mint julep, then dragged her off into the dungeon after she'd finished it. Time went by in a flash. They talked to Doms and subs, and watched couples play. Some scenes were very arousing, while others made her blush and want to run for the door.

Kyle just chuckled at her discomfort.

"I may want to try that some time," he said, amusement gleaming in his eyes.

She glared at him, to which he raised an eyebrow.

"Maybe I'll try that tonight."

Her eyes flared wide at the thought, and the eagerness in his voice. He laughed out loud. For a moment she pretended to be insulted that he was making fun of her, but his deep laugh was too contagious. She couldn't help but join in.

"Don't worry, babe." He grinned. "I got something better in mind for you."

She smiled at him, until she saw he was serious.

Back to discomfort. Genuine worry was more like it. This was nerve-racking. Lighthearted, dominant, lighthearted, intimidating, lighthearted, worrying. The bastard had her on tiptoes, and judging by the smile on his face, he knew it too. Her pussy enjoyed it. The constant change in vibe had gotten her soaking wet. The glint in his eyes told her he was aware of that as well. *Bastard!*

She was almost relieved when he was called away because of some issue. Before he took off, he walked her to a quiet area where a few submissives were seated. Some of her friends were there too—Kate, Melissa, Rebecca and some others she'd talked to before.

"Stay here, sweetie. I'll be right back." Kyle pressed a kiss on her lips and stalked away.

The girls greeted her and Rebecca patted the sofa she was sitting on.

"Sit with us, Sellie," she said with an inviting smile.

Getting off her feet would sure as heck be nice, but it would expose her pussy. Rebecca looked at her short skirt, understood her dilemma and grabbed a blanket from a pile. Grateful, Sellie accepted it, wrapped it around her hips and sat down.

"God, this is good! These boots are killing me," she sighed.

Soon she was engaged in girl talk, enjoying herself. At some point the conversation shifted and the women started sharing stories of what they'd done to their Doms and Masters to sass them. Most of them giggled at what the others had come up with while some looked downright shocked.

"You girls are bad!" Melissa said, then she chuckled. "I'm taking mental notes."

One of the subs was in the midst of a funny anecdote when the skin on the back of Sellie's neck began to tingle. A sense of warm pressure that set goose bumps in her skin. The tingling ran down her spine in a longing shiver. She raised her head and looked straight into Kyle's blue eyes, which shimmered with desire. It brought a spasm to her clit. It was unbelievable how strongly her body reacted to him, each and every time. Just the one look or word were enough to stir up a fire in her core. Would she ever not want him?

"Are you taking notes as well, sweetie?" Kyle sounded casual, but Sellie didn't miss the glint in his gaze.

For a moment she wasn't sure what to reply. She sure as hell was going to try and remember some of the things she'd heard. And she'd put them to the test on him as well. But telling him that was not the smartest thing in the world. Not when he acted like Mr. Charming and I'm-so-cool-about-it. Looks could be deceiving, and when it came to Kyle they usually were. She could lie, but that wouldn't go down well either. If there was one thing he hated, it was lying. *How wonderful to be put on the spot.*

Kyle raised an eyebrow, waiting for her reply.

Sellie decided to bullshit her way out and cast him a sexy smile.

"I was merely paying attention to learn how I can be a good sub, Sir," She fluttered her lashes at him as she tried to hold a straight face under his probing gaze. But she lost it when one of the other girls giggled, and she burst out in laughter.

"I'm...I'm s-so fucking s-sorry." She hiccupped. "But some of it is just too good to ignore."

A corner of Kyle's mouth curved up.

"I don't think you're sorry at all," he said, smiling at her. "But we'll talk about the fun side of it later."

Although he sounded nonchalant, there was a smoky gleam in his eyes. Her laughter stuck in her throat.

"I'm sorry," she said, and hastened to add, "Master."

Kyle nodded. "Better. Time for your full body inspection. Now!"

The command in that last word almost made her jump to her feet. The blanket she'd wrapped around her hips slid off and she hastened to pull the hem of her skirt down to cover herself.

After an approving look-over he said, "Follow me, sub."

Rebecca mouthed a *good luck*, then Sellie followed Kyle as he stalked through the dungeon. As she tried to keep up with his long strides, she cursed her high-heeled boots.

"Do you have to walk so fast?" she mumbled under her breath, then barged into him as he stopped.

"What's that, sub?" he asked without even turning around.

"I'm...I-I c-can't keep up, Sir," she stammered. How had he even heard that?

Kyle nodded and continued with Sellie in tow, but he did slow down a bit. They got to a circular scene area and he motioned for her to stand in the middle of it. Sellie knew it had colored lights overhead, which made for beautiful effects during play. There were sofas right next to the circle so people could watch the scene. *Thank heavens those are roped off now.* She wasn't quite sure what a full body inspection meant, but she was certain she didn't want an audience with it. Then Kyle clicked a footswitch and she was flooded in bright white light. *White light? Seriously?* She glanced down and saw that her red sequin corset looked great with the light sparkling off it. The man knew his aesthetics and had good taste, she had to give him that. But she still didn't want to be lit up like a football field during a championship match. She cast him her most evil look. *Why settle for a small audience when you can stand out like a sore thumb for the entire dungeon to see?*

Kyle chuckled as he came back to her.

"Problems, love?"

"Not at all, oh Lord and Master." Sarcasm dripped from her voice. "But I think I prefer pink."

"As do I." He smiled. "Your pretty ass a deep pink, with the proper light on it for me to enjoy."

She gave him a defiant look. "A spanking? But what about the inspection?"

"What about both?" he retorted.

"Why do you always have to..." she started, then swallowed the rest when he treated her to his lethal Master-look that made her want to melt in a puddle at his shiny boots. Her *"I'm sorry"* stayed glued to her vocal cords. All that came out was some kind of croaking sound.

"You're tongue-tied. Good for you!" he said. "I was beginning to think I'd have to tongue-tie you for real."

Sellie blinked, then her jaw dropped as the words sank in. Kyle stroked over her tongue before she could snap her mouth shut, just missing his finger.

"T-tongue-tie?" she stammered. "You can't, you wouldn't!"

Knowing she was staring at him like a puppy begging for a pat on the head didn't do much for her confidence levels.

Laughter shone in his eyes, and instead of giving her the reassurance she needed, he flashed her a broad smile.

Oh. My. God. I really don't want that. Ever! Instinct made her clench her teeth together.

"Don't worry, babe. Some other time."

She let out a sigh of relief as he stroked her cheek and brushed a kiss across her lips. Then he lowered his gaze to her breasts and slowly traced a finger over the upper curve.

"Now for this inspection. Let's start with your boobs." His voice had gone low and a bit husky as he began to undo her corset.

* * * *

Not much later, Sellie was trembling in her high-heeled boots with sheer need. Her head was spinning, her pussy soaking wet, and her nipples ached.

After he had loosened the corset enough for her breasts to be exposed, he had caressed, kneaded and pinched every bared inch of her skin. He'd bitten her sensitive neck, her ass and her inner thighs. Then he'd moved up to nuzzle her pussy, lap over her throbbing clit and taste her juices. She'd tried to suppress her moans, not wanting to attract attention and an audience, but she couldn't help herself. The man was way too good with his tongue. He'd toyed with her nipples and had given her mouth and pussy a thorough inspection with his cock, until she'd been begging him to make her come. Then he'd stopped and gotten up to bore his gaze into hers.

Now she was craning her neck to look at him as he loomed over her. Dominant, powerful, dangerous and horny as hell.

"You want to come, and you want pink light?" he asked, sounding hoarse with lust. "Anything for my girl. But it comes at a price. A very sexy price."

Sellie tried to clear her brain while he wrapped a soft blanket around her. Before she could speak, he'd swung her up in his arms and carried her toward a private room.

Oh Lord, have mercy on me!

Chapter Twenty-Four

Sellie could see herself in the mirror, bathed in pink light that made her skin appear soft and delicate. Her breasts, hips, even the curves of her shoulders looked beautiful. She would've been happy with the view if it weren't for the fact that she was gagged, tied up, bent over some narrow type of bench, and had an anal hook up her bottom.

The hook was attached to a rope that Kyle had tied to her ponytail, limiting her choices of movement.

Option one was to look at herself in the mirror, which made her feel humiliated. Option two was to bend her head to avoid looking in the mirror, but that pulled on the anal hook. That annoyed her, because in spite of her humiliation about the damned thing, it turned her on.

She couldn't quite decide what infuriated her more — seeing her naked body and dangling breasts in the mirror or getting more aroused, wet and excited by that thing up her ass.

Whatever she did, she felt vulnerable, exposed, humiliated. And she didn't like it one bit. Looking like a pig on a skewer was not her idea of a good time. Her rectum begged to differ. It seemed to like the stimulation, starting a wildfire of pleasure that radiated up and out.

No matter how good it was, Sellie wasn't willing to surrender to the sensations and admit she liked it. Loved it. Excitement flooded her like a tidal wave. Her pussy was throbbing and her nipples had turned into hard peaks.

Sellie would have cursed him if it weren't for the gag. Instead, she cast him a furious look via the mirror. He smiled, which rattled her cage even more. Then Kyle slid a finger through her pussy. Slow and teasing. Under different circumstances, she would've enjoyed that. Right now, feeling as embarrassed as she did, she'd rather hide within than admit to being aroused by it all. Him playing with her soaking wet pussy took away the option to pretend the scene didn't affect her.

"Let's see how excited you are," he muttered and thrust his finger inside her slick vagina. "You are very wet, darling. You love the anal hook, don't you?"

Her angry, muffled protest didn't score much effect with him—he continued to play with her. He pulled his fingers out of her pussy and circled her clit, wetting it with her juices. Her sensitive nub pulsed as he teased it, so slowly it was agonizing, stroking the sides, going over the hood. Enough stimulation to drive her wild, not enough to come. She started to writhe and wiggle. She couldn't help herself—the bastard knew how to stimulate her inside and out. Her movements made the anal hook shift. A moan welled up in her throat as jolts shot out from the tender tissues inside her rear end. Her clit throbbed in symphony.

Sellie wanted to cry out for more as he kept working her up with his fingers, higher and higher, but not allowing her to plummet over the edge.

All that came out were muffled sounds. *Damned gag!* She moved her hips to get the desired stimulation, which, without intending to do so, made the ball on the hook slide up and down her ass. The sensitized nerves sent heat waves through her core. Her ass was having a real good time, and her pussy was swollen and wet, her clit almost aching.

Sellie glanced up, a plea in her eyes, to let him know she was in dire need. Instead of meeting his eyes, she found herself looking at her own reflection in the mirror.

Her breasts were swollen, her nipples hard, her cheeks red with excitement, her eyes dazed.

No! I don't want to look like this. Like a slut in need!

A sob welled up, yet her body kept screaming for more. Even her mind joined the party now, stirring wanton thoughts and desires. She could live with that, but seeing herself like this, not so much. It was impossible for her to face it. She refused to do it.

Bending her head wasn't an option — it'd pull on the hook and instead of bringing relief it'd add to the overwhelming dark desires that flooded her mind and body. She chose the only other way out and closed her eyes.

Kyle's chuckle resonated in her ears. The thought that she'd outsmarted him almost made her giggle.

She knew she had a smug look on her face. Maybe not the smartest thing to show her Master.

"Open your eyes."

Sellie almost obeyed. Almost. But her embarrassment was stronger than his command. She refused.

"Open. Your. Eyes!" The steel in his deep voice cut through her resistance. A shock went through her and she opened her eyes, only to close them again the second she saw herself in the mirror.

Kyle waited. Sellie knew she'd obey, even though everything inside her screamed to resist him. She had to. The bond between them ran deep and she wasn't able to defy it. It took her less than ten seconds to open her eyes again and meet his in the mirror.

"Good girl!" he said, caressing her cheek with his fingers. "Let's give you a reminder to keep them open."

A few minutes later, he had adorned both her nipples with clamps with weights on them.

"I'll add more weights if you close your eyes again," he warned. The spark in his gaze when he said that, as if he hoped she would disobey him, sent a longing shiver up her spine.

It was incredible how she now wanted to please him, even if that meant more weights and more discomfort. The urge was overwhelming.

Seeing her own reflection changed her mind. Her nipples were stretched by the weights and it looked horrible. Horribly sexy and slutty. It made her feel that way too. A whine escaped her.

Their gazes met in the mirror and sparks flew across the room, the connection so strong it made her head spin. A sense of loss filled her when he broke the eye contact.

Sellie moved her head down and back up, alternating between easing the tension on the rope with the anal hook and watching herself in the mirror. Her neck muscles were getting a bit tired and she needed to let her head hang down, even if just for a moment, but that pulled that wretched thing up in her ass, and she didn't want that. As she was struggling with her predicament, she got more and more turned on, and something inside her shifted. Through her haze of arousal, she found that she craved to look in the mirror, to see herself in that humiliating position.

Oh my! I really am a bad, bad girl!

When Kyle again started playing with her pussy, moving a finger in and out and stroking around her swollen clit, she almost came. Almost—the bastard made sure he kept her on the edge, making her wiggle and squirm, until her mind went numb. All that remained was ecstasy and the rush of sensations that turned into tongues of fire, searing her body, feeding the heat in her core that was getting ready to explode.

Her moans and whimpers turned into a constant whine of need. She begged him with her eyes to give her the release she so wanted.

Fire was smoldering in Kyle's eyes. Seeing and sensing his arousal added to her own. The ordeal got worse—or was it better?—when he made the weights on the nipple clamps dangle.

A long-winded, muffled "Please!" broke from her.

"You want more?" Kyle's deep voice sounded hoarse with desire. He added more weights to the nipple clamps.

Her nipples stretched further and the sight was awful and slutty but arousing nonetheless. Her eyes burned with lust now—her resistance had melted away.

"You've been a good girl. You deserve a reward," he said. "Keep your eyes on the mirror."

Knowing he'd allow her to come this time put her system in overdrive. She was delirious with need—her entire body was alight. He moved faster around her clit, then over the hood, down toward the bundle of nerves.

Her leg muscles trembled and the heat in her core reached unbearable levels, then he rubbed over her clit and the fireball exploded. Her mind blanked and her vision swam as the fire raged through her body until sparks seemed to shoot out of her every pore. Her entire body shuddered. Then it slowed down to pleasurable ripples, but the dangling weights tugged at her nipples and the sliding hook in her ass sent jolts to her pussy. The combined sensations ignited a new fire in her lower body. One stroke over her clit sent her over right away, and a muffled scream tore from her as she was thrown in rapture.

Her vagina clenched, hoping—needing—something to clamp down on. Nothing. Her pussy kept convulsing as she rode the last waves of her orgasm. Being left empty almost hurt. She so needed to be filled up, to have him inside her. To be completed, fulfilled. To not get that almost made her cry.

Sellie wasn't sure if Kyle was unaware or undeterred. But when he started to play with her pussy again, she knew he was aiming for another orgasm.

She fought it. She didn't want to. Not another clitoral orgasm and having her vagina ache for his cock and not getting it.

The gag stopped her from telling him. She could only communicate with her eyes. She let them convey an angry "No way!"

He smiled at her.

"You will." There wasn't a shred of doubt in his words, nor in his voice.

The "I will not!" she put in her gaze lit a blazing inferno of dominance in his that hit her via the mirror.

"You will. Because I want you to."

The reply she sent him with her eyes made a corner of his mouth curve up.

"Stubborn little thing," he mumbled. "Excellent time to get the Hitachi out."

Her eyes got wide.

He had used it on her before and she remembered all too well what a Hitachi felt like. She knew she was going to lose this battle, but she'd put up one hell of a fight regardless.

Kyle attached the Hitachi to her leg then walked around her and pressed a kiss to the top of her head. He played with the weights on the nipple clamps. Electric currents of pain and pleasure zinged over her nerves, straight to her core. She tried to resist it, but her clit throbbed.

He caught her gaze in the mirror.

"Ready for it, darling?"

She cast him a death-look, and although her mouth was quite full with the large ball gag in it, she managed to produce a nonstop rant with a great many F-words. She watched as Kyle walked toward her rear end and switched on the Hitachi. A shock went through her body and she stopped ranting.

Her stomach muscles tensed as she fought the vibrations that were shooting through her core at the speed of light.

No, no, no! I do not want to come, dammit! I want you in me, you bastard! I do not want to... Oh God, please no! Oooh, pleeeaseyesss!

In her mind she was cursing, swearing and fighting, but her body betrayed her. She couldn't stop it or fight it. The orgasmic explosion blew her away. Shattered her world. Flashes of color blinded her as she shook out of control. Again her vagina clamped down on nothing, and it hurt so bad that she started to cry through the last waves of her orgasm.

Kyle removed the vibrator and ran his hand over her back as he walked around her to remove the ball gag.

Sellie was exhausted, sated and yet not sated at all, irritated because of it, and crying. Her pussy was still clenching.

Having been aroused beyond belief and only getting clitoral orgasms wasn't enough. It was infuriating. Her body was screaming for fulfillment that could only be gotten by having him penetrate her, and even more so, having him come inside her. The ancient primal instinct of "man takes woman and shoots his seed in her womb" overtook her and mingled with her urgent desire to be sexually fulfilled.

Not getting that satisfaction frustrated and angered her. It made her feel like a pressure cooker and she couldn't help but let off steam.

"You prick! Bastard for doing that! I do not want…" Her voice sounded shrill as she kept ranting.

The fact that Kyle ignored her didn't help. He disappeared from her sight.

When she heard him unzip his leathers, she glanced in the mirror, just in time to see him behind her, then he buried his cock to the root inside her wet cunt. Her cry got drowned out by his low, rumbling groan. He curved his hands around her hips and took her. Hard.

"Yes! Oooh, yesss! More!"

Her brain shut down and instinct took over. Her vagina muscles clamped down on his cock, which filled her again and again.

"That's it, baby," he growled.

He hammered into her, hitting her deep, and she whined. Hot fire and pain rushed through her, making her clit pound and her nipples tingle and ache. Warmth crept up from her feet through her legs and her thigh muscles started to tremble. She was hovering over the precipice of release and somehow sensed he was too.

"My sexy slut. I'm going to fill your cunt with my cum." His voice had gone low and throaty.

Then he thrust into her sweet spot. The delicious torture pushed her over the edge and she came so hard she almost passed out. Lighting shot up her spine and flashes of heat coursed through her in exhilarating waves. Her shrill cries echoed through the room, mingled with his roar. Her cunt convulsed around his cock as he fucked the aftershocks out of her while shooting his cum deep inside her, leaving her happy and sated at last.

* * * *

After their scene in the private room, they'd left the club in the capable hands of Master Rafe and retired to Kyle's private quarters.

Kyle had gotten the hearth going, poured them a drink, and had pulled Sellie close on the sofa. He'd shut his eyes, fully enjoying the moment and the glowing aftermath from their scene.

The next night they'd spent in the dungeon again, but they hadn't played. They'd mingled while he'd kept an eye on her to make sure she was all right. But he didn't have to worry, she was having a great time. It pleased him to see that she was starting to get acquainted with a few other submissives. She'd been talking to Kate and Ruth — and Rebecca, of course. He could tell it did her a world of good to be in the club, and to make new friends. Making gal-pals among submissives was important. Having people to turn to for advice, a giggle and support could help her a lot. And it might help her to eventually face Peta, the woman who had triggered her that awful night.

Yes, Saturday night had been great. He found that he had needed it more than he'd thought. Being with his friends, the members, the vibe, had settled something inside him. Peace. Home, and a lot of fun. It had been amusing to see how shy Sellie could get when another Master addressed her. Strong and fiery as she was, she still felt out of her depth when there was an abundance of dominant men around. Master Luke seemed to scare her the most. Not a surprise — the man had that effect on many subs. He'd feel sorry for the man if it weren't for the fact that he knew that Luke enjoyed freaking subs out. And scary or not, it turned many on just the same. Kyle was certain many submissives got wet panties when Luke put his pale blue gaze on them. His Sellie wasn't one of them. She'd burrowed closer when Luke had come over to talk to him, and he knew her well enough to be able to tell she wasn't aroused. Not one bit.

It had been a good night in more than one way. They'd gotten to know one another even better.

Now, on a lazy Sunday afternoon, Kyle was sipping a beer on the patio. Sellie was washing her car. He'd helped her out with the hose, then left her to her own devices. The carwash wasn't all that far away, but since it was so warm, she'd wanted to have some fun, and splash and dash with water.

His eyes closed and he smiled when he heard her sing. He loved her voice, sweet and tingly. Everything about the woman was great. Her personality, her body, the way she came, how her green eyes could spit fire when she was angry. And damn, had she been angry Friday night during the scene with the anal hook. Thinking about that got heat going in his groin.

He'd enjoyed her predicament with it. It had turned him on, made him hard as rock.

He appreciated most forms of predicament bondage. Seeing a sub struggle, and eventually surrendering, was one of the most beautiful things in the world to watch.

And fuck, had she looked beautiful! Bent over, wearing those sexy red thigh boots, her pussy exposed. The way her breasts had swayed when he'd loosened the corset and they'd spilled free.

The minute he'd put the anal hook in place, she'd started to swear and call him names. That didn't bother him. If nothing else, he had counted on it. Any excuse to gag her was good enough for him. He had chosen a large ball gag, a red one to match her outfit. He'd loved it. She'd hated it. He'd loved how she hated it. Kyle chuckled as he remembered the way Sellie had looked at him via the mirror, fire shooting from her eyes.

Yes, his little vixen had been livid. And very excited as well. Her pussy had glistened with her juices, her nipples had turned into hard buds and her breathing had been ragged.

He thought of the muffled protests that had come from her when he'd played with her pussy. Her clit had swelled against his fingers and her cunt had clenched around them as he'd finger-fucked her.

He was fully erect now. He unzipped and pulled out his dick. He began stroking himself — slow moves, letting his hand work its way up and down, taking his time to build it up as he enjoyed the erotic images in his head. The way she had mentally fought the slide of the anal hook. The exquisite mixture of fury, lust and humiliation in her eyes. It had almost robbed him of his self-control.

His breathing got faster. As he kept stroking his shaft, he slid his other hand down to his testicles and cupped them. A groan welled up in his throat when heat ran through his balls at the touch, at the same time loving the sensation of cupping them with his hand.

More arousing pictures came to mind. Her helpless gaze when their eyes had met in the mirror. He'd have loved to make her tell him that she wanted to be a slut, his slut, but that would've meant removing the gag. Easily done, but he'd liked it. So did his cock.

Then, and now.

Stroking turned to motion. His cock was pulsing now, blood flowing through the veins on his shaft, making him harder. Engorged. His testicles tightened and drew up. He knew that if he continued, he was going to come. Hard.

He hauled in a deep breath. It would be good to come, but sharing it with Sellie would be better. A helluva lot better. He wanted her. Badly.

A hard, sensuous ride in her slick cunt was what he craved. Just fucking her, and seeing lust bloom in her eyes as he drove deeper would make him even harder. Until his balls ached with need and glorious release took his head off.

He zipped up and stalked to where she was washing her car, oblivious of what was to happen. She truly was gorgeous. Wearing shorts, legs a mile long, and a tight tank top that hugged her breasts.

"Lose the shorts." His voice easily carried to her.

Sellie whirled around, their eyes locked and she dropped the garden hose. Pressure made it twist and turn on the ground and she got sprayed with water. She yelped as the cold liquid soaked her head to toe. Kyle groaned. The now wet tank top clung to her breasts, showing off her hard nipples and areola.

"My own wet T-shirt girl. I like it!" He sounded throaty. "Lose the shorts. Now!"

Shock was still clear in her eyes as she got out of her shorts. Kyle walked over to her, turned the nozzle on the hose so he didn't get soaked as well then faced the woman in front of him. Her hair was glued to her skin, tracing over her collarbones and the swell of her breasts toward her nipples. Water dripped from her locks over the taut peaks.

"You look just like a mermaid," he mumbled. "So sweet and innocent."

Before she had time to reply, he grabbed her tank top and tore it to shreds.

Her eyes flared wide.

"Much better," he said, and flashed her a wicked smile. "I don't want innocent and sweet. I want to fuck a wild siren."

She shrieked when he lifted her up, put her ass on the hood of her car and draped her legs over his shoulders.

"Kyle, you can't—" she started.

"I can. I am," he interrupted. He kept her pinned with his gaze as he slid his fingers under her thong toward her entrance. When he found her aroused, he growled. "A wet, slutty woman. Exactly what I need right now."

Without further ado he unzipped, moved her flimsy piece of underwear out of the way and swirled the tip of his cock through her juices. Her breath hitched when he slid up, around and over her clit. Little tremors shook her, making her breasts wobble and her legs muscles quiver.

"Oh, you're ready for me all right," he mumbled, sounding husky.

He pushed himself inside her pussy inch by inch, enjoying how her silky soft and wet tissues enveloped him. He tilted his head back.

"You're a dream to fuck, baby," he groaned. Her pussy clamped down on his shaft in reply.

After a few slides she was wet enough for more action, and he curved his hands around her hips.

"Brace yourself, girl."

He buried himself to the root inside her cunt. His balls slapped against her buttocks.

"Yesss, oooh, Kyle, yess!" she whined.

Kyle didn't need more encouragement and he gave in to his desire. Her breasts bounced with each thrust, the sight making his cock jerk. His gaze dropped to her pussy, her labia spread and swollen. He groaned as he watched his shaft move in and out, her inner pussy lips slick and tight around him. The visual was almost too much to bear.

Liquid lava coursed through his veins, searing him. He was so close, almost at the point of no return. His balls and scrotum were pulsing, pulling up. Warmth spread out in waves from his core, down his legs and up his shaft. It intensified, and heat flooded his belly and stomach. The mind-boggling rush heightened all his senses. Smell, taste, sound, touch, vision. Each sensation got stronger. Her tight pussy tugging and clenching around his throbbing cock, her mewls as he pounded into her. Her cries of sheer joy when she came, shocking and thrashing, her satiny cunt trying to milk him, and succeeding. He couldn't hold it any longer — didn't want to either. His testicles tightened to the point of pain — sheer bliss — then pushed up his cum from deep inside his balls, through his shaft. The erotic feeling made him growl and his vision blurred. He slammed into her with short, swift thrusts as his semen neared the head of his cock. Then it shot out of the tip in mind-shattering spurts until the force of his ejaculation began to fade. The waves of sexual pleasure turned to ripples and his muscles began to relax. He surrendered to the warm afterglow and the divine sense of emptiness in his balls.

"I damned love you, girl," he whispered.

Sellie wrapped her arms around his neck.

"I love you too, Kyle."

Chapter Twenty-Five

Another couple of months had gone by, and Sellie was doing great. She still went to her coach, Diana, but not quite so often anymore. Diana wanted to make sure Sellie wouldn't slip back into old patterns and they'd agreed to continue the sessions for a bit longer.

Things with Kyle had progressed as well. They'd gotten to know each other on a deeper level. In spite of that, or because of that, they hadn't done many scenes in the club anymore. At first Sellie hadn't understood why, so she had asked him. Kyle had smiled and told her that he wanted her all to himself. He felt that what they shared was too precious, and he preferred to keep that private.

Sellie had been surprised and had giggled.

'So, in other words...you are too damned possessive?' she'd asked with a smile.

The Dom death-look he'd given her had made her swallow. He'd pulled her head back by her hair, his piercing eyes sharp enough to cut.

'Do you have a problem with that, sub?' The words had been spoken oh-so-soft and polite, but the threat in his voice had been clear. And very arousing. Her nipples had tightened into hard peaks.

She'd been intimidated all right, and it hadn't been a great time to taunt him. Not when he looked like that. But she couldn't help herself. If he gave her enough rope to hang herself, she would, again and again and again, even though it sometimes scared the bejesus out of her. The buzz of it was too good. She loved the thrill. Sass him, annoy the hell out of him, only to be dominated and controlled. Forced onto her knees, literally or figuratively. She needed that feeling of tranquility that filled her being when she submitted to him. That state of being that allowed her to let go of everything and anything. Besides, it was too much fun to rile him up. Most of the time.

That time he had forced her on her knees. It had infuriated her, but he'd held her in place with ease, unzipped, and had taken her mouth. Her objection had turned him on more, and his resolve aroused her. The way he'd fisted his hand in her hair and had just used her mouth was somehow sexy as sin.

Until the bastard had come on her face. She hated that, and she'd wanted to swear, but one look at him had shut her up. His hand was still tangled in her hair and he had kept her pinned with his eyes. She'd so wanted to avert her eyes, but he wouldn't let her. Then something inside her belly had shifted, opened up and absorbed the dominance that oozed out of him, accepting it. Her muscles relaxed as she surrendered to his will. A wonderful sense of safety and total trust had enveloped her and mingled with a deep inner peace.

'Still having problems with me being possessive?' he had asked.

'No. Sir,' she'd whispered.

He'd gotten on his knees before her, the hug he gave her so full of love and care that tears pooled in her eyes. She'd buried her face in the crook of his neck, breathing in the moment of intimacy.

After a while he'd stood up, pulled her to her feet as well.

'Let's go get cleaned up,' he had said. *'I want to take you out to dinner.'*

They'd had a wonderful time. They always did. Sometimes they didn't see each other for more than a week—as they both had busy jobs, it couldn't be helped. But they did get in touch as often as their schedules allowed.

Today she'd gotten a peculiar message from him though. An email.

My sweet, meet me tomorrow night. My place, come to the patio, 9 pm sharp.

"Talk about vague," she mumbled. "Odd, but exciting.".

Just as she was thinking about what to do, what to expect and what to wear, the doorbell rang. A delivery from Kyle. The parcel was wrapped in shiny red foil and had a fragrant white rose on it. *Sexy!*

Her fingers trembled a bit when she read the card that was on the box.

Wear this, and only this.
xx Master Kyle

Excitement buzzed through her and her heart thumped with sweet expectation. She was dying to find out what he had bought her. The box and wrapping were quite romantic. Maybe it was a negligee. It could also be that he had bought her a fancy dress to take her out. Then again, he had signed the card with 'Master', so it had to be something kinky.

Sellie opened the box, looked at its contents and sucked in air. *He has to be kidding? Black high heels and a blindfold. That's it?* She rummaged through the box, hoping there was at least a flimsy something she could wear, hidden under the pumps. Nothing. Except for a handwritten letter. She read it, gasped then read it again. It told her exactly what she had to do when she got to his place, the instructions unequivocal.

"This is too much," she whispered.

In her mind she could hear his reply — "No, it's just right."

She sighed, knowing she wouldn't be able to shake her nerves or stop the mild excitement that put a glow in her lower belly. No matter what Kyle was going to do, he'd make sure it was good. And awkward as hell.

Finally, the time arrived for her to leave. She had bathed, sprayed herself with her favorite perfume and packed a bag with clothes and toiletries. Then she was ready to leave, meaning she had to change into nothing much. Kyle's instructions had said she had to wear what he had bought her when she got there. A fancy way of saying she had to be naked.

She stripped out of her jeans, top and underwear, and slipped on her coat. The pumps would have to wait until she got to Kyle's. She didn't like driving in high heels. Barefoot would do.

It was odd to walk out of her house in nothing but a coat. No one could tell the difference, but she knew, which was enough to stir mild exhibitionist sensations. The way the lining brushed over her skin and nipples was very erotic.

The half-hour drive went by in the blink of an eye. Sellie sat in the car for a few more minutes after she'd parked, nervous and excited.

Why was this so difficult? She trusted Kyle — that wasn't a problem. Being naked shouldn't be an issue either. He had seen her skyclad a gazillion times and had explored every inch of her body. And her mind. She was safe with him, no doubt about that. The premises were known territory to her. They'd spent many hours on the patio and in the gardens. She was comfortable there. That wasn't a problem either. Yet being naked on the patio without any prelude or foreplay seemed off. Having to wear a blindfold made things worse. Not being able to see what was going to happen would be scary, even when the man and surroundings were familiar. The idea was arousing nonetheless. Butterflies fluttered in her stomach and her pussy dampened.

She grabbed her bag and got out of the car. Her gaze roamed over the mansion.

It was impressive. And huge. Light yellow walls, solid window frames, the ornate wooden front door sporting wrought iron handles and ornaments. Rustic black lights with amber glass on either side of the entry cast a warm glow on the porch. Pink flowers in pots made it look inviting and friendly.

The building was a reflection of its owner. Tall, warm and charming at first sight, while radiating a steadfast power underneath. A power that would meander gently, unobtrusive, inexhaustible. Almost like a purring kitten nuzzling someone's ankles, only to spring into action like a roaring lion when the occasion called for it. One hundred percent masculine power.

Sellie had witnessed that change in Kyle a number of times. A daunting experience, especially when she was at the receiving end of it.

Now she had to enter the mansion, his lair, not knowing whether to expect the adorable kitten or the wild animal. Her mind hoped for the first — her pussy was definitely more interested in the latter.

Then the front door closed behind her, and she took a deep breath. Parts of her body seemed to receive messages from her nervous brain. Her knees were wobbly, her hands trembling. Other parts seemed more in sync with the vibe her core was emitting. Like her glowing clit, and her nipples that had hardened into tingling buds.

A quick glance at her cell phone told her it was almost nine p.m.

She shoved her bag to the side, put the blindfold in her coat pocket and toed her feet into the pumps, the softness of the leather remarkable, the stiletto heels so high that walking would be difficult.

For a minute she stood there, mentally going through the instructions he had given her. Then she started to walk, through the hallway and the living room, toward the patio doors. She stepped onto the veranda and stood still to take in the scene. Soft music, the scent of roses and incense, candles and tea lights, a vase of peonies on the table. Two beautiful wineglasses and a bottle in a cooler. It would've been very romantic if it weren't for what she had to do next.

High heels are all you will wear when you get to the patio.

The coat would have to go. Now. *So much for romance.* And where was Kyle anyway? Somewhere in the dark of the garden no doubt. Hiding behind a bush as he ogled her. No, that would be pathetic. Nothing about the man was pathetic. More likely he was standing somewhere in the open, dressed in black, camouflaged by the night. He could be standing directly opposite her, a mere few meters away. No way she could tell—it was too dark. But even though her eyes couldn't distinguish him, her instinct did. A fuzzy, warm feeling deep inside her belly told her he was close.

She tried not to think of that as she fumbled with the buttons of her coat. It was very awkward to undress, aware of the fact she was being watched. Even if it was by Kyle. Her man, her Master.

The last button came undone, and she took the blindfold from the pocket and let the coat slide down. Her heart was racing, her chest heaving. Knowing his gaze was on her almost made her moan. She'd had no idea how much this would turn her on. It made her horny as hell to stand there naked in the semi-dark, her Master invisible but present. The heat in her core turned up a notch and gave her the courage to continue. She sashayed to the other side of the patio, walking tall, making sure her breasts bounced.

Then she got to the side table where she was supposed to wait for him and put on the blindfold. Her courage crumbled at the thought.

She licked her lips and swallowed hard. Then she did as her Master had ordered, slipped the blindfold over her head and put her hands in the small of her back. Her entire body was trembling as she waited. She pricked up her ears, but all she could hear was music and the bubbling of the stream in the garden.

Where is he? How long had she been waiting now? A few minutes? Twenty? She couldn't tell anymore. Her jumbled-up emotions were playing tricks on her mind.

After what seemed like an eternity, footsteps approached and stopped a few meters short of her. Fear washed through her. Would it be Kyle? Just as she was about to yank off the blindfold, he spoke up.

"My beautiful girl." Kyle's deep voice was a whispered caress.

Sellie's eyes brimmed with tears behind the blindfold. Relief flooded her and her shoulders relaxed. She hadn't even been aware of how tense she had gotten. A sob welled up in her throat. She really, really needed him to hold her right now. Then his body was against hers, warm and solid. Comforting. His arms strong, holding her tight. Sellie basked in his embrace. Her emotions settled and her breathing got back to normal. He lifted her face and kissed her. A warm, soft kiss, exploring and tender, making her feel safe, comfortable almost. He moved his hands over her back, caressed her behind and kneaded it. The warmth of his flesh on hers reminded her of her nakedness and she stiffened in his arms. He deepened the kiss. No more gentleness—he took her mouth with unbridled passion. One hand got tangled in her hair and kept her head still. Instinct made Sellie try to break free, but she found she couldn't. He had her restrained against his hard body by his embrace, hands and lips. Her own hands were still on her back, pinned there by his arms, leaving her front side vulnerable and naked. His erection pressed against her lower belly and his chest flattened her breasts. The touch of his hands got rougher, greedier, his mouth and tongue more demanding. The sheer lust that oozed from him made her head spin. Her body reacted to him and waves of heat coursed through her. Her pussy was soaking wet and her clit pulsed. Need made her want to writhe, but he didn't let her. She could do nothing but allow him to take his pleasure from her. A sense of complete helplessness came over her, which aroused her even more. It made her horny as hell.

She moaned in his mouth.

Kyle pulled back, stabilized her, then let go, the warm night breeze all that now touched her. The sudden withdrawal had Sellie off-kilter. She was in a state of passion and her head swam as if she was drunk. Just when she was about to keen a protest, a soft finger was put over her lips, reminding her of her instructions. *'No talking until after the scene.'*

The urge to express her disagreement was too high, and an exaggerated sigh came from her.

Kyle chuckled. "Don't taunt me too much, girl."

She giggled. And got her nipple pinched. Real hard. *God. Damn. It! Doesn't he know how much that hurts?*

He did nothing to ease the pain or to distract her from it, which forced her to get through the full extent of it by herself. She focused on breathing, doing her damnedest not to curse. Finally, the sharp sting wore off to a dull throbbing. Her shoulders relaxed, and she prayed he'd leave her nipples alone for the next half hour. Or next three days, rather. Maybe she should've told him to leave her sensitive nips out of the punishment zone. She wondered if he'd pay heed to that.

Sellie's mind was off and she frowned behind the blindfold, thinking about what she was going to tell him after the scene.

A tremor shook her when Kyle put his finger on her clit.

"Focus, sub," he said, his voice almost a whisper.

Without hurry, he slid toward her entrance, swirled through her wetness, and back to her clit. Her breathing quickened as he went around her nub, pressing against the sides, over the hood. Little shocks shot through her, and before long she arched her hips toward him, loving the stimulation, but it wasn't enough. Too soft, too slow.

How she wanted to beg for more. Or maybe swear because he didn't give it to her. All the while he fingered her, swirling around her throbbing nub, stroking over it.

Her over-sensitized clit swelled against his finger as he continued the sweet torture. Too good to ignore, not enough to get off..

To hell with begging, she wanted to curse now. It took all of her willpower to not plead, or scream, or rant. Anything. This mental gag was worse than a real one.

His soft, husky laugh made her want to hit him. Dig her nails into his back. The bastard deserved it for doing this to her.

Again, he moved toward her now soaking wet entrance, but instead of going back up, he thrust a finger inside her. She jerked at the unexpected entry, yet her vagina muscles clenched, welcoming the intrusion. A mewl broke from her when he put two fingers inside her pussy and started finger-fucking her. Not the deep and fast thrusts that could make her come, but slow slides that were agonizing, and not the full length of his fingers either. In and out, in and out. Sellie tilted her hips, craving more, much more. Not getting it was infuriating. Hot waves washed up and out from her lower body. Her nipples were so hard they ached. The tiny pain added to her arousal, but it still wasn't enough to get off.

She longed for him to knead her breasts and to make her come, but he did nothing of the kind — just continued what he was doing.

In and out, in and out, the rhythm steady. Then he thrust his fingers deep into her pussy and brushed his thumb over her clit. A long whine welled up in her throat as electricity zinged across her nerves. Her legs muscles trembled out of control. She was swaying on her feet, delirious with need.

"Time for chains, baby," he whispered.

She almost let out a protest when he withdrew his fingers, leaving her empty, which was almost painful. Her pussy was swollen inside and out. While she was wallowing in self-pity, she heard the clanking of chains somewhere behind her. Then Kyle made her step back.

"Give me your hands, Sellie."

She complied and rubbed her cheek against his as he put cuffs on her wrists. After he'd made sure they weren't too tight, he cupped her head and held her for a minute. The brief moment of loving connection made her heart sing with joy. A kiss was pressed to the top of her head, then he let go. Kyle attached the handcuffs to the chains and pushed her feet apart. The chains got pulled up, raising her arms in the air. It wasn't comfortable, but the support from the chains was nice. Her limbs were heavy, her feet aching. *Damned high heels.*

"You may get out of your shoes if you like."

Oh yes, she did like! Very much so. She let out a sigh of relief as she kicked off her shoes, only to find she was now forced to stand on her tiptoes.

Oh yes, this is so much better! Thank you, Master Asshole!

Her hope that he'd lower the chains a bit went out the window when she heard him huff a laugh.

She started to wiggle her feet closer together to get more slack on the chains. Fingers crossed he wouldn't notice.

"Sellie." The power he managed to put in that one word stopped her dead in her tracks.

"Damn you!" she spat out.

Smack! Smack!

Sellie shrieked when he slapped both buttocks. How could she forget he had a very hard hand?

"Behave, sub." The warning in his voice made her shudder.

She swallowed a whispered "I'm sorry," as she remembered the no-talking instruction.

Her mind was still searching for its equilibrium when he put cuffs around her ankles and attached them to rings. Sellie knew he had solid steel rings hidden everywhere throughout the garden, but she'd never seen any on the patio floor. *Sneaky bastard.*

There she was, outdoors, blindfolded, naked, spread-eagled, on tiptoes. And her ass hurt like hell.

She sensed him behind her, his warm breath caressing her skin. A sweet kiss on her nape sent a shiver down her spine. He reached around, cupped her breasts, kneaded them and bit her neck. Her breathing got a bit faster and hitched when he swirled his tongue through her ear. At the same time, he drew erotic circles around her nipples with his thumbs, rubbing over them. She moaned and pushed her breasts forward, wanting more. He inched toward the taut peaks and teased them, rolled them between his fingers. Then he pinched and pulled, and sizzling jolts raced over her nerves straight to her core, rekindling the fire in her pussy. He increased the pressure, and she whimpered, arching her chest to counter the pain. He released her now aching nipples, only to continue to sensitize the rest of her body until her legs quivered and her knees wobbled.

"Put your feet flat on the ground, love." A whisper in the air. She complied, wondering when he had loosened the chains enough for her to get off her tiptoes.

She forgot about that when he kissed the oh-so-sensitive curve of her neck. Tiny tremors shook her and she let out a soft mewl. Then he removed the blindfold, stroked through her hair and brushed his knuckles over her cheek. She kept her eyes closed, enjoying his touch.

"You may speak now."

Speak? Was this it? Disappointment put a dull ache in her gut. Her feet were tired and her skin was tingling from his hands and whatever else he had used. Her pussy was very wet and her clit was pulsing. And this was it?

"Are we done?" Her voice sounded flat.

"No, sweetie. We're only just beginning," he said.

"Oh." Sellie wasn't sure what to say.

"Fuck, I love this view," he mumbled behind her. "My siren at the seaside."

Not knowing what to expect, she opened her eyes and blinked a couple of times to focus. Her jaw dropped when she saw what he was talking about. She shook her head as if that would erase the image, but nothing had changed. She was staring at the mural she had worked on for so many hours. Candlelight lit the beautiful, painted columns, arches and the seascape. She had meant for it to enhance the vibe on the patio. Something peaceful and romantic to look at, not to be part of a BDSM scene. And now he had chained her up in front of her painting. Her work of art. *'My siren at the seaside,'* he had said. As if she were part of the mural? *The audacity!* Fury bubbled up inside her.

"You...you...bastard!" she shrieked, and futilely yanked on the chains.

Whack!

Leather fingers painfully hit her right ass cheek, and she inhaled sharply, caught off-guard by the unexpected blow of a flogger.

"Ouch! This is all wrong, you idiot!" she ranted.

Whack!

He hit her other buttock, then waited.

"Blasphemy!" she squeaked.

"What do you expect? I'm a pervert, baby," he said, sounding throaty.

Whack! Whack! Again, he waited.

The stings registered now and cut through her anger. The searing blaze of heat that shot out from her ass was overwhelming and she sucked in air. He'd used a flogger on her before, but it had never stung like this. A piercing hot flash of pain.

Sellie decided it'd be best to shut up.

Kyle flicked his wrist, and as Sellie heard the movement of the flogger through the air, her muscles tensed. But the tails felt soft now, teasing. They landed on her back, her thighs and ass. The mild thuds were so pleasurable, she wanted to lean into them. The rhythm was steady, predictable. Her skin started to glow, and she yielded to the sensation, even when the thuds got a little more intense. Her skin got warmer, the heat in her core hotter, her pussy wetter.

Just as it got good, he eased off and went back to light and gentle teasing. The tails danced against her thighs and calves as he twirled the flogger. She mewled, loving the cool leather falls on her tingling skin.

Then he went back to flogging with a regular rhythm, building it up. Her skin was burning now, and the heat seemed to pool in her pussy, making her clit pulse with need. The steady pace and sensations made her head dizzy, but he slowed down before the fluffy clouds and bliss of subspace could envelop her. A protesting moan fled her lips.

Kyle put his chest against her back and reached around. He started kneading a breast with one hand, played with her pussy with the other. Drawing slow circles around her clit, switched to figure eights through her pussy. Around her swollen nub, over her inner labia, back up, pressing against the sides of her clit, sliding over the hood. She whined and her hips jerked out of her control.

"Pleease!"

He increased pressure, stroked faster, kneaded her breast harder, tugged at her nipple.

"Yess, please, yes!"

Everything in her center coiled tighter as her climax approached. Her leg muscles quivered. The pressure in her core increased and the fire got hotter, almost unbearable. Something had to give. One more stroke over her clit and she went over the edge.

"Oooh!" She wailed as she exploded. A tidal wave of inexplicable pleasure flooded her, filled her entire being from head to toe. Wave after glorious wave made her body shake and thrash.

Kyle drew out every aftershock, and she was hanging heavily on the chains. He patiently waited and held her until her legs could carry her again. Her breathing got more regular as she landed. She was almost back to normal, except for the tingling sensation of her back and ass.

He circled her and brushed his knuckles over her cheek. "Are you ready?" he asked.

"Hmmm. A beer would be nice," she said, her voice still husky.

Kyle smothered a laugh. "I've got just the thing for you, only better."

Something in his voice made her insides quiver. He had sounded lighthearted, but there was an undertone to it that she couldn't quite place. Like the base notes in a perfume that weren't easy to distinguish. Her inner sub-alarm went off, but she hadn't a clue what it was exactly that had triggered it. She lifted her face to look at him. Her heart started to pound in her chest when she saw the darkness in his eyes. Shivers ran up and down her spine.

Time stood still as his gaze bored into hers, penetrating her very essence. There was no way she could stop it. He was too strong, and the after-orgasm buzz had left her open and vulnerable. The thing in his eyes flowed through her and settled in her lower belly like a throbbing ball of forbidden pleasures. An unexpected wave of deep, dark desire engulfed her.

His eyes released her, and she let out her breath, unaware that she'd been holding it. His gaze raked over her, breasts to pussy to legs and back to her pussy, lingering there. A jolt shot through her clit as if he had touched it. She knew she was getting wet, in spite of coming only minutes earlier. Then his gaze caught hers again, and she blinked to try and hold herself under the power in it. Part of her wanted to rip her eyes away from his and hide. Another part reveled in the darkness that gleamed in his gaze. A part that made her want to challenge him, defy him. Her wanton desires won the inner battle with ease, bursting up and out from her lower body until every fiber of her being was pulsing with an insatiable hunger for more. Much, much more. She'd never felt this way before — it blew her mind and melted her spine. Adrenaline coursed through her veins and her muscles trembled with excitement. Yes, she craved more, but no way in hell was she going to roll over and play sub. Damned if she was going to be tamed. If he wasn't willing to work for her submission and prove his worth, he wouldn't get her. Ever. She'd fight him, resist him. God, how she wanted to bite him, dig her nails into him, scratch him. Her defiance oozed out from her every pore. She knew her eyes reflected her thoughts and emotions when his gaze began to burn with possessive fire. One so hot that it seared her. She'd never seen him like that, and she was quite sure he had never seen her like this either.

He gave her a devilish smile that turned her core to liquid and fueled her resolve and strength.

"Yes, I think you are ready." His voice was low and hoarse with lust. "Tonight, I will take everything."

A husky growl welled up in her throat and she glowered at him, fully aware that she was about to put all her stakes into this game. Holding nothing back, giving it her all. she lost, she'd have nothing left. She'd submitted to him before, but she had never allowed him access to this small part that she kept hidden, even from herself. Like a vault that held all her vulnerabilities and deepest, darkest desires. For the first time ever, she had opened it, and if he won, he would see and know everything she was. Everything she stood for. Her very essence. And he could enter that place whenever he wanted. It was a terrifying thought. Not daunting enough to stop her, though. She was not going to lose. *Unacceptable!* She wouldn't let him.

His piercing eyes told her he understood, and that he wasn't going to back away from it. He accepted the challenge.

"My little tigress." His throaty tone arousing, the words jarring. Being compared to a little tigress when she was feeling this strong was insulting.

"Fuck you!" she spat.

"I will do that too."

Fury welled up inside her, along with a weird animalistic lust that made her pussy and clit throb with anticipation. His deep laugh only made it worse.

"Are you ready?"

"No. Yes. Fuck you." Sellie yanked on the cuffs so hard the chains clanked.

Kyle circled her and let his hand graze the skin of her back.

"Resistance is futile, baby," he whispered.

Before she could reply, he hit her with the flogger. Not too bad, although her skin was still sensitive from the earlier session.

Whack! Whack! Whack!

He hit her lightly. The mild thud from the multiple strands didn't bother her much. If nothing else, it was quite pleasant.

"That all you got?"

Kyle just chuckled. Gradually the impact increased, the rhythm never changing. It started to get to her brain and she felt herself starting to slip into subspace.

Whack!

Sellie yelped as the unexpected sting brought her back to full awareness. He began to alternate stings and thuds, stopping her from going to her happy place.

"Damn you," she said through clenched teeth, desperate to try to anticipate what the next blow would be like and failing abysmally. Her hazy brain and body couldn't even work out what she liked more. Hated more. Sting or thud. The stings were white hot flashes of pain whereas the thuds were deeper penetrating blows. She hated both. Then liked both.

Her pussy wasn't partial. Every heated blaze of pain seemed to gather between her legs, and her clit pulsed with joy. The burning of her back and ass added to the party.

Overwhelming, painful, arousing, a bit more painful, but she could handle it.

Then, without the blows stopping, the feel changed, got sharper. A moan fled her lips.

No no no! Not a whip!

Her heart was racing. She could safeword, but it wasn't too bad. Different—more of a bite, but okayish. She'd bear and grin it. The next blow was a bit harder. As was the next one. The fourth made her shriek. The rhythm didn't falter and nor did the strikes. The impact built up from okay, not so okay, bloody painful, to fucking unbearable. Again and again and again.

She fought the pain, groaned and huffed. It didn't change a thing—he continued whipping her, unrelenting, the rhythm the same. The turmoil inside her increased, needed to go somewhere, had to be expressed. Her body started to squirm and writhe by itself. She yanked on the cuffs, struggling with the restraints and the pain. The first didn't budge and the latter didn't cease. Tears ran from her eyes and she started to cry out loud. Then her mind gave up, her body gave in and she accepted the pain. Embraced it. Then she finally drifted off to her happy place.

Sellie was floating, enveloped by fluffy clouds that embraced her. Her skin burned and ached, vying with the fire between her legs.

The strikes had stopped. When, she did not know, nor did she care. Just as long as she could float. Butterfly touches winged over her hips, legs, ankles. An appreciative hum came from her. The butterflies went up over her legs, teasing and tickling, then they fluttered over her labia. Her legs shook at the touch and she mewled. The light feel of the wings turned up the heat in her pussy, but it wasn't enough. Not nearly enough to quench the fire down there and satisfy her pounding clit.

"Please!"

Her eyelids were so heavy, and she struggled to open them a bit. She saw Kyle kneeling in front of her, his hands between her legs. The sight sent a jolt through her.

"Pleease. I want... Need..." Her tongue refused to work.

Kyle bent his head and licked through her pussy. A long whine bounced off the patio walls. Through her haze she realized it was her own, but didn't give a toss. All she cared about was the urgent heat in her core that needed dousing. The pain and burning of her backside let her float in her happy place but kept fueling the fire in her pussy as well. It was almost too much to handle.

Again and again, he lapped over her clit, the sensation wonderful, but it wouldn't give her the sweet release she craved. She needed his full mouth on her cunt, his firm lips around her clit, hot and wet, sucking and licking.

A groan welled up in her throat. If only she could push his head against her pulsing pussy, but her arms seemed to have gone.

Then his mouth was on her. She wailed and thrust her hips forward. His tongue slid through her labia, flicked her nub, pressed against the sides. Hot waves of pleasure rolled through her, each wave stronger than the last, driving her closer and closer to the zenith. Her nipples swelled and tingled, added to the mind-boggling sensations of his swirling tongue.

Just when she was about to explode against his mouth, he pulled back.

"Noooo! You bastard!" She almost started to cry. Being cut off like that hurt like hell. Her cunt clenched, her clit pulsed, and everything was tight and swollen.

Whack!

A whip landed on her wide-open pussy, and she moaned. She didn't want to be whipped there, but it felt good. And she so had to come.

"Beg me to let you come." His voice was thick with lust. "Beg your Master."

Whack! Whack! The whip hit her labia, her clit, her entrance. The strikes were aimed with care that didn't allow her to come, but were enough to keep her on the precipice.

"Beg me," he grunted.

She didn't want to. If she did, he'd win, and he'd have her all. But even through the fog in her brain, she knew he already had her all. This was just the last threshold. And she couldn't not beg — her need was too high, the pressure in her core unbearable, as if she was going to burst.

"I fucking hate you," she whispered, breathing heavy.

"I don't fucking care. Beg me." No leeway. She knew he was not going to relent.

Again the whip hit her, on her now engorged clit. Jolts of electricity shot up her spine. The next blow trashed the last shreds of resistance and she yielded with her entire being.

"Pleeease! Please let me come, my Lord!"

He groaned as he gave her the pleasure. Her cries of joy filled the air as she rode the waves of mind-shattering release.

A minute, an hour, or maybe a week later, she more or less came to her senses. On the wooden table on the patio. She opened her eyes, saw candles, the posh wineglasses and the peonies she'd seen ages ago. Before he had flogged and whipped her to paradise. Everything hurt. Her back, her ass, her pussy. And her arms from bearing her weight when she'd been hanging on the chains, delirious with passion.

Sellie sighed, glad she could rest her aching body on the table, even though the surface was hard. Her eyes closed again and a soft mewl of contentment fled her lips.

"Don't get too comfortable, darling."

Her eyes flew open when she heard his voice behind her, and the edge of lust in it.

Her ass cheeks were pulled apart and a cold blob landed on her back hole. She was wide awake now.

He swirled the head of his cock through her crack, and the muscle of her rear entry puckered tighter as he rubbed over it.

Kyle growled, fisted his hand in her hair and pulled her head back.

"Do not fight me, sub. You are mine."

Her mind was churning, her breathing shallow and fast. She'd given him everything she had to give, had granted him access to her most secret inner spot. Now he wanted to take her ass, which she also considered a private place. But not nearly as much as that place deep inside her soul. She belonged with him. He knew her, kept her safe. He was her man, her Master. An intense desire to please him washed over her. All of a sudden, she wanted him to take her there—as if that would mark her as his own. And she needed that. Craved it.

Her muscles relaxed.

"Please, take me. Make me yours." Her voice was soft but clear.

He kept his hand in her hair as he pushed inside. Inch by careful inch until his full length was sheathed. More lube landed on her ass and he thrust, moving slow still to lubricate her. The slick slides roused nerves that sent fiery messages to her clit. A glow began to spread upward and out from her rear end. The delicious pressure of his cock inside her ass made her whimper.

Kyle groaned, curved his hands around her hips, yanked her deeper onto his shaft and started a steady rhythm.

"Make yourself come," he said, sounding hoarse with lust and need.

She slid her hand between her legs and started stroking her clit. Still oh-so-sensitive after the whipping, but the glorious sensations from her ass made it throb back to life. It swelled against her finger and she moved faster, swirling, flicking, rubbing.

Kyle grunted and pounded into her, impaling her with his cock, the feeling so good it almost made her cry.

"Come with me, baby, now!"

His cock seemed to swell even further and blew her over the edge. Her high shriek of ecstasy got drowned out by his roar as he shot his cum up her ass. He kept slamming into her thrashing body until he was spent. Both their bodies relaxed at the same time, and his hand slid out of her hair.

After a while he stirred and pressed soft kisses to the delicate curve of her spine.

"I love you, I really do," she muttered. "But can I please get that beer now?"

Kyle chuckled.

"I may have something better."

Sellie let out an exaggerated moan.

"I'm going to safeword to anything that isn't a beer."

He laughed. "Then your wish is my command. For now."

He withdrew from her, pulled her up and took her in his arms. She melted against him like a lazy cat. Kyle lifted her face and she looked in his eyes. "Promise me one thing, Sellie," he whispered.

"Hmm?"

"Don't ever change."

"Never!"

He tightened his hug and buried his face in her red hair. The words he mumbled made her heart sing.

"I goddamned love you, my fiery siren!"

Want to see more like this?
Here's a taster for you to enjoy!

The Playgrounds:
The Words to Bind
P. Stormcrow

Excerpt

What the hell am I doing here?

Luna Weir stared at the mirror above the sink, tapping the porcelain rim as she bit her lower lip, studying herself. The woman in the mirror looked almost sickly, her features lost in the pale complexion framed by almost-silver hair. The only spots of color were the startling blue of her eyes and the red lips that were bruised from being chewed raw. Nervousness was making her twitch this way and that.

She was in no shape to meet new people.

Outside the public washroom she was in was a group of pure strangers sitting down to have a nice Sunday brunch together. If it were any other networking event, Luna would stride out there with all the confidence of an ambitious newbie in the industry.

But this was not a professional meetup—and the topic at hand wasn't what she would call work-safe.

Eating with strangers... Talking about kinks and fetishes...

Why am I doing this again? Right... She'd said she would give this one last shot.

'We're done, Luna. I get you want my opinion, but stop making me make all the decisions. It's exhausting. You're just too intense. Look... I wish you luck, but I'm not the guy for you.'

She winced at the memory. He'd also expressed other choice words, like what he thought about her lack of enthusiasm in bed. It was true. She had a low libido. And yet, she couldn't reconcile the earlier memories of how turned on she'd been by even the faintest idea of something kinky. *That's why I'm here, right?*

Luna startled as the toilet flushed behind her. A woman emerged from the stall, a bounce of impossible red curls matched with impossible stilettos. She was stunning, with brilliant hazel eyes lighting up at the sight of...something.

Wait... She can't be looking at me, can she?

"Hello, sweetie. Luna, right?"

Oh God. Oh God. Oh God.

Luna mustered a smile, watching as the woman walked up to the sink next to her with a sway of hips and washed her hands. A pang of envy stabbed through her. The woman oozed confidence and swagger in a way she only wished she could emulate.

"I'm Lani, the hostess for the munch this month." She smiled, glowing with warmth, and Luna could not help but relax just a smidgen.

"Yeah, I'm Luna. Nice to meet you." *Always be nice to the hostess.*

"Let me guess... You've come up with a case of nerves and that's why you're hiding in here?" Lani leaned forward, but before Luna could protest, she added with a lowered whisper, "It's okay. My first time, I hid in here most of the munch and kept peeking out until the last person had left." She winked and tilted her head toward Luna, as if sharing a conspiracy.

She couldn't imagine the self-assured woman in front of her afraid of anything, but somehow, it made her feel better.

"Now, if you're feeling lost, why don't you come sit with me? I can point out who's who."

Luna stared at the offered arm, beginning to wonder why she had been so scared before. They were just people—people like her. Okay, she was nothing like Lani, the indomitable force, but Luna found her easy manner hard to resist. She looped her arm around the other woman's and nodded. "All right, I can do this. Lead the way!"

Lani tossed her head back and laughed. "That's the spirit!"

The waiter was just arriving to take people's orders just as they made their way to the long table in an alcove at the back of the restaurant. As Luna sat, the waiter came around with a friendly smile.

"And what can I get for you today?"

It was an easy decision for a sugar fiend like her. "French toast, please, with the whipped cream and strawberries."

"Sure."

Surprise made her turn with as much discretion as possible to study Lani as she ordered the same. The woman flashed her a quick grin and nodded toward the rest of the table, an invitation to look.

Luna ventured to observe the people around the group. Seven, including herself, rounded the table—three on each side with Lani at the head. She was seated to Lani's left, while to her own right was a lanky man with a mop of light brown hair and rimmed glasses. Across from her was another woman about her age, a slim Asian who was built like a ballerina. A couple sat farther down the table across from her, but she could only catch an occasional glimpse of the last person on her side. From what Luna could tell, the three at the other end of the table were deep in discussion about the best flogging techniques. She bit her lower lip, memories surfacing before she clamped down hard on them. A distant echo of a sensation — the pain — and the sheer lack of pleasure.

"Luna, I'd like you to meet Cassandra and August."

Thankful for the distraction, Luna gave a little awkward wave.

"Oo-o, fresh meat," the girl across from her squealed.

"Cassie, stop trying to scare her off. Not everyone's competition," August cut right in.

"Was not!" she protested in return.

The man ignored her and turned toward Luna instead with a cordial incline of his head. "So, Luna, what brings you to the munch?"

Although she appreciated the save, *wow...biting*. To the question he'd directed at her, she answered without hesitation. "Curiosity." It was the answer she'd prepared before she'd left her apartment.

Lani's eyes sharpened with interest and Luna braced herself for more questions. Instead, Lani grinned and clapped her hands together. "Excellent answer." She lifted a long-stemmed glass of orange liquid to her lips and Luna wished she had ordered a mimosa too. She could use some liquid courage.

"So, has anyone heard about the private play party Erica and Dominique are throwing in a few weeks?" Lani was quick to open the topic.

She had heard about these play parties before in her chat room.

"I heard it was invitation only?" August asked with a lift of his brow.

Cassandra—or Cassie, as everyone else seemed to call her—grinned like a cat with a large bowl of milk. "Guess who already got an invitation?"

August ignored her again and instead turned to Lani. "Ma'am, would you happen to know who would be attending?"

Ma'am. Things snapped into focus. Lani was a Dominant and August was likely submissive. Or did their relationship go deeper than that? *Wait...* Did they have a relationship of any sort?

"Well, Jacob and Darryl are both going to be there, I believe, though I think Jacob may be working as a dungeon monitor. Erica mentioned she also invited a shibari master to come to demonstrate."

Dungeon monitor, shibari... These were all terms Luna knew, in theory. A voice in her head suggested that she should make a hasty exit right about now. It was one thing to keep things online. Words were easy, sexy. The one time it had spilled to real life... Luna opened her mouth to make her excuse to leave.

"French toast for the ladies." The waiter set the plates down and Luna snapped her mouth shut, lest drool escape. *Okay, maybe after the food.*

Decadent pieces of brioche, dipped and fried in batter, were layered on top of each other, with bright red syrup drizzled over them. Slices of fresh strawberries spilled from the top, held in place by a generous mound of whipped cream, which was topped by a single large strawberry. A light dusting of powdered sugar provided the finishing touch to the delectable dish.

Heaven on a plate.

Luna licked her lips, beholding the indulgence set before her. Given the choice of food or sex, she would pick food...every time. Tempted to dig right in but aware that manners dictated that she should wait, she reached for her glass instead, to take a sip of water.

"Is it just me or does that look like a boob with a red nipple?"

Oh God. Luna's eyes watered and she started coughing as liquid went down the wrong way. She turned from the table and bent over, struggling for breath as her face was likely turning red as a tomato, or in this case, the strawberry in the discussion.

"Cassie!" Lani exclaimed, though she was stifling a giggle. She turned to Luna after realizing she was choking on the comment and the hostess patted her back. "Oh dear. Here. Breathe, sweetie. Drink more water."

"What? It's true!"

Recovering, Luna sat back up in her chair and eyed her plate. Now she couldn't unsee it. Her gaze traveled to Cassie, who gave her a quick wink, and she wondered if the woman had made the crass comment on purpose in an attempt to help ease her nerves. Well, that would be what Luna chose to believe.

As the food arrived for everyone else, Luna took her fork and knife in each hand. Inhaling to summon her humor, she grinned, mischief tugging the corner of her lips upward. "Well then, let's deconstruct this boob!"

It earned her a round of laughter and helped silence her nagging doubts for a moment.

Over the meal, chatter ranged from the mundane to the kinky. Content to just listen, Luna adopted the strategic approach of pacing her eating so that there were no expectations for her to join in on the conversation. Even when Lani moved to the other end of the table as part of her hostess duties to mix, Cassie and August kept her entertained with their antics.

Before long, people were settling their bills and saying their goodbyes. Satisfied that she had done what she had set out to do, Luna did the same and attempted an inconspicuous exit.

"Luna!"

She paused and turned, one hand already at the door. Lani approached, a light coat in one hand, a handbag in the other. "Got any plans after this? Wanna grab a coffee?"

Home of Erotic Romance

Sign up for our newsletter and find out about all our
romance book releases, eBook sales and promotions,
sneak peeks and FREE romance books!

About the Author

Born and raised in the Netherlands, Dani Rose moved abroad as an adolescent for a few years where she fell in love with the English language. She spent some time in Australia and picked up a lot of new words, and a nice Australian accent. The love for English remained, the Australian accent didn't.

Dani's always had a love for writing. Her first work was published when she was barely six years old. Okay, it was published in the kiddie section of a newspaper, but that's not the point! At the time she couldn't even write herself so she dictated the short story to her mother who then sent it in. Little Dani was ecstatic when it got printed! A writer-to-be was born.

As a teen she wrote romantic love stories for her best friend and became known by all her classmates as a wannabe-author of short love novels. More projects were started, some never got finished. Then, around 2006 Dani became intrigued by the realms of BDSM. Now there was a subject she could — and wanted to — write about!

Unfortunately life got in the way and it wasn't until 2015 that Dani found her mojo again and could be seen writing for days, weeks, months on end, working on several stories at the same time.

Finally, in 2016 her first book was finished! The first of a series that loosely evolves around an exclusive BDSM club.

Today Dani lives in the Netherlands with her four-legged furry creatures that occasionally meow to let her know they need food and she has to take a break from writing.

Dani loves to hear from readers. You can find her contact information, website details and author profile page at https://www.totallybound.com